Third Time's a Charm

Third Time's a Charm

VIRGINIA SMITH

This book is dedicated with much love to
Sarabeth Graham and Tori Smith—
the youngest sisters in my family's next generation.

A Note from Ginny

When I wrote *Third Time's a Charm,* I was so aware that this would be the last novel about the Sanderson sisters. Writing their stories has been a tremendous joy. I've poured my own family relationships into the Sister-to-Sister books, and when I first started on this fictitious journey, Joan, Allie, and Tori bore more than a passing resemblance to me and my sisters. But as their stories developed, the Sandersons took on personalities and thoughts all their own. It has been delightful—and sometimes surprising—to record their journeys to a place of ultimate peace and happiness with their heavenly Father.

This book was first published in 2010. The version you're about to read is nearly identical to the previous one, but I've updated the technology a bit. As I re-read Tori's story, I remembered why I've always secretly thought this book is the best of the three. In the first two books Tori sometimes appears to be a bit shallow. But once I dug beneath the surface, I realized she has depths and layers of personality I hadn't seen before. Her character is complex, and the changes she goes through in this story are imminently satisfying.

I thought something else when I read *Third Time's a Charm* – there's a lot more to discover about the Sanderson sisters. Maybe this book isn't the last in the series after all.

Chapter One

One sign was certain to drive even the most pressing appointment right out of a girl's head: Today Only—All Shoes 15% Off. The bright red letters snagged Tori Sanderson's gaze as she speed-walked through the mall toward the exit, an elegantly wrapped box clutched in her arms. She skidded to a halt before the exclusive store. The last time she shopped here, she'd tried on a darling pair of Bournes that had haunted her dreams since she walked out without them. If her sister Allie hadn't been with her at the time, she would have bought them in addition to the two pairs that went home with her. But Allie wasn't here now. Tori glanced down at the pumps on her feet. They looked okay with this new dress, but those Bournes would be perfect.

She glanced at her watch. Two o'clock. The bridal shower started in one hour, and the drive from Lexington to Danville would take about forty minutes. If she'd known about the sale, she would have left the office at noon. Or maybe she would have skipped work completely. Some people didn't come in at all on Saturday.

But, of course, those people didn't work for Kate Bowman.

Tori thrust thoughts of the office out of her mind. She spent far too much time at work, and even more time worrying about her job when she wasn't there. Anybody who worked as hard as she did deserved a reward. And was there a better reward anywhere than a new pair of shoes?

She tucked her sister's shower gift under her arm and tilted her chin in the air as she pressed her way into the crowded shoe store.

Ninety minutes later Tori marched up the sidewalk and mounted the stairs to Allie's front door, then paused to examine the dim reflection in the storm door glass. With nervous fingers, she plucked at her hem and guided a stray ringlet back into the Shirley Temple mass on her head.

What was the matter with her? Why didn't she just dash into the mall, pick up Joan's gift, and run straight back to the car? She aimed a smile at the shoes on her feet. They *were* absolutely adorable, and the matching belt had been on sale too. But she should have ignored the sale sign. Then she could have gotten here in time to pretend to be enthusiastic about Joan's wedding and help set up for this party.

No, it wasn't the shoe store. It was her job. If she had a normal job, she wouldn't be working every Saturday. She would have been here this morning, blowing up balloons or something, and she wouldn't feel like such a loser of a sister now. Kate's constant demands were taking over her personal life lately, and she didn't like it one bit. But what else could she do? Advertising was a fiercely competitive business. If she slacked off even a little bit at work, she'd find herself removed from the prestigious customer accounts and assigned to something dull and unimportant, like Lawton Lawn Service.

Besides, Allie probably didn't need her help planning a bridal shower. No doubt her super-organized oldest sister had everything under control, as always. She probably recruited

Gram to bake cookies or other goodies, much better than the bag of Oreos Tori would have grabbed at the store if she'd been put in charge of snacks. Allie could handle anything: the food, the decorations, those silly games you had to play at showers. Besides, both Joan and Allie knew she'd been working on a big project the past few months. They didn't expect her help.

And hopefully they didn't suspect her lack of help with the shower was because of her lack of support for the wedding. They wouldn't think that, would they? No, they wouldn't.

Tori clutched at the shoulder strap of her handbag. So why did she feel like such a slouchy sister?

A burst of muffled laughter sounded from inside the house. The party was under way, and she was missing it. Tori squared her shoulders and opened the door.

Inside, a jumble of clutter and chatter greeted her. Folding chairs lined the perimeter of Allie's tiny living room, each one occupied. Wall-to-wall women, all of them talking and laughing and sipping something orangey out of plastic punch cups. Tori stopped just inside the doorway and scanned the room for a familiar face.

"Tori!"

Joan jumped off the sofa and crossed the room in two steps. Tori found herself pulled into an embrace.

"I'm sorry I'm late." She held on to her middle sister for an extra couple of seconds.

Joan returned her hug. "You're just in time. Allie has been hinting at some embarrassing game she's planning to play, and I need an ally." She pushed Tori back, hands clutching her arms as her gaze swept downward. "Look at that dress. On most women it would look like a baggy T-shirt, but on you it's fantastic."

A rush of warmth for her sister thawed the edges of Tori's discomfort. Nobody could spend more than a minute in Joan's company and feel uncomfortable. She exuded happiness, especially since she met her fiancé, a doctor who moved to town last year. Of course, the guy's good looks were spoiled by an over-the-top attitude about religion, in Tori's opinion. An attitude that seemed to be spreading through the Sanderson family at an alarming rate.

"This is for you." Tori thrust her gift into Joan's hands. "I hope you like it."

"What a gorgeous package." Joan ran a finger over the elaborate silver bow. "Go grab some punch while I put this in the other room. Allie and Gram are in the kitchen."

Tori picked her way across the room, nodding a smile at the chatting women. She recognized a few faces. Most of these women went to the church where Tori and her sisters had been raised, and where they still attended.

"Hey, long time no see." Eve Tankersley scooted her folding chair sideways a few inches to allow Tori to squeeze through. "We've missed you at church. Where've you been lately?"

Tori shrugged as she angled through the opening. "Working, mostly."

She escaped to the kitchen without having to offer any further excuses. When she stepped through the doorway, Allie pounced on her.

"There you are! It's about time. Here." She thrust a plastic container into Tori's hands. "Get a tray out of the cabinet above the dishwasher and arrange these brownies on it."

Tori stuck her lower lip out and sniffed loudly. "It's nice to see you too."

Allie paused in the act of reaching for the sink. She returned to squeeze Tori's shoulders in a quick hug. "Sorry, I'm doing the headless chicken dance right now. It is good to see you." She whirled away.

"Hello, Tori." Gram started to rise from her seat at the small table, but Tori hurried to her side to save her the effort. Gram had recovered enough from breaking her hip last year that she no longer used a walker, but she still winced often and moved more slowly than before.

Tori pressed a kiss into a soft cheek. "Hi, Gram."

Wrinkled eyelids drooped over the blue eyes turned up toward her. "We missed you again last week. Sunday dinner isn't the same without the whole family there."

"I missed you too." Tori sidestepped Allie to retrieve the tray. "My job is crazy busy right now. Sundays are the only day I seem to be able to get any work done, when the phone isn't ringing constantly and someone isn't poking their head into my cubicle every few minutes."

Gram's mouth drew into a puckered line. "You shouldn't work on Sundays. It's supposed to be a day of rest."

Tori had a flash of irritation over the lecture, but it evaporated as quickly as it came. Gram meant well. "I know, but apparently my boss doesn't believe in rest." Work wasn't a subject she wanted to discuss right now, certainly not with Gram, so she changed the subject. "Where's Mom?"

"In the nursery, rocking the baby."

Tori brightened. Ten-month-old Joanie could sweeten even the sourest mood. "Oh, goodie! I want to go play with my niece."

She tossed the tray and brownie container onto the table. Before she'd taken half a step toward the doorway, Allie gripped her arm and pulled her to a stop.

"Oh, no you don't. Mom's trying to get her down for a nap. If you go in there, you'll just get her all riled up again and we'll never get anything done." She gave Tori a gentle shove toward the table. "Now get cracking on those brownies. We have to hurry up in here so we can go wrap Joan in toilet paper."

"Wow, Joan, you pulled in quite a haul." Tori stooped as she shuffled across the living room in her bare feet, her finger held firmly in a chubby little hand. Seemed like Joanie had grown two inches since she last saw her. Bright blonde wisps of hair were starting to curl over her collar and above her ears, and she was a lot steadier on her feet. Not quite ten months old, and she was close to walking already. She turned a happy grin upward and giggled. Tori could feel her stress melting away at the sound.

Mom had left with the last of the shower guests, apologizing for not staying to clean up, but she had just enough time to get to the hospital before her nursing shift began. Tori tried not to think of the piles on her desk back at the office. She'd stuffed a report in her briefcase to work on at home. It was due Monday, and since this afternoon was shot, she'd have to do it tomorrow. That would mean missing the traditional Sanderson family dinner three Sundays in a row, but it couldn't be helped.

Allie wadded up a piece of wrapping paper and shoved it into a bulging plastic garbage bag. "I don't know where you're going to put all this stuff in that tiny little house of Ken's. And this is just the shower. In another month the wedding gifts will start pouring in."

Joan balanced a box on top of an already unsteady pile near the door, ready to be loaded into the car. "Gifts won't be *pouring in.*" She slid the band off her long brown ponytail and combed a couple of stray locks back into place with her fingers before replacing it. "We're only having a small wedding."

Joanie toddled toward the chair where Gram sat dozing. She released Tori's finger and clutched the padded chair arm. Tori straightened and arched her back to stretch muscles stiff from bending. "Three bridesmaids is not a small wedding."

Joan's head dipped in acknowledgment. "True, but I had to have my sisters with me, and I couldn't leave Ken's sister out."

She gave a short laugh. "We're going to have more people in the wedding party than guests."

"You might not be sending out a lot of invitations, but I think you'll be surprised at how many people from church show up." Allie gave the contents of the garbage bag a flat-handed shove to make room for more trash. "If you ask me, issuing a blanket invitation to the entire congregation is a mistake. How are we going to estimate a number for the reception?"

To save money, Joan had asked her family to help prepare the food for the wedding reception. And the church sewing circle was making the bridesmaids' dresses. Tori was skeptical about the outcome of *that,* but it wasn't her wedding.

"We'll work it out." The bride-to-be seemed entirely unconcerned as she dropped to her knees and opened the top of a box. She lifted out a cream-colored cable knit throw blanket and rubbed it on her cheek. "Tori, this feels absolutely glorious. Where in the world did you get it?"

Tori crossed the room and fingered the soft cashmere. "At the mall. The store ordered it in special."

"A Ralph Lauren blanket." An almost fearful look crossed Joan's face. "I'm sure it cost a fortune. Do we dare use it, or should I lock it in a safe and save it for the next time the Queen of England comes for a visit?"

Tori laughed. "Use it. You deserve it more than any old queen. Nothing but the best for *my* sister." She sobered and gave Joan a stern look. "But keep that giant mongrel away from it."

The thought of the slobbery horse Ken passed off as a dog lounging on her expensive gift sent a shudder rippling through Tori's shoulders.

"Don't worry. I won't let Trigger near this." Joan stored the cashmere throw back in the box and replaced the lid.

Allie thrust the garbage bag into Tori's hands and pointed toward the coffee table, where an array of plastic cups and plates and forks littered the surface. As Tori perched on the edge of the couch cushion and began clearing the trash, Joanie dropped to her hands and knees and crawled across the carpet toward Aunt Joan with surprising speed, her plastic diaper crinkling. A pile of brightly colored bows diverted her attention, and she veered toward them. She cooed a soft "Ooooohhhh" and reached for one with a chubby hand. Laughing, Joan pulled the little girl onto her lap and covered them both with bows.

"I wish you were old enough to be my flower girl." She planted a kiss on top of the baby's head.

Tori kept her smile guileless. "You could wait until she is. Another two years and Joanie will be the perfect age."

Allie paused in the act of folding a chair to send a scowl toward Tori, but Joan's laugh held no trace of hurt feelings. "Oh, I can't do that."

You could if you wanted to. Tori avoided both sisters' gazes and picked up a plate with a half-eaten piece of cake.

"So, have you decided who's going to give you away yet?" Allie leaned the collapsed chair against the wall and reached for another.

Joan's smile dissolved. "No. In fact, I'm thinking about walking down the aisle by myself."

Allie shook her head. "Not a good idea. Trust me, you'll need someone to lean on. My legs were shaking so badly Uncle Edward had to practically carry me down the aisle. I wish he was still alive."

Tori glanced toward Gram at the mention of her deceased brother. The elderly lady's head had nodded forward until her chin rested on her chest. Her shoulders rose and fell in an even rhythm.

"I wish Grandpa was still alive," Joan said quietly. "He's the one who ought to give me away."

Nobody mentioned Daddy. Tori scooped up the last crumpled napkin and shoved it in the bag. He'd lost the right to give the bride away fifteen years ago, when he deserted them after his divorce from Mom. The jerk.

"Mom would do it," she said.

"I know, but…" Joan plucked at a blonde curl on Joanie's hair. "I don't know. It just doesn't seem right. Mom deserves to be escorted herself, and sit in the place of honor as mother of the bride."

Allie collapsed the last of the folding chairs. "Eric will be glad to walk you down the aisle, you know that."

"But I want him to escort *you*, not me." Joan heaved a sigh and stuck a bow on the top of Joanie's head.

Tori stood and picked up the garbage bag. "Can we rent a little old man somewhere? Just for a couple of hours."

Allie's eyes twinkled. "Can't you see the ad? *Wanted: Distinguished-looking man to give away bride. Must have graying hair and a tux.*"

Joan laughed. "I don't need anyone to give me away—I'm giving myself to Ken." A pretty blush colored her cheeks. "It's getting me down the aisle I need someone to cover. I'm sure I can find someone at church who'll be happy to do it. I just haven't decided who to ask yet."

It wasn't right, asking someone who was practically a stranger to escort a girl on the most important walk of her life. But what choice did Joan have? Tori clutched the top of the bag and gave it a quick twirl. Some day she'd meet Mr. Right herself, and then she'd be in the same position as Joan, looking for a substitute father for her wedding day.

She hefted the bag and headed for the back door and the big garbage can outside. Allie followed her, and when they stepped onto the back porch, grabbed her arm.

"You have got to stop scowling every time the wedding comes up." Her hiss buzzed in Tori's ear. "This is a happy time for Joan, and she doesn't need her little sister spoiling it for her."

"I'm not spoiling anything. I'm entitled to my opinion, and I think they're moving too quickly." Tori tossed a quick glance toward the door. "She's known him less than a year. It's not right."

"They were made for each other, anybody can see that. Ken and Joan are both mature, intelligent adults who have thought this through. And they're in love. There's no reason to wait."

"There's only one reason they're rushing into marriage." Tori lowered her voice. "They just want to have sex legally. If you ask me, they ought to go ahead and do it. Get it out of their system."

Allie's jaw dropped. "I can't believe you said that."

"Oh, why not?" Tori lifted the lid on the trashcan and stuffed the bag into it. "You're not going to stand there and tell me you and Eric waited for your wedding night. It worked out for you okay."

A deep flush colored Allie's fair skin. "That's not the point. Joan and Ken are doing this the right way." She lifted her chin. "God's way. And He'll bless their marriage because of it."

Here it comes. Why did every conversation with her family always turn into a sermon? Well, she didn't have the patience to listen to another one today. She had too much work to do back in Lexington.

Tori slammed the lid down. "Whatever. I'm not going to say another word."

She started to step around Allie toward the house, but stopped when her sister put a hand on her arm.

"Be happy for them, Tori. Joan is your sister, and she deserves your support. Don't spoil her big day."

Looking into Allie's earnest eyes, something twisted inside Tori's chest. Allie was right. If anyone deserved her support, it was Joan. Who came to every football game all the way through high school to watch her cheer when Mom was working second shift? Who helped her practice by reading the part of Li'l Abner to Tori's Daisy Mae about a thousand times before the school play? Who taught her to drive a stick shift, even at the risk of her own car?

A movement inside the house drew Tori's gaze through the window in the back door. Joan bent down to help Gram stand from the chair. The old woman leaned heavily on her middle granddaughter, just as Tori had leaned on Joan for years.

She drew a slow breath and looked back at Allie. "You're right. I'll be good from now on. I promise."

Allie smiled and drew her into a hug. "I know you will."

She released Tori and reached for the door. Her hand paused on the handle. "I'm dying of curiosity. How much did you pay for that Ralph Lauren cashmere throw?"

Tori hesitated. "You won't tell, will you?"

"No. But when we visit Joan and Ken, I want to know how much luxury I'm wrapping myself in while I munch popcorn in front of a ball game."

Tori chewed the inside of her lip. Her entire family already thought she was far too extravagant and teased her about the price she paid for clothes and shoes. And really, she'd spent way too much on Joan's present, even though it was exactly everything Tori liked in a gift—luxurious, attractive, unique. But she'd never be able to deceive her big sister. Allie could spot a lie like she was looking through binoculars.

"Six hundred dollars," she admitted. "But don't tell Joan, or she'll be afraid to use it."

Allie gave a low whistle. "Don't worry. She wouldn't believe me if I told her." She shook her head. "Girl, I wish I had your job." She grinned. "Or at least your paycheck."

Tori flashed a quick smile in return. "It's my credit limit you want. American Express loves me."

Chapter Two

"That's the last load." Tori closed the trunk of Joan's car and stepped backward on the sidewalk. The warm June sun still shone high in a bright blue Kentucky sky. "When it comes to kitchen towels and potholders, you're set for life."

"But not a single bath towel so far." Joan hefted a bow-covered Joanie higher on her hip. "We might have to dry ourselves off with dishtowels."

On the sidewalk next to Allie, Gram stood with her arms crossed, her age-spotted hands absently rubbing her sleeves. "Nonsense. I have dozens of towels and other linens at the house. You and your mother can divide them between you. Whatever you don't want will just have to be donated to Goodwill soon, anyway."

Tori whipped her head toward her grandmother. The ringlets surrounding her face bounced in her peripheral vision. "What do you mean, donated to Goodwill?"

Gram's eyes went round and her mouth snapped closed. A quick glance passed between Joan and Allie, which sent a shaft of alarm through Tori. Something terrible was going on, and they were keeping it from her.

"What?" She looked from one guilty expression to another. "You guys know something you're not telling me. Come on—out with it."

She marched over to stand toe-to-toe with Allie and glared up into her oldest sister's face. They used to do this when they were kids, the two older sisters keeping secrets from the baby. Well, she wasn't a baby anymore, and she deserved to know everything they knew, especially if it involved the family. Allie's lips formed a tight line, but worry settled on her forehead.

Softhearted Joan caved first. "Gram is selling the house after the wedding, when I move next door to Ken's house." A blush colored her cheeks. "I mean *our* house."

Tori's alarm turned to stunned disbelief. That house had been their home for almost fifteen years, since Mom's and Daddy's divorce. Tori barely remembered the series of apartments and rental houses they lived in prior to moving in with Gram and Grandpa. A vague memory here and there, but not one of them had meant anything to her. Not like Gram's house. Forget the fancy apartment she rented in Lexington. That was just a place to live. Gram's house was *home*.

"But...but..." Questions crowded for attention in her mind. "But where will Mom live?"

"She's going to buy a condominium," Allie said. "They're building some really cute ones not too far from Waterford, so she'll be close to Gram."

Her mother was going to live in a *condo*? Mothers didn't live in condos. They stayed at home, where they belonged, and kept things exactly as they had been.

"Why? Is it a money thing?" Tori whirled toward Joan. "Because if it is, why doesn't Mom buy Gram's house instead of some old condo?"

"Because the condo costs half what Gram can get out of the house," Joan said. "Mom can't afford it."

"So you and Ken buy it," Tori shot back. "He's a doctor. He makes tons of money."

Joan's lips twisted. "Not as an ER doctor in a small hospital. And we can't afford to buy anything until he pays off his student loans."

Tori's teeth ground together. If they'd quit spending all their money on mission trips, they might be able to buy a house. Or even take a normal honeymoon. But *noooo*. Joan and Ken were scraping pennies together to go off to Thailand or Taiwan or somewhere dirty like that to hand out Bibles to poor people, like good little missionaries. Which was *not* Tori's idea of a honeymoon. A Caribbean cruise would be so much more romantic, and wouldn't cost nearly as much. Even a trip to Myrtle Beach would be better.

Tori folded her arms. "So rent Gram's house instead of that cracker box next door. Ken could just move in after the wedding. Then Mom wouldn't have to buy a condo, and everything could stay the same."

Allie laid a hand on Tori's arm. "Ken and Joan need their own home, Tori." She cast a sideways glance at Gram, whose thin shoulders drooped as she watched them argue. "And Gram needs to sell the house for financial reasons. It's the right thing to do."

Tori didn't stop her lower lip from protruding. Apparently everything had been decided—without her. "Where will we have family dinners?"

"We'll take turns," Joan said. "Even Gram's assisted living center has a community kitchen families can reserve."

Gram nodded. "Eula Jane Foster's family did it just last week when she turned ninety. I peeked in while they were cooking and her granddaughter gave me a taste of the best scalloped potatoes. I'm going to try the recipe someday soon."

Tori sniffed. "But what about holidays? Where will I stay on Christmas Eve?"

"With me." Joan stepped closer.

Allie gave Joan a mock-scowl and put an arm around Tori's shoulders. "No, with me. That way you can be here Christmas morning to see what Santa brings Joanie."

"You can sleep on my sofa," Gram said. "I have plenty of room."

"Actually," Joan told her, "Mom's condo will have two bedrooms. You'll probably stay there."

Tori's shoulders deflated as she looked at the ring of beloved faces surrounding her. "You have this all worked out. You've discussed it." She sniffed. "Without me."

"Oh, don't talk like that." Allie squeezed her shoulders. "It's not like we've been purposefully keeping secrets from you. We've been working out the details for a while, and you're too busy to talk on the phone for more than a second."

She was right. Today was the first time Tori had seen her family in weeks. She'd been so busy at work she had barely seen her own apartment other than to sleep and shower. And while she was chained to her desk, her family's lives were going on without her.

"Well, I'll be here tomorrow." She held out her hands to Joanie, and felt a warm thrill when a grin lit the toddler's face and she came willingly into her aunt Tori's arms. "Set my plate at the table and I'll be here in time for dinner."

"What about church?" Joan asked. "It's been a long time since we've all been in church together."

Tori tickled Joanie's toes, delighted when the little girl chortled. She had to finish that report before Monday. But she had all night. If she worked until she got it done, surely she could finish in time for church in the morning. Then she could focus on participating in important decisions with her family.

"I'll try."

A car pulled up to the curb and parked in front of Joan's. The minute the vehicle stopped moving, the two doors on the passenger side opened. Allie's husband, Eric, got out of the back-seat and Joan's fiancé emerged from the front. Joan rushed across the grass to throw her arms around his neck and welcome him with an enthusiastic kiss.

Tori plucked a bow off of the baby's head and crushed it in her fingers. *Great. If I'd gotten out of here thirty seconds earlier, I could have missed the peep show.*

It's not that Ken wasn't a nice guy, and he was certainly handsome. In fact, when he first moved into the house next door to Gram's, Tori had entertained thoughts of a relationship with him herself. Except he made no secret of the fact that he clearly preferred Joan. Still, something about the guy set her teeth on edge. He was too nice, too eager to please. And way too religious. In fact, the recent upsurge in the fanaticism level in the Sanderson family could be traced directly to Dr. Ken Fletcher, and that bugged Tori no end. What was wrong with keeping things the way they were? It's not like they were pagans or anything. Through Tori's whole childhood they attended church every single Sunday. They still did, and she joined them whenever she could get away from work long enough. But in waltzed Ken last year, looking down his nose at them as if they were heathens. Next thing she knew, her whole family was spouting religious talk like they were learning a new language, and praying out loud at the drop of a hat. It was unnerving.

A sharp pain struck her toes. Allie had stomped on her foot. Outraged, she jerked her shoe away and opened her mouth to protest, but her big sister's hiss cut her off.

"Stop scowling at him."

"I'm not scowling." But she was. Tori quickly schooled her expression into something pleasant.

"Da-da-da-da!" Joanie caught sight of her daddy, and Tori had to hold tight when she tried to throw herself toward him.

"There's my girl." Eric swept the baby out of Tori's arms and swung her upward. Joanie's delighted laughter rang in the air.

A movement on the other side of the car drew Tori's attention. The driver stood, his eyes fixed on her. Ryan Adams, from the singles Sunday school class she attended when she was in town. Nice-looking guy. Didn't talk much, but she liked the way his eyes betrayed the fact that he found her attractive. She smiled and turned her right cheek—the one with the deepest dimple—toward him.

"Ryan, how nice to see you. What a surprise."

Beside her, Allie angled her head so Ryan couldn't see her face, and rolled her eyes expansively.

What? Nothing wrong with a little flirting between consenting adults. She sidestepped around Allie and headed toward the front of the car, where Ryan was just rounding the bumper.

"Hey, Tori. Haven't seen you around lately. Where've you been?"

He shoved his hands in his back jeans pockets. She couldn't help notice the muscles flex in his shoulders. Not the overdeveloped bulging of those body-worshiping gym rats she couldn't stand, just firm and fit. And sexy, in an outdoorsy lumberjack sort of way.

"My job keeps me pretty busy." She tossed her head so her curls bounced just a tiny bit as she looked up at him. "But I'll be at Sunday school tomorrow. Will I see you there?"

His throat moved as he swallowed. He opened his mouth to say something, then closed it again, and gave a nod instead. Tori deepened her smile with warmth in an attempt to put him at ease. Ryan always seemed charmingly tongue-tied around her.

Ken stepped forward, pulling Joan along with an arm around her waist. "It'll be good to see you at church. Joan and I don't have too many more Sundays before they kick us out of the singles group, you know."

Behind him, Allie gave her the evil eye, a silent warning to be nice. Honestly, she acted more like a mother than an older sister. Like she didn't trust Tori to act pleasantly.

With steel control, Tori did not allow her smile to go cold. "Well, you won't be going far, just down the hall to the couples class." She gave Allie a look that said, *See? I can be good when I want to.*

That report wasn't getting done by itself. With an exaggerated sigh, she said, "I'd better get back to Lexington. I've got a ton of work to do tonight." She narrowed her eyes and looked from Joan to Allie. "Don't make any important decisions after I leave. Save them for tomorrow."

Joan grinned. "Bring some work clothes to change into. We need to start going through the boxes in the attic."

"Not until after lunch," Gram said. "I'm fixing fried chicken and mashed potatoes."

"I can't wait." Tori brushed a final kiss onto Gram's soft cheek, then headed for her car.

Ryan found his voice as she waltzed past him. "I'll see you tomorrow, Tori."

She flashed a dimple and wiggled her fingers in the air. "Looking forward to it."

Ryan watched Tori's car disappear around a curve at the end of the street. The faint sound of her horn reached his ears as she beeped twice in farewell, a slender arm waving out the open window. Why did he always act like an idiot in front of her? One look at those smiling pink lips and rational thought flew right out of his head. No doubt she thought he was a country bumpkin, incapable of intelligent speech.

Heck, she was probably right.

A hand on his shoulder gave a playful shove from behind. Eric said, "Pull your tongue back in your mouth, dude. You're drooling on your shoes."

Ryan turned to find everyone staring at him. Ken's grin mimicked Eric's, and Tori's sisters both wore that pitying look women reserved for guys who'd just made fools of themselves.

Heat suffused his face. "She's, uh, done something to her hair, right?"

Joan's smile was painfully kind. "She started wearing it curly about a month ago. Guess she hasn't been to church since the perm. I think it suits her, don't you?"

"Yeah." He swallowed. "It does."

Ken shook his head, his grin crooked. "Why don't you ask her out? You obviously like her. I don't think she's seeing anyone else right now." He looked at Joan for confirmation.

Joan shrugged. "She hasn't mentioned anyone."

Allie stooped to pick up a red bow that Tori had dropped in the grass before she left. "I don't think she has much time to date."

Mrs. Hancock, the Sanderson girls' grandmother, folded her arms. Worry deepened the lines on her forehead. "Tori works too hard. And I don't think she's eating properly. Did you see how thin she was?"

Actually, Ryan thought she looked good. Great, even. She was short, what his mom would call *petite;* the top of her head barely came up to his chin. Nothing big about Tori. Except she had curves in all the places a woman ought to have curves. Heat rose in his cheeks again at the thought, and he cleared his throat. "She wouldn't be interested in going out with me anyway. I'm just a farm boy from out in the county. She probably goes for the big city suit-and-tie type."

Joan's eyes narrowed, her head tilted. "I don't think Tori really has a 'type.' In college she went out with a law student for a while, and with a guy who was studying engineering a couple of times. In high school she dated jocks."

"There you go, buddy," Eric said. "Didn't you play football in high school?"

Ryan scowled. "Yeah, but I was a country bumpkin even back then." He gave Allie and Joan a sour look. "Girls like you from the city were too good for hicks like me."

Allie tilted her head in acknowledgement. "But that was a long time ago. We've grown up since then."

An engine erupted to life nearby. They turned at the sound and watched a man next door disappear around the far side of his house, pushing a shiny red lawn mower.

"You should ask her out, Ryan," Joan said. "If you could coax her out of that office for an evening, it would be good for her."

Coax her? He didn't have the slightest idea how to convince an elegant, professional woman like Tori Sanderson to go out on a date with a guy who worked in a hardware store. Seemed like a sure ego-buster if there ever was one.

"You could come to dinner tomorrow after church." Mrs. Hancock's eyes held the same twinkle as her youngest granddaughter's. "That's the way my husband and I got to know each other, over my family's kitchen table. Papa wouldn't let me go out with him until he'd courted me with a proper chaperone."

There's an idea. But Ryan intercepted an uncomfortable glance that passed between Allie and Joan.

"I don't know." Uncertainty drew out Allie's words. "She's going to see that as a set-up. It'll turn her off for sure."

"I agree," Joan said. "Tori doesn't like to be forced into anything. It might be better if you ask her out to dinner in a restaurant, like a real date."

Allie snapped her fingers, her expression bright. "How about coffee? He could suggest a latte tomorrow evening before she heads back to Lexington."

Latte? He never touched the stuff.

Joan considered Allie's suggestion for a moment, then spoke slowly. "Coffee's good. Nonthreatening, informal. That would work."

Nonthreatening? How could a beautiful girl like Tori ever consider him threatening? He opened his mouth to ask, but Allie cut him off.

"But don't make a big deal out of it." Her pointer finger shook in his direction. "Keep it casual. Engage her in conversation. Then if she's enjoying herself, take the next step."

Joan's head dipped in agreement. "Dinner."

What were they, Dear Abby for the dateless and desperate? Ryan shoved his hands in his pockets. Well, he wasn't *that* desperate. He could handle asking a woman on a date without advice from a couple of matchmakers.

But they *were* Tori's sisters...

"So, she likes coffee?" he asked.

"Not just any coffee." Allie reached over to take the baby from Eric's arms. "Tori's a latte girl, through and through. Feed her mocha-flavored coffee with lots of froth and she'll love you forever."

Great. Five bucks for a cup of fancy coffee. His budget couldn't afford many of those. But if that's what she liked...

He'd been interested in Tori Sanderson for three years, since his first Sunday at Christ Community Church when he saw her sitting with the rest of the college students. She'd always been friendly, even flirted with him. But he'd known from the start she wouldn't go for a farm boy from Junction City, even if he did have a plan to work his way off the family farm. But if Tori's sisters thought he had a chance, what harm was there in asking her out for coffee? Provided, of course, he could manage to untangle his tongue and form a coherent sentence when she smiled at him.

Maybe he'd better figure out what he was going to say *before* he got to church tomorrow.

"Thanks for the tip." He nodded a general farewell to the group. "I'd better get going."

"See you in the morning," Ken called as Ryan rounded the car.

He slid into the driver's seat and turned the key. Good thing he'd promised to help his brother with those wall studs this evening. Otherwise he'd spend all night thinking about Sunday school in the morning and worrying about Tori's answer to his invitation.

Thoughts paraded through Tori's mind during the drive from Danville to Lexington, each one pulling her mood lower than the last. She didn't turn on her radio like she normally did. Instead, she rolled all four windows down and let the warm June breeze thunder through the car's interior, tickling her nose with the smell of freshly cut grass.

Their family home, sold. So many important milestones in her life had happened there. She'd baked her first cake in that kitchen with Gram. Greeted her first date in that living room. She could still see Grandpa scowling at the poor guy as he listed the rules that must be followed for the honor of escorting his granddaughter to the movies. She couldn't walk down the hallway without remembering the day after she was named homecoming queen, when she'd worn her crown to the breakfast table and Joan and Allie teased her and called her Queen Victoria.

Without the concrete reminder of Gram's house, would the most important events in her life be reduced to memories that would eventually fade? They had tons of pictures, but pictures didn't capture the whole story. One day would she have trouble remembering the unique smell of Gram's kitchen, where mingled odors of her cooking over the years had seeped into the very wood of the cabinets? Or the sound of the mantle clock ticking late at night?

Just like she could no longer remember Daddy's voice?

A sudden rush of tears blurred the oncoming traffic. She blinked hard. It was silly to feel this way about a house. Her family was still around, they'd just be spread out a little more. That was bound to happen anyway, first with Allie marrying Eric, and then Gram moving to Waterford Assisted Living Center, and now Joan getting married.

Tori tightened her grip on the steering wheel. Why did Joan's fiancé bug her so much? Her dislike made no sense, because he was a nice guy. A doctor, no less. Intelligent and kind and handsome. And he was obviously good for Joan; she'd blossomed since he moved in next door. Of course, she'd also become as super-religious as he was.

A strain of symphonic music, almost masked by the sound of the wind roaring through the car, interrupted her thoughts. It took her a second to recognize her cell phone's ringtone. With a one-handed grip on the steering wheel, she fished in her handbag for the phone, then raised the windows so she could hear.

"Hello?"

"Kate Bowman here."

Tori straightened in the seat. Her boss. The woman was one of the smartest executives in the advertising business, and Tori was lucky to have the opportunity to learn from her. Everybody said so.

She forced herself to reply with an even tone. "Hello, Kate."

No sense asking how she was, or if she was having a nice Saturday. Kate did not believe in chitchat.

"What time will you be in the office tomorrow?" Though posed as a question, Kate's voice held a touch of command.

"Um…" Tori glanced at her briefcase in the passenger seat. The correct answer was *I'm not,* but Kate wouldn't appreciate hearing that one. "I've got the data for the Harmon traffic ana—"

"Tomorrow." Her bark cut through the cell phone. "What time?"

Being interrupted before she could finish a sentence drove Tori nuts. She drew in a calming breath. "Tomorrow's Sunday, Kate. I wasn't going to—"

"I know what day it is. Don't you usually come in on Sunday?"

"Sometimes. I was planning to work at home tomorrow, though."

"Change your plans. I'm flying to Chicago Monday morning for that conference, and I need to meet with you before I go."

No fair! Couldn't she at least have one day without meetings? Sunday was the only day of the week when her schedule was her own, and she could actually get some work done without being ruled by the departmental meeting schedule. Not to mention the plans she'd just made with her family. What if she said no? Could they fire her for refusing to come into the office on Sunday?

Kate's voice snapped with impatience. "I just spoke with Mitch, and he'll be here at ten."

Tori's spine stiffened. She was pretty sure Kate wouldn't fire her if she refused, but there were other ways to make her life miserable. One of them was letting Mitch Jackson in on a project with one of the firm's prestigious accounts. No way in the world would Tori let Mitch attend a Sunday meeting without her.

She tightened her grip on the steering wheel. "I can be there by ten."

"Good. Shouldn't be more than a couple of hours."

The line went dead. Kate didn't believe in saying goodbye.

Tori slid the cover down and slipped her phone back into her bag. So much for church in the morning. But being with her family tomorrow afternoon in her family home was the most important thing anyway. Sunday dinner would be served at one o'clock, as always. If Kate's meeting ended by noon, she could make it to Danville with twenty minutes to spare.

Ryan would be disappointed when she didn't show up for Sunday school. Actually, she was a bit disappointed herself. He was a nice guy. His quiet demeanor had a calming influence on her while Allie was glaring and Joan was beaming up at Ken. She enjoyed watching him become flustered when she flirted. Nothing could ever happen between them—they were way too different—but she'd looked forward to seeing him in the morning, maybe even sitting beside him in church.

Oh, well. There was always next week.

The truck in front of her slowed as they approached the first major intersection in the city of Lexington. Tori raised the signal lever to indicate a right turn, toward her apartment. The evening stretched long and dull before her. That analysis for the Harmon account would be time-consuming, but it held little challenge for her. She'd done dozens just like it since she took the job as a marketing research analyst for this firm. A soft sigh escaped her lips. It wasn't fair. This was so not what she'd envisioned when she walked into Connolly and Farrin with the ink still wet on her marketing degree.

At least she had a job in her field, even if it was doing dull analyses instead of the fun stuff, like creating campaigns and overseeing strategies. Some of the friends she'd gone to school with had settled for jobs outside of marketing altogether. She'd been lucky to find a job as a marketing research analyst. One that paid well too.

And if she wanted to keep her job, she needed to have the Harmon report on Kate's desk before she left for Chicago Monday morning. Since tomorrow's meeting would probably result in another big project that would suck up her Sunday night, the sooner she got the Harmon analysis out of the way, the better.

But surely she deserved a few minutes' pleasure. After all, it was Saturday night. The mall was just a few miles away…

She flipped off the turn signal and headed straight through the intersection. A little shopping before she dove in to all those dull numbers was just the mood lifter she needed.

Chapter Three

The tree-covered hill on the other side of the cornfield tossed back a sharp echo with each blow of Ryan's hammer. Walt held the stud in place as the brothers knelt together on the subfloor. The smell of raw timber mingled with the rich odor of tilled soil that had been ever-present from Ryan's earliest memories being raised on the farm. Thank goodness the wind was blowing from the west this evening. At times the smell of the hogs from Pop's farm next door could get pretty rank.

One last pound and the nail sank flush with the stud. Ryan sat back on his ankles and stretched his spine as he spoke to his older brother. "Hand me that level, would you?"

Walt grabbed the tool from behind him and held it next to the stud. Ryan leaned forward onto his hands and knees to check their work. The bubble was hard to see in the rapidly dimming light. One more stud and they'd have to call it a night whether this wall was finished or not.

Walt squinted at the level. "Looks good." He climbed to his feet and crossed the subfloor to gulp from a bottle of water at the edge of the platform, in front of what would eventually become the back door. "The weather looks good for tomorrow afternoon. With luck we'll be ready to raise this one by midweek."

A trickle of sweat ran from Ryan's temple to his jaw, and he lifted his arm to wipe his face on his sleeve. He glanced down the

length of the unfinished wall. With just the two of them working tomorrow after church, they'd probably finish the framing
in a couple of hours and get started nailing on the sheathing.
One exterior wall stood braced in place on the south side of the
subfloor. Maybe when they got this second wall in place the
building would look more like a house-in-the-making and less
like a pile of lumber on a platform. But at the rate they were
going, Walt and Loralee and the boys would be in that singlewide trailer at least another year. He glanced toward the front of
the property, where a light shone dimly in the small window of
the place his brother's family called home.

Ryan crawled sideways and checked the position of the next
stud in the frame. "I can work for a few hours right after church,
but I may have something going on tomorrow afternoon." He
focused on lining up the two-by-four with the marking they'd
made earlier, aware that Walt was studying him.

"Yeah? You have a date or something?"

Ryan shrugged a shoulder. "Maybe." *If all goes well tomorrow
morning.*

"With who?"

"You don't know her." He picked up his hammer.

"'kay, so who is she?"

Ryan lifted an eyebrow at his brother. Walt wasn't normally
all that inquisitive about the girls he dated. "Does it matter?"

A grin hovered around his brother's lips. "Loralee will want
to know."

Walt's wife had been trying to fix him up with a friend from
the restaurant where she worked since last fall, when the girl
from church he'd been sort of going out with took a job out
of town and moved away. Loralee meant well, but the idea of a
blind date held about the same amount of appeal as cleaning out
Pop's hog pen. She was becoming increasingly pushy lately, so
much so that Ryan wondered if her persistence had something to

do with her pregnancy. Some sort of misplaced nesting instinct that extended to others or something.

"She lives in Lexington." He didn't mention Tori's name, or the fact that she'd grown up in Danville, just a few miles from here. Actually, even though they'd gone to different schools, it was possible that Loralee did know the Sanderson sisters, since they were all approximately the same age.

"Okay." Walt's grin deepened. "Just asking."

Ryan centered the nail on the bottom plate and began a rhythmic hammering. The familiar echo answered his efforts, *pound-tap, pound-tap.* Before he'd finished the second nail, a shout mingled with the sounds.

"Dad! Hey, Dad!"

He looked up to see his nephews racing around the edge of the cornfield from the direction of the trailer. Seven-year-old Cody trailed his older brother, spindly legs pumping hard to keep up. Even from this distance, and in the waning sunlight, Ryan recognized the fierce determination in the younger boy's face. How often had Ryan nearly killed himself to keep up with Walt? Though with five years difference in their ages, he'd never had a chance. Cody, only sixteen months younger than Butch, might one day actually be a match for his brother.

Ryan tossed the hammer to the deck as the pair tore across the grass, Butch in the lead. His oldest nephew leaped up on the subfloor, and Ryan braced himself just before Butch tackled him like a linebacker. Even so, he was knocked backward on his rear.

Walt's roar echoed like the hammer had done moments earlier. "Boy, what have I told you about running up here? There's nails and tools laying around all over the place. If we have to take another trip to the emergency room, your mother will have my hide."

Butch immediately rolled off his uncle. "Sorry, Dad." The impudent grin he shot Ryan was anything but repentant.

Ryan pulled himself upright and gave the scamp a good-natured shove just as Cody arrived and climbed up onto the platform.

"Mama says it's time to quit." He high-stepped quickly through the studs they'd nailed in place as though they were tires on an obstacle course. "Uncle Ryan, she says for you to come have a piece of pie."

Nine-year-old Butch gave him a grin full of oversized permanent teeth. "It's cherry, from real cherries. Grandma brung it to us."

"Grandma *brought* it." Ryan ruffled the mop of dark red hair that the boy got from his mother's family. It still amazed him that Walt was a *dad*. A good one too, even though the boys came along when he was younger than Ryan was now. Ryan couldn't even imagine carrying the weight of responsibility for a pair of scamps like his nephews, and soon another baby too.

But Ryan and Walt were living different lives. Walt never wanted to do anything except farm, just like Pop. He didn't seem to mind having his life controlled by the seasonal cycles of planting and harvesting or his income dependent upon the vagaries of the weather and the market price of livestock. Nor did Loralee. They both loved the life of the farmer, just like Mom and Pop. Whereas, as far back as Ryan could remember, he'd itched to discover something different, something *better*.

"Yeah, come on in for a piece of pie." Walt slapped him on the back as they walked toward the edge of the platform.

Ryan caught a gleam in his brother's eye. No doubt he couldn't wait to get inside with news of Ryan's date. Nerves twitched in his stomach. *If* he managed to actually get a date with Tori, which he didn't think all that likely. He really didn't feel up to his sister-in-law's cross-examination tonight. Because if Tori said no, which she probably would, he didn't want to look like a loser in front of his family.

"Thanks, but I think I'm just going to head on home." He hopped down to the grass. "I'll see you tomorrow after church."

Walt gave him a shrewd glance, then shrugged. "Suit yourself. See you around one, one thirty?"

Ryan nodded, and lifted a hand in farewell as Walt and the boys headed for the trailer. He opened his car door and stood for a moment, watching their retreating figures. Walt, in the center, rested a hand on each of his sons' shoulders as they made their way along the edge of the field's dark soil toward Loralee and a thick slice of cherry pie. Yeah, Walt was one lucky guy. He was living the life he'd always envisioned.

Not for the first time, Ryan envied his brother. It would be nice to know what you wanted out of life. Someday maybe he'd figure out what he wanted to be when he grew up.

Tori guided her car into the parking garage and zoomed up to the row of reserved spaces. She slipped into a visitor space close to the building's elevator with a thrill of satisfaction. A choice parking spot was little enough reward for giving up her Sunday morning.

Of course, the closest space was already occupied by a familiar silver Lexus. Kate's car.

"I'll be there for dinner, Mom." She switched the cell phone to her left ear, freeing her right hand to shift the car into Park and turn off the engine. "Kate said the meeting should only last a couple of hours. If we get out early, I might even be waiting for you when you get home from church."

Possible, but unlikely. Meetings with Kate usually ran over, not under. Still, she could hope for the best. Since her boss was leaving town in the morning, maybe she'd want to get out of the office quickly today.

Yeah, right.

"That would be good." Mom's voice sounded pinched, a sure sign of worry. "I feel like I haven't seen you in months."

Tori tossed the keys into her purse. "We saw each other yesterday."

"That doesn't count. There were too many people around to have a real conversation."

"Like about selling Gram's house and buying a condo?" She tried to keep the irritation out of her voice, but failed.

Mom's sigh sounded in her ear. "Joan said they told you after I left the party yesterday. She said you seemed upset. I'm sorry, honey. I wanted to talk to you about it myself in person, but you've been working so hard lately there hasn't been a good time."

Tori's irritation evaporated and she wilted against the seat. Mom was too nice to say it was her own fault for ignoring her family. "I know. It's hard to have a conversation with me when I'm never around."

"I'm worried about you. You're working too hard. You need to find a balance."

A yawn took Tori by surprise. Through sleepy eyes, she stared up at the concrete ceiling where, six floors up, Kate was already in her office. Balance? Tori had worked until after five in the morning to finish the Harmon report. "I don't think there is such a thing as balance in marketing, Mom."

A movement drew her eye to the rearview mirror. Another familiar car had just pulled into the parking garage. Mitch had arrived.

"I've got to go. Tell Joan and Allie not to be mad at me for skipping church."

"I will, honey. See you this afternoon."

"Bye."

Tori slipped the phone into her purse and gathered her briefcase. The heels of her new boots touched the pavement as

Mitch's car glided to a stop beside her. His head appeared over the roof almost immediately, and a low whistle cut through the June warmth.

"Look at Miss Victoria Sanderson, all dressed up for a Sunday meeting." His admiring glance traveled the length of her new slacks and blouse.

Tori paused in the act of punching the lock button on her remote to turn a dimple his way. Mitch flirted outrageously and without partiality, but at least he appreciated an attractive outfit when he saw one. They'd hired on at the firm within a month of each other two years ago and performed the same function, though for different clients. He was extraordinarily handsome, and she'd seen enough of his work to know he was smart, but both attributes were spoiled by an ego that blotted out all else the moment he opened his mouth.

He fell in beside Tori on the walkway, his hands swinging freely at his side. "Any idea what this meeting is about?"

She glanced at him sideways. "I was about to ask you the same question. It must have something to do with her trip tomorrow."

Mitch shook his head. "She's going to a conference, not a client meeting. This is something else." They walked on a few steps. "Since she wants us both there, I figure it must be a new account with a tight deadline."

That made sense. On a few occasions, Kate had assigned Tori and Mitch to work on a rush project together. They worked well in partnership, especially when the work required long hours at the office when the rest of the staff had gone home and Mitch had no audience but her. After a few hours alone, she'd actually seen that smirky mask slip once or twice as he got into a project.

"Great." Tori aimed a winsome scowl at him. "And to think, I was looking forward to a week without a boss breathing down my neck."

"Are you kidding?" They arrived at the door, and he leaped ahead of her to open it. "You know Kate can breathe through the phone just as well as in person. Even her emails reek of Tic Tacs."

Tori giggled as she swept by him through the doorway.

The hum of the elevator motor began the second Tori pushed the button. Another good thing about working on Sunday: no waiting for the world's busiest elevator.

Mitch followed her inside and pressed the button for the sixth floor. As the doors closed, he leaned a shoulder casually against the polished metal wall. His gaze swept her once again, and the admiring gleam returned to his eye. "So, after we're let out for recess, you want to go out and play with me?"

His tone held just enough insinuation to be flattering without being offensive. Tori's stomach gave a delicious flutter in response. She never really knew how to take Mitch. Was he seriously asking her out, or just flirting like he always did? They'd grabbed the occasional lunch together, but only as co-workers. She always wondered how he'd respond if she accepted one of his playful invitations. She'd even gone so far as to check the policy manual for rules about dating, and discovered that as long as one of them didn't report to the other, nobody cared. A relationship between the two of them would probably cause tongues to wag, but at least neither of them could lose their job.

On the other hand, Mitch always made insinuating comments like that, and not just to her. Best not to stick her neck out and be embarrassed by him backing off.

She turned her dimple grin toward him as the doors slid open. "Sorry, but my play date calendar is full for the rest of the day."

They passed the empty reception desk with the shiny metallic logo for Connolly and Farrin on the front, and wound their way around a row of cubicles. Tori slipped inside her own cube long enough to drop her purse in the bottom desk drawer and pull the Harmon report out of her briefcase. She took an extra moment to glance through the neat stack of papers, careful not to bend the edges beneath the paper clip. The colorful pie charts the client liked didn't give enough detail to make a financial decision, in Tori's opinion, so she'd supplemented the analysis with a couple of line graphs and summarized the supporting data in easy-to-read charts that had taken her hours in front of the computer screen. Kate would appreciate the extra effort when she discussed the results with the Harmon people.

Kate's office was one of the few that overlooked Triangle Park, the beautiful wedge-shaped grounds nestled in the heart of downtown Lexington. Every time she entered the room, Tori's gaze was drawn to the stunning site of the cascading fountains that curved along Vine Street. This morning the sunlight sparkled on the line of water that shot high into the air and plummeted to the churning pool beneath while cars circled the park on all sides of the triangle. One day, Tori intended to have an office with a view like this.

Apparently the view was lost on her boss. Kate sat facing her computer on the heavy credenza against the wall, her back to the wide desk with the neat piles of papers and magazines placed evenly across its surface. Mitch stood in front of the desk, trying to look casual as he strained his neck to read the screen over Kate's shoulder. He jerked when Tori stepped up beside him, then gave her an unrepentant cocky grin.

"Close the door and have a seat," Kate said without turning. "Be with you in a minute."

An odd request. Typically a closed door at Connolly and Farrin indicated a confidential conversation was taking place, but they were the only three in the entire office. There was nobody out there to overhear. But Kate was like that—overly paranoid when it came to discussing client information. Tori did as requested and then slid into one of the two padded chairs while Mitch took the other. The *tap-tap-tap* of Kate's keyboard filled the room.

After what seemed an eternity, the printer on the corner of the credenza hummed to life. A series of papers emerged from the front, and Kate snatched each as soon as the machine released it. When she had six in her hands, she swiveled the chair around.

Made up to perfection, as usual. She'd pulled her dark hair back this morning, the line of her white scalp stark where she'd parted it in the center. She laid the papers face down in the center of her desk.

Tori held her report toward her boss. "Here's the Harmon analysis you asked for."

Kate took it and tossed it on the top of a pile to her right without a glance. Tori swallowed a flash of resentment. After she'd stayed up all night to get the thing done, the least Kate could do was look at it.

Instead, her boss planted her elbows on the desk and entwined her fingers. She slid a sharp blue gaze from Tori to Mitch. "Dan handed me a new prospect on Friday."

Tori straightened in her chair. Dan Farrin, one of the firm's founders, had intimidated her since her second day on the job, when he reamed out an executive in front of the entire staff. She was pretty certain he liked her, or at least she'd never given him a reason to dislike her. Actually, she stayed out of his way as much as possible. Not hard the past few months, because Mr. Farrin had spent more time out of the office than in. Rumors had been doing the rounds about health problems, but Rita, his longtime administrative assistant, remained tight-lipped.

"That's great," Mitch said.

Tori nodded. "Terrific news, Kate."

The account must be a really big one. Potential new clients weren't all that unusual at Connolly and Farrin, certainly not enough to justify a Sunday meeting. The firm handled a large number of marketing campaigns for various businesses around Kentucky. When a business owner wanted to run an ad, or film a commercial, or design a new logo, Connolly and Farrin almost always got the job.

When a new account came along, the competition among the firm's three account executives to sign the client could get fierce. For Dan to hand Kate a new prospect was a feather in her cap.

It also meant a lot of work for her staff. Tori couldn't imagine how she could squeeze one more client into her workload. But she did have a couple of projects that were nearly wrapped up. As long as the deadline wasn't too tight, she'd find time.

"Tell us what we can do to help," Tori said.

A secretive smile hovered around Kate's mouth. "You two are not going to be helping me this time."

That made no sense. Kate had no other staff. "But you just said the prospect was yours."

"It is."

Mitch cocked his head, his expression cautious. "Are you transferring us to another AE?"

"No." Her lips twitched. "Well, in a way. One of you will be transferred."

Tori refused to meet the startled glance Mitch shot in her direction, but kept her gaze fixed on her boss. Irritated words rolled around in her brain, and the only way she managed to keep them from shooting out of her mouth was to clench her jaw. She was not in the mood for Kate's games today, not when she'd only had a couple of hours' sleep working on a report that apparently wasn't as important as she thought it was. But she knew better than to express her frustration in front of her boss. Instead, she folded her hands in her lap, leaned against the padded seat back, and waited.

Kate held her gaze for a moment, then relented with a brief dip of her forehead. "This is confidential, so please keep this news close to your chest. Dan is going to announce his retirement next month, and I've been asked to take his place as a full partner in the firm."

Tori managed not to gasp, while beside her Mitch's head jerked upward, his eyes round. Kate Bowman, a full partner with Mr. Connolly. This news would rock the office to its foundations. Most wouldn't be happy about it, either. Kate's single-minded focus and workaholic tendencies hadn't made her a favorite of the office staff.

"Congratulations, Kate," Tori said when she could speak without stuttering. "A partner. That's terrific."

"Yeah, wow." Mitch actually rubbed his hands together. "Just imagine what Osborne's going to say."

Kate's promotion would be a public slap in the face to Phil Osborne, one of the other two AEs. He'd been around from the early days, when the firm was just a start-up company with offices in a strip mall, or something like that. Without a doubt, he would assume he'd be tapped to step up if one of the founders left. Tori felt sorry for him when he found out.

"That's one reason you need to treat this news with the utmost confidentiality." Kate's gaze hardened as she held Mitch's. "Dan and Stephen want to sit down with him and explain the situation."

"Do you think he'll quit?" Tori asked.

Kate shook her head. "He's been with Connolly and Farrin since the early days. He's got too many years in with this company to bail out now." The secretive smile returned as she rocked backward in her chair. "But my promotion presents an interesting opportunity for one of you."

Tori widened her eyes as the impact of Kate's words hit her. The firm had more than enough work to keep three account executives busy. They'd have to replace Kate, and there were two ways to do that. Either they'd hire someone from outside the company to take over her accounts, or they'd promote someone inside. Tori stole a sideways glance at Mitch. The only two who knew Kate's clients inside and out were sitting right in this room.

Mitch had obviously reached the same conclusion. The narrow-lidded glance he gave Tori held a note of speculation that hadn't been there a moment before. She returned it without flinching.

"Either of you would make an excellent AE." Kate's words drew their attention back to her. Tori straightened, her senses suddenly more alert. "Which is why I've decided to give you an equal shot at the promotion. I want you to design a campaign." She picked up the papers she'd printed a moment before. "You've heard of Maguire's Restaurant?"

"Sure. Who hasn't?" Mitch's voice held more than the usual level of suck-up, the weasel.

Tori ignored him. "It's an upscale restaurant over in Twin Creek Center. They have a small menu that features mostly steaks and signature sauces. Prices are moderate to high." She'd been there on a date last year with an attorney she met through a client.

Kate's forehead dipped in acknowledgement. "They're expanding, and looking for a marketing firm to design a campaign to help them launch their new location."

"They're building?" Mitch asked.

"Renting. They're negotiating to rent a building not far from downtown. The opening is projected at six months out."

Tori did a mental calculation. "Is December a good time for a restaurant opening?"

"That's your job—to make sure it is." Kate's smile stretched wide. "The Maguire people are ready to sink some money into their business, and they're looking for a firm to help make this launch a success. So we need to wow them. I want to see a situation analysis, strategy, a multifaceted ad campaign, even branding recommendations."

"So, how are you dividing the work between us?" Mitch asked. "Is one of us going to take lead on this?"

Kate tapped the papers' edges on her desk with a loud crack. "You didn't understand me. You won't be working together. I want each of you to come up with a plan for Maguire's independently. That's the job of an account executive. You'll make your presentations to me, Dan, Stephen, and the other AEs. Whoever comes up with the most effective and comprehensive plan will become Connolly and Farrin's new AE."

Tori swallowed. She'd studied all of those things, and of course she'd worked with Kate long enough to know what the firm expected in terms of deliverables for a client marketing plan. But she'd never developed an ad campaign on her own. And branding a restaurant? She slid her eyes sideways toward Mitch for a split second. At least he didn't have any more experience than she did.

Only one of them would get a promotion out of this. Which meant the other one...

She cleared her throat. "What happens to whichever of us isn't promoted?"

Kate peeled off two of the pages and extended them across the desk toward her. "That person will report to the new AE."

Her, report to Mitch? She turned her head to lock gazes with him, and her confidence slipped a notch. He wore one of those stupid smirks she was accustomed to seeing from him, but his eyes glinted with something new. Determination.

Tori set her jaw and took the papers from Kate's hand. Hard work didn't bother her. She'd throw herself into this project and produce the best darned marketing plan this company had ever seen.

"When's it due?" she asked.

"You'll make your presentations on July 11." Kate handed a set of papers to Mitch. "Now, let's go over the information I've put together on the Maguire account."

Tori stared at the printed page without seeing the words. July 11 was only one month away, not much time to put together a full-blown marketing plan for a business she knew nothing about. Her mind reeled with all the work she had to do. Where to start? She might as well forget about sleep until after the presentation. It would take every minute of every day between now and then to get this project done. She wouldn't have time for anything else.

And then something hit her.

Joan's wedding was July 19. Her sister was getting married eight days after the biggest presentation of her life. The next few weeks were jam-packed with pre-wedding stuff, especially since she'd promised to help with the food and decorations. No way could she get out of those things, not and keep her place in the Sanderson family.

Good thing she didn't need much sleep, because she wouldn't be getting any for at least five weeks.

Tori bit back a sigh as she forced her attention to the details Kate outlined.

Chapter Four

The chairs surrounding the long table in the young adult Sunday school room at Christ Community filled up quickly. Ryan sat next to an empty one, his arm casually draped across the back in an unspoken claim. When Tori arrived, maybe she'd sit beside him, and he could get the coffee question out of the way.

When Joan and Ken appeared in the doorway, he straightened and craned his neck to see behind them. Instead of Tori, he caught sight of the oldest Sanderson sister. Allie's head moved as she scanned the room and when she saw him, she crooked a finger in his direction to beckon him into the hall. He stepped past Ken, who entered the room to grab a couple of chairs, and joined Joan and Allie outside.

"She's not coming," Joan said as he stepped through the doorway. "She called Mom this morning and claimed to have a meeting at work."

Disappointment deflated Ryan's tense muscles. Disappointment, and maybe a touch of relief. Tori probably wouldn't go out with him anyway. Embarrassing situation avoided.

Allie scowled. "She didn't even have the nerve to call one of us, not after she promised to be here. And of all the lame excuses."

Ryan cocked his head. "You don't think she really had a meeting?"

She grimaced. "On Sunday?"

Joan plucked at his sleeve to move him out of the way so someone could enter the Sunday school room. "I believe her about the meeting. Tori's boss is a real slave driver. Mom said she sounded upset at having to go into the office this morning."

Allie folded her arms. "Still. She could have called me."

Ryan hid a smile. Seeing the fierce grimace on Allie's face, he didn't blame Tori one bit for wanting to avoid her oldest sister.

In the next instant the grimace faded, replaced by a calculating smile. She patted Ryan's arm. "But this doesn't change anything. She's still coming to Gram's for dinner. Just call the house this afternoon to ask her out."

Ryan scuffed his heel on the thin carpet, doubt nagging at him. It was one thing to sit beside a girl in Sunday school and casually suggest a cup of coffee later. If she said no, he could always act like it was no big deal. But if he called her on the phone specifically to ask her out and she turned him down, that cranked the humiliation factor upward a ton.

"I don't know," he said. "I sort of promised my brother I'd help him work on his house this afternoon. Maybe I should just wait until next week."

Allie's hand gripped his forearm. "No. Today's the perfect day. We're going to be working up in the attic, so she'll be here all afternoon."

Joan nodded. "Call the house around four. By then she'll be ready for a break."

"We'll make *sure* she's ready for a break." Allie grinned. "By the time we finish with her, she'll be begging you to rescue her."

He looked from one intense face to the other. They wore nearly identical expressions that put him in mind of his sister-in-law when she was trying to convince him to go on a blind date with that girl at the restaurant. Joan and Allie were playing matchmaker, trying to fix him up with their sister. Even though he shared their goal where Tori was concerned, the feeling of being manipulated didn't rest easy with him.

He narrowed his eyes. "What's going on here? Why are you two doing this?"

Both pairs of eyes went round.

"What do you mean?" Allie asked. "We thought you wanted to ask our sister out."

Joan nodded. "We're just trying to help."

Actually, he was feeling the same reaction he'd had to Loralee. The harder they pushed, the more he wanted to dig his heels in. In fact, maybe asking Tori Sanderson out wasn't such a good idea after all. He edged toward the classroom. "Well, thanks, but I've got it covered on my own."

Allie stepped in front of him. "So are you going to call her or not?"

Irritation flickered in the base of his skull. "I'll think about it."

Joan moved to stand shoulder to shoulder with Allie, blocking his path. "Ryan, please don't be upset with us. We're just trying to look out for our little sister."

By manipulating him into asking her on a date? He cocked his head. "What do you mean?"

"Like we said yesterday, she's working too hard," Allie said. "She needs to go out, relax, have a little fun."

"And not only that, but there are some pretty unscrupulous men out there." Joan's smile was soft. "We know you'll treat her well."

"And besides," Allie said, "I think she likes you."

Ryan's back straightened. "She does?"

Their nods were enthusiastic.

Just then their Sunday school teacher, Mr. Carmichael, shuffled down the hall toward them, a stack of books in his hands. He stopped long enough to peer first into Ryan's face, and then Joan's. "If you're ready to get started, Mr. Adams, Miss Sanderson." His gaze slid to Allie. "Are you joining us this morning, *Mrs. Harrod?*"

The disapproval he managed to pour into the title let them know exactly what he thought of a married woman attending the singles Sunday school class.

Allie awarded him a broad smile. "No, sir. I'm just on the way to my class with my husband." Before she stepped away, she looked at Ryan and mouthed, *Call her.*

Ryan ignored her and gestured for Joan to precede him into the classroom. He liked Tori, but being the object of a pair of scheming women's plans was a bit unnerving. He wasn't sure he was willing to play along, even if it meant a date with the youngest and, in his opinion, the prettiest Sanderson sister.

After a delicious fried chicken dinner, the women chased the guys into the living room and Tori joined her sisters for cleanup duty. They each took their places in the familiar kitchen where they'd spent their teenage years, and settled into their routine. The sound of a cheering crowd drifted their way from the television, Eric's and Ken's voices an accompanying low murmur as they commented on some boring old ball game.

Tori ran a fork across a dirty plate, shoving chicken bones and a few stray green beans into the trashcan. "It's an amazing opportunity, but it's going to be a lot of work."

She set the plate on the counter. Joan picked it up and plunged it in the sink full of soapy water. "Well, you're used to that. I don't know anybody who works harder than you do."

On the other side of the kitchen Allie snapped the lid on a plastic container full of leftover mashed potatoes. "Maybe once you're the boss you'll be able to take a weekend off every now and then. You know." She raised her eyebrows. "Get a real life."

Tori scowled and reached for the last dirty plate. "I doubt it. Kate works every weekend."

"Is that because she has so much work to do, or does she choose to work all those hours?" Joan asked as she took the scraped plate.

Actually, Tori had often wondered the same thing. Kate seemed to have no life outside the office. Unmarried, no steady boyfriend. As far as anyone knew, the only time she went out socially was when she was entertaining a client. All her energy went into her career, and that was one reason the clients loved her. Which, of course, was why she was being made a partner at Connolly and Farrin when she couldn't be much over thirty years old.

Tori shrugged. "Doesn't really matter. She'd still be my boss. I'm sure she expects whoever takes her place to give 120 percent in the job, like she has."

On the other side of the kitchen counter, Mom sat in a straight-backed chair at the dining room table while Gram ran a damp dishcloth across the gleaming wooden surface. Beside Mom, Joanie was still picking at the food on her highchair tray. Mom selected a green bean from the plastic tray and held it up before the child, but instead of taking it with her chubby, mashed potato-covered hand, she leaned forward and ate it directly from her grandmother's fingers.

The overhead light glinted off Mom's glasses as she turned her head to look into the kitchen. "Are you sure you want this job, honey?"

"Mom's right." Allie stacked the leftover container on top of an identical one containing buttered corn, then picked them both up and opened the refrigerator. "Would it be so terrible to let this other guy get the promotion and report to him?"

Her, work for Mitch? Tori shuddered expansively. "I'd rather quit the company."

Joan half turned to look at her. "Seriously? Would you consider going somewhere else?"

Tori didn't answer immediately. She stepped up beside Joan, rinsed her hands under the faucet, and picked up the dishtowel. "I don't know," she finally said. "I wouldn't make near as much money anywhere else. Connolly and Farrin is the biggest marketing firm in this part of the state. Besides, I might not even be able to find a job in my field without moving to a big city. I was lucky Kate hired me right out of college."

Gram approached and set the dishrag on the counter, then placed an arm around Tori's waist and hugged. "I wouldn't want to see you move away."

Allie snorted. "I don't know, if she went to work for a company that actually unchained her from her desk every so often, even if it was a couple of hours' drive from here, we might see her more."

Tori dried off the big potato pot and crossed to the cabinet where the pots and pans were stored. There had been a few times she'd considered leaving Connolly and Farrin and had even quietly checked out the want ads in the local newspaper. That confirmed her suspicions of good marketing jobs not being all that easy to come by.

She bent down to stack the pot in the cabinet, then straightened and turned. "You guys don't seem to understand what a great opportunity this is. To be an AE for a respected firm like Connolly and Farrin at *twenty-four years old*?" She shook her head, curls bouncing in her peripheral vision. "Chances like this don't come along very often. I have to go for it."

"Then of course you'll get the job. I can't imagine you not accomplishing anything you set your mind to." Mom's smile held the confidence that had soothed Tori's insecurities from the time she was as young as Joanie.

"Thanks, Mom."

"One thing, though." Joan turned from the sink, her expression worried. "You won't be too busy to help with the wedding, will you? And you have to make time for the dress fittings with the church sewing circle."

Tension threatened to turn the good food in Tori's stomach sour. She returned her sister's anxious stare with a broad smile. "Of course I won't be too busy. Food, decorations, whatever you need me to do. You don't think I'd let you down right before your wedding, do you?" *Even though I think you're rushing into this marriage just so you can have sex with a religious nut.*

She flashed a glance in Allie's direction and saw from her expression that her older sister knew exactly what she was thinking.

Allie narrowed her eyes, then gave an almost imperceptible nod. She drew herself up and spoke in her bossy big-sister voice. "Tori, I know you're going to be really busy between this job thing and the wedding, but it's important that you take care of yourself too."

Allie looked toward Joan, who wore a blank expression.

Then Joan's eyebrows rose. "Oh. Yes, she's right. You can't neglect yourself. You know what they say about all work and no play."

"So if you have the opportunity to, you know"—a smile flashed onto Allie's face—"go out or something, you should take it."

Joan nodded vigorously. "Definitely. Take every opportunity that comes along."

What in the world were they talking about? She glanced toward Mom for a clue, but Mom looked as confused as she felt.

"O-kay," she told them. "Not that I get invitations all that often." Unless she counted Mitch's suggestive comments, which would surely stop now that they were in a heated competition for their boss's job.

Allie planted her hands on her hips. "You don't expect us to believe that the biggest flirt in the state of Kentucky isn't fending off prospective dates with a baseball bat."

Tori shook her head. "Seriously, I don't have many opportunities to meet interesting men."

Joan exchanged another glance with Allie. "What about somebody at church? Like, maybe"—her eyes went innocently wide—"Ryan Adams."

Allie snapped her fingers. "Now *there's* an idea. He's obviously into you."

Ryan's ruggedly handsome face swam into focus in her mind's eye. He and Mitch Jackson were as opposite as two good-looking guys could get. Where Mitch was suave and professional and more than a little sarcastic, Ryan was down-to-earth and, well, *real*. But at least Mitch spoke her language. Ryan wouldn't know a DMA if it slapped him in the face. "I don't know. He's cute and all, but…" She lifted a shoulder.

"You don't like him?" Joan and Allie asked at the same time.

Too quickly. Suspicion stirred as she examined first Joan's suddenly blank expression, then Allie's. What were those two up to? "Why do you want to know?"

"No reason, really." Joan's smile was guileless. "Just that he was so disappointed this morning when you didn't come to church."

"Hmmm. Well, like I said, he's cute and all." She wrinkled her nose. "But I don't think we have anything in common."

"Don't assume that without getting to know him," Allie said.

Tori didn't filter the skepticism out of the look she turned on her oldest sister.

Allie spread her hands. "I'm just saying."

Those two didn't fool her for one minute. They wanted to push her toward Ryan because he went to church regularly. They probably figured if she started going out with one of their church buddies, she'd be one step closer to their particular brand of fanaticism. Which wasn't anywhere on her To Do list. She didn't have time to deal with church, or guys, or anything except the Maguire campaign and this wedding she couldn't generate any enthusiasm for.

She brushed her hands together as though wiping off the effects of this conversation, which was going nowhere fast. "So, are we going through boxes today or what? Because if not, I've got plenty to do back in Lexington."

"Oh, no you don't." Allie looped an arm through hers and dragged her toward the hallway and the pull-down stairs that led up into the attic. "Mom, would you keep an eye on my baby, while I put *your* baby to work?"

Mom grinned at Joanie. "I'll be happy to."

Tori let out an audible groan as she was pulled from the room, but she flashed a quick grin in Mom's direction. Weird, but she was looking forward to digging in all those boxes with her sisters. That attic was dark and dusty, but at least the three of them would be working together. And this way she knew they weren't making any important family decisions without her.

"Ohmygosh, would you look at this." Tori reached into the box and pulled out a small cocoa brown jumper. "It's Allie's old Brownie uniform. And here's the tie."

"Let me see that." Allie crawled on her knees across the dusty wood floor, hand outstretched. "Gosh, can you believe they dressed us in *orange* ties? Isn't that considered child abuse or something?"

Tori giggled. "If it isn't, it should be. So, do you want to keep it?"

"What on earth for?" Allie tossed it into the box labeled Donations. "Maybe they can sell it as a costume or something. Anything else in that one?"

Tori pulled out the last few garments from the box in front of her. "Just some more of our old clothes."

Joan scooted further beneath the rafters. "Allie, are you sure you don't want to keep some of them for when Joanie gets older?"

Tori had a box of the clothing she'd worn in high school pushed off to one side, ready to be loaded in her car and taken back to her apartment. It wasn't likely that she'd wear many of them again, but she couldn't bear to give them away.

Allie obviously didn't feel the same. "Definitely not. My child is not wearing hand-me-downs from her mother." She blew her bangs off her forehead. "Besides, she won't be able to wear those for years, but there are orphans all over the world who need them now."

Tori compressed the garments in the Donations box and folded the flaps to seal it. She slid it toward the opening in the floor, then stuck her head down and shouted, "Eric, here's another one." Then she sat back and looked around the attic. The few pieces of furniture stored up here—a lopsided floor lamp, a single bed frame, a couple of mismatched end tables— had already been hauled downstairs by Eric and Ken and loaded into the back of Eric's pickup to be taken to the Salvation Army. Their old toy box was in the truck too and would be taken back to Allie's house along with an old trunk of Gram's, filled with sewing supplies and fabric scraps. All that was left were a half-dozen boxes, filled mostly with clothes and a few odds and ends. Hopefully Mom and Gram were making similar progress with the stuff stored in the basement.

"Here's a whole box of blankets and stuff." Joan shoved a box out from beneath the slanted rafters toward the center of the open space. "I think they might have been from before the divorce."

Tori pulled it into the ring of light from the naked bulb that swung above their heads. "Ug. That's pretty heavy. There's something other than blankets in here." She folded back the top flaps and pulled out a fuzzy blue blanket, and beneath that, a thick comforter. The musty smell grew stronger. She looked inside. "Well, that explains the weight. There are a bunch of books in here."

She lifted out a thick hard-back tome and squinted at the cover. "It's a textbook. *General and Social Psychology.*" She extended the book toward Allie. "Is this yours?"

Allie shook her head. "My old college textbooks are in my garage."

Joan crawled over and pulled out another one. "Look, here's *Psychology: The Key Concepts.*" She fanned the pages. "I wonder if these are Mom's."

Tori rose up on her knees and dug through a layer of books. Beneath them lay a couple of file folders with what looked like old tax forms inside, and then—"What's this?" She pulled out a shoebox, its sides creased and the top crushed.

Allie gasped. Her eyes had gone round. "I know what that is."

Tori lifted the lid and looked inside. "It's full of pictures." She pulled one out and flipped it over. Her heart gave a lurch. Staring back at her was a face she hadn't seen in fifteen years. The familiar smile, aimed straight at the camera—straight at her— made her breath whoosh out of her lungs.

"It's Daddy," she whispered, unable to tear her eyes away from the snapshot. He wore cutoffs and a pair of flip-flops, his bare chest tanned and gleaming in the sunlight. He held a big sponge in one hand, a garden hose in the other, and soapsuds covered the hood of a red car behind him.

Joan reached into the box and pulled out a stack of photos. She flipped through them one at a time. "They're all of Daddy."

Allie nodded. "I'll bet Mom forgot this box was up here."

Tori looked up at her. "What do you mean?"

"She put it here shortly after their divorce." Allie waved at the textbooks. "Packed up all his stuff and shoved it up here. All the stuff he left behind, that is. He took most of it with him when he split."

Tori picked up another snapshot. "Hey, I remember this. It was taken at the fair. Look, Joan. There's you and Daddy on the Ferris wheel." Excitement gleamed in young Joan's eyes as she snuggled beneath the arm of her father in the metal seat.

Joan took the picture from her fingers and looked at it a long time. Her throat moved as she swallowed. "I look around twelve there. That couldn't have been too long before he took off."

Allie flipped through a stack of photos. "Just a few months. Don't you remember? Mom and Daddy were separated, and Daddy picked us up and took us to the county fair. Tori cried because she wanted Mom to come too."

Yes, Tori remembered. Mom stood on the front stoop and waved goodbye as they backed out of the driveway. Though Mom hadn't shed a tear, the look on her face made Tori's stomach ache as they drove away, leaving her behind. Even now, a shadow of that fifteen-year-old ache threatened to send tears into her eyes.

Allie upended the shoebox on the floor between them and sifted through the photos with a finger. "I took that picture with Daddy's camera. And here's another one."

She extended another photo, this one with Daddy standing in front of a tilt-a-whirl with Joan on one side and nine-year-old Tori on the other. Tori examined her younger self, the familiar dimple, her small hand engulfed in her father's large one. The sight of those clasped hands brought a lump to her throat.

"Boy, there's an old one." Joan tapped the pile with a finger. "Tori, you couldn't have been more than two months old there."

Allie laughed. "Joan, do you remember those dresses? We called ourselves twins when we wore them."

Joan's smile was wide. "I do! And those matching tights and shiny black shoes too. I can't believe I remember that. I was only three."

Tori stared at the portrait. Mom was seated and holding a ruffle-covered blonde infant that held no resemblance to the woman Tori had become. Allie and Joan, in identical polka-dot dresses, stood on one side of her chair, blonde Allie a head taller than her brunette sister. Towering above them all, the head of the family stood behind Mom's chair. Daddy's left hand rested casually, almost possessively, on Mom's shoulder. Gold gleamed on his third finger.

Looking at that hand, acid surged in Tori's stomach.

She scooped up the pictures and began shoving them back in the shoebox. "So, this stuff goes in the trash, right?"

Joan and Allie looked startled.

"We can't throw these away." Joan's fingers tightened on the photo of her and Daddy at the fair. "This is all we have left of our father."

"Our *loser* father." Tori slapped the lid on the box. "And who cares? He deserted us. Why should we want any reminders of him? He's obviously forgotten all about us."

Tori was surprised at the sharpness of her tone. Apparently Joan and Allie were too. They both watched her stuff the shoebox back in the bigger box, concern etched on their faces.

When Allie spoke, her tone was the even one she used when she was getting ready to play armchair psychologist. "Listen, we're all dealing with anger over Daddy. That's completely normal. But I think Joan is right. One day each of us will have to come to terms with our parents' divorce and our father's actions. When that day comes, we might want—"

"Oh, cut the psychobabble, Allie." Tori tossed a textbook in on top of the shoebox with force. "We don't have to *come to terms* with anything. It wasn't our fault our father was a jerk. We didn't do anything to drive him away. At least, that's what you've said in the past." She challenged Allie with a direct gaze.

"Of course we didn't do anything wrong. We were children."

Allie's placating tone only served to fuel Tori's irritation. "That's right. We were kids. And you know what? Lots of people get divorced and they manage to keep a relationship with their kids. But not our father." She replaced the blankets and slapped the flap over to close the box. "So I don't see where we have anything to *deal* with. Our father didn't want to be bothered with his kids." She jerked a shrug. "It happens. Life goes on."

Joan placed a hand on Tori's arm. "Life does go on. But sometimes in order to *move* on with life, we have to forgive the people who have hurt us. Otherwise our pain holds us back."

Oh, great. In another minute one of them would start spouting Bible verses, and they'd join forces to gang up on her with a sermon on forgiveness. Well, she didn't intend to sit around for that.

"All this dust is making my throat dry. I need some water." She climbed to her feet, stooping so she didn't bang her head on the sloped rafters, and brushed off her slacks. "You guys do whatever you want with the stuff in that box. I don't care one way or the other."

She didn't wait for them to say anything else, but hurried down the pull-down stairs into the hallway below. On the way to the kitchen she peeked into the living room. The volume of the television set had been turned down low, the golf game going unwatched. Ken had left earlier to report for work at the hospital. Eric lay back in the recliner, sound asleep with Joanie snoozing on his shoulder. From the basement she heard the quiet drone of Mom's voice and Gram's answer.

Brrring. Brrring.

She hurried into the kitchen to grab the phone before it woke the baby.

"Hello?"

A moment of silence was broken by a throat being cleared. "Is this Tori?"

A guy's voice. Vaguely familiar. "Yes, it is. Who's speaking?"

"It's Ryan Adams."

She turned and leaned against the counter. "Hi, Ryan."

"Hi. Uh, I missed you in church this morning." A pause. "I mean, *we* missed you. The whole class."

Tori grinned. "Thanks. Trust me, I would have rather been there. My boss called an unscheduled meeting, so I had to go in to work for a couple of hours."

"Yeah, that's what I heard." Another pause. "Uh, listen. I was wondering. Since you're in town, do you want to go somewhere? Like, maybe get a cup of coffee or something?"

Tori glanced at the clock on the dining room wall. Almost four o'clock. "You mean today?"

"Well, yeah. But it's okay if you don't want to. I know it's short notice and all. I'm sure you're busy with your family, but I thought maybe if you had a few minutes before you head back home."

A scraping noise came from overhead. Joan and Allie were moving boxes around upstairs. Maybe they were moving *the* box around. Tori's insides tightened. Suddenly, returning to the attic held little appeal. Who wanted to go through a bunch of boxes of old stuff? No decisions were being made up there. None that she wanted to be a part of, anyway.

She spoke into the phone. "You know, coffee sounds good."

"It does?" Surprise flooded Ryan's tone.

"Yes, but I do need to get back to Lexington before too long. When did you want to go?"

"Well, whenever you want."

The eagerness in his voice brought an answering smile to her face. "What about now?"

"Sure. I'll come right over to pick you—"

She cut him off. "Oh, don't bother. If I've got my car I can just head on home from there. How about we meet at The Hub Coffee House in, say, twenty minutes?"

"The Hub it is. See you then."

"By-eee." She drew the word out into two syllables before she pressed the button to disconnect the call.

As she returned the receiver to its cradle, a thought occurred to her. Ryan calling to ask her out wasn't a coincidence. She'd probably just played into her sisters' hands. She tilted her head to scowl at the ceiling. Well, she wouldn't give them the satisfaction of telling them where she was going. And anyway, Ryan's call couldn't be more perfectly timed. It would feel good to spend time with a handsome man who found her attractive, even though there was no way she could consider a serious relationship with him. Their worlds were too far apart. She went to work every day in a business environment, surrounded by professionals. He worked in a hardware store. Their lives and goals couldn't be more different.

But what harm was there in having a cup of coffee? None at all.

Now where was her purse? She'd better freshen up her makeup before she left. After crawling around in that dirty old attic, she probably looked like a homeless person.

Ryan disconnected the call and tossed his cell phone through the open car window into the passenger seat.

"What's The Hub, Uncle Ryan?"

Cody squatted on the ground beside him, tearing up handfuls of grass to make a pile. His head cranked all the way back to stare up at Ryan.

"A restaurant where they serve fancy coffee." Ryan leaned down to look into the side mirror and brushed a bit of sawdust out of his hair. No time to shower, but he'd better at least wash his hands. He straightened and called over the top of the car. "I'm taking off, Walt."

Walt knelt on the grass measuring a piece of plywood. "You coming back Wednesday? I'll get some guys to help us raise that wall."

"I'll be here."

He opened the car door and Cody jumped up. "Can I drive to the house? Please?"

The kid had a snaggletooth grin that never failed to bring an answering smile to his uncle's face. Ryan glanced over at Butch, whose attention was fixed on the measuring tape he held for his dad. With luck, he wouldn't notice the privilege his younger brother was getting, or they'd have a fight on their hands. "Yeah, sure. Come on."

Ryan slid into the driver seat and let Cody climb onto his lap. The boy gripped the steering wheel with both hands and, while Ryan operated the pedals, steered the car down the dirt drive. The kid executed a perfect turn at the far end of the corn-field and guided the car to a place not far from the front door of the singlewide mobile home.

"Thanks, Uncle Ryan!" He didn't wait for the door to open, but planted his sneakers on Ryan's jeans and launched himself through the window.

Ryan got out of the car and brushed at a footprint on his thigh. "Hey, you little rat. Now I've got to go see a girl with dirty clothes."

The boy's high-pitched giggle floated behind him as he pounded up the metal stairs and jerked open the door. "Mom, Mom! Uncle Ryan let me drive, and now he's gonna go drink fancy coffee with a girl."

Great. If that didn't get Loralee's attention, nothing would.

Sure enough, his sister-in-law appeared in the doorway, a look of delighted interest on her face as she wiped her hands on a kitchen towel. Her belly looked bigger today, rounder than the last time he saw her.

Meddlesome interest sparked in her green eyes. "You have a date? Anybody I know?"

Ryan shook his head. "She lives in Lexington. Hey, could I use your bathroom to clean up a bit? I'm supposed to meet her in twenty minutes."

"A'course." She waved the towel toward the bathroom, and when Ryan headed that way, she trailed him. "Where y'all going?"

Cody's shout came from the small bedroom the boys shared. "The Hub!"

Ryan rolled his eyes. "No secrets in this family."

He closed the bathroom door and rummaged in the narrow closet for a clean washcloth. While the water warmed, he buried his fingers in his hair and shook, dislodging a shower of sawdust. "Great."

He brushed the dust off of his shoulders. Why hadn't he thought to bring a change of clothes? No time to run by his apartment, so he'd have to meet Tori Sanderson covered in saw-dust and sweat.

But hey, brothers share, right? He opened the medicine chest and rummaged among the bottles and tubes for a comb. There it was, right next to a bottle of Walt's aftershave and a stick deodor-ant. He lifted an arm and shoved his nose underneath.

"Phew!" The June sun had done a number on him this after-noon while he'd helped his brother work on the house. He raised his voice and called, "Hey, Loralee, does Walt have a clean shirt I can borrow?"

The closed door muffled her voice. "Yeah, sure. I'll get it."

He peeled his T-shirt off and did the best he could quickly with a wet washcloth. He even ran it over his jeans and made them look almost clean. When he opened the bathroom door, Loralee stood in the hallway with a shirt in each hand.

"You can go casual"—she held up a blue University of Kentucky T-shirt—"or dressy." The golf shirt had a Wildcat basketball insignia over the left breast, but at least it had a collar. Walt never went to college, but that didn't stop him from joining in the rabid fanaticism enjoyed by every Kentuckian who lived within a hundred-mile radius of Lexington—U.K. basketball. His closet was full of blue and white.

Ryan took the golf shirt. "Thanks." He pulled it over his head, then stepped back into the bathroom to run the comb through his hair.

Loralee leaned against the doorjamb. "So if she's from Lexington, what's she doing here?"

"Her mom lives in Danville."

"Really? What's her name?"

Ryan didn't answer immediately. He put Walt's toiletries back in the medicine chest and closed the door. When he turned,

Loralee had folded her hands atop her protruding belly and stood watching him without any sign of moving to let him pass until he satisfied her curiosity.

Where was the harm? "Her name is Tori Sanderson. Her mom's a nurse at the hospital in Danville."

Loralee's mouth flew open. "You mean Joan Sanderson's sister? I know her!"

Great. "Yeah? How do you know Tori?"

"Well, I don't *know* her, but I used to know Joan a little. She played the clarinet, just like me. We were at band competitions together."

Joan and Ryan and Loralee were all the same age, though they'd attended three different high schools. Ryan had been vaguely aware of Joan during school, but only as someone with whom he occasionally crossed paths when he hung out with the guys at the Sonic or in the shopping center parking lot. Loralee had grown up fifteen miles away, in Harrodsburg, and Ryan had never even heard of her until Walt introduced them. And he didn't know Tori at all until he met her at church.

"Okay, so you know her." Ryan put a hand on each of Loralee's shoulders and pushed her gently backward so he could squeeze past. "Now I've got to go. It isn't nice to leave a girl hanging out at a restaurant by herself."

Loralee followed him to the front door. "Have fun. Do you want to fetch her out here for supper sometime?"

Ryan trotted down the metal stairs and then turned to give his sister-in-law an exasperated grimace. "I'm taking her for *coffee.* We're a long way away from a family dinner, okay?"

Loralee raised her hands. "Just asking!"

Yeah, right. And the next thing he knew, she'd be *just fishing* for details about his coffee date, and then *just nagging* about the next date, and then *just insisting* that he bring Tori home to meet everyone. Which was exactly why he hadn't wanted to mention her at all.

"Goodbye, Loralee." He used the sternest tone he could to put an end to the discussion. Hopefully, she'd get the point. But he doubted it.

Chapter Five

Tori stepped through the door of The Hub Coffee House on the corner of Main and Third Streets, and paused on the mat to inhale the rich aroma of freshly brewed coffee. Hmmm. Was there a smell anywhere in the world better than that? The dark mustard-colored walls held giant chalkboards displaying the various coffees and teas, as well as specialty sandwiches and soups. An industrial-sized espresso machine hissed on the other side of a wood counter crowded with wrapped biscotti and pastries on display. Behind a cash register, a barista in a maroon shirt punched buttons as a customer on this side of the counter spoke in a voice low enough to be drowned out by the gurgle of the milk steamer.

Tori scanned the shop's interior and experienced a flash of irritation. She'd beaten Ryan here. Which meant she'd be the one waiting for him, when it ought to be the other way around. Hard to make an impressive entrance when the audience hadn't arrived yet. She pressed her lips together and felt them slide with the layer of shiny pink gloss she applied in the car at a stoplight on the way over. When she turned her head, a stray curl bounced at the corner of her eye. She grasped it between a thumb and forefinger and carefully tucked it back in place.

The lone customer stepped away from the counter and the barista turned a questioning glance her way. Tori flashed a quick smile and focused her attention on an old-fashioned sideboard covered with a display of tea canisters and mugs. Where was he? She couldn't even step through the connecting doorway to the Centre College Bookstore to browse while she waited, since it was closed on Sundays.

She'd moved to another wall and stood examining a collection of framed photographs and artwork when the door behind her opened. She arranged her smile and turned. Ryan swept inside, bringing a rush of warm air with him. When he caught sight of her, an admiring smile lit his features. An answering thrill brushed away Tori's irritation. Okay, maybe they had nothing in common, but he sure was nice to look at.

He crossed the distance between them with three long-legged strides. "Sorry I'm late. Have you been here long?"

"Just a minute or two." Standing beside his muscled frame made Tori feel dainty and feminine. She flashed her eyes sideways up at him and affected a teasing tone. "Just long enough to worry that I was about to be stood up for the first time in my life."

A grin eased the worry off his face. "Not by me. I was out at my brother's farm in Junction City and got trapped behind a tractor pulling a load of hay on the way in to town." He placed one hand at the small of her back and gestured toward the counter with the other.

Tori let him guide her, enjoying the warmth of his fingers through her blouse. They stood side by side examining the menu boards on the wall behind the counter, close enough for her to feel the heat radiating from his body and catch a spicy whiff of some sort of cologne. Strong enough to have been freshly applied, which meant he took the time to slap on some cologne before coming to meet her. Because he wanted to make a good impression, maybe?

She was still smiling at the thought when he looked sideways down at her. "What do you recommend? I've never been here."

"But this is *the* place to go in Danville." She raised her eyebrows. "Don't you drink coffee?"

"Sure, normal coffee. I have no idea what half that stuff is." He waved a hand at the board. "I mean, I know what Rattlesnakes and Honeybees are, but they aren't something you pour in a mug. And a Jitterbug is a dance, not a coffee. Maybe I'd just better stick with the regular stuff."

She put a hand on her hip and tossed her curls. "Well, I don't know if I can go out with someone who's never drunk a Jitterbug."

Oops. She shouldn't have mentioned going out. No reason to pretend this was anything more than a spur-of-the-moment conversation between friends. Good looking or not, she needed to remember that they were just friends, and they'd better keep it that way.

He looked startled for a moment, and then a slow grin spread across his lips. "I'll try anything once, and I'm highly motivated."

O-kay. Obviously he'd like it to be more.

A blush at his blatant compliment threatened, and she looked purposefully at the menu board. "If you like caramel, the Jitterbug is good. Or if you like vanilla..." Her voice trailed off as the blush warmed her cheeks. The vanilla latte was called a French Kiss. Better not go there.

"It all sounds good. Hey, look at the Depth Charge. Four shots of espresso?" He gave a low whistle. "I'd be awake for a week if I drank that."

"Amateur." She pretended to heave an exasperated sigh. "Maybe you'd better leave this in the hands of an expert." She stepped up to the counter. "We'll have two Temptation Lattes." She gave him a sideways glance and added, "Extra whip."

He read the description. "Hazelnut, white chocolate, cinnamon." Nodding with approval, he said, "Good choice."

Tori considered paying for her own, but he whipped out his wallet before she could do more than reach for her purse. Okay, this was his idea, his invitation. Let him pay this time. She left him at the counter and wandered over to pick out their seats. Maybe the comfy leather sofa? Too hard to look at each other if they sat side by side. The matching oversized chairs? No, too cozy. A regular table, then. That way they could face each other and have the barrier of a surface between them. She selected one against the window.

A few moments later, Ryan set a steaming mug piled high with whipped cream and a couple of napkins in front of her. "Here you are. And I just want you to know, I'm expecting big things from this. My supper last night cost less than one of these cups of coffee."

"Really?" Tori wrapped her hands around the warm mug. "Where in the world can you eat a meal for under four dollars?"

"Are you kidding?" He looked at her through narrowed eyes. "You obviously don't indulge in fast food. I would die of starvation if it weren't for the ninety-nine-cent menu at the restaurant near my apartment."

"I'll tell you a secret." She leaned toward him across the table. "Sometimes on the way home from the office at night, I run through the drive-thru and get a super-size order of fries. I love them. I just can't eat them as often as I like or I'd be as big as a house."

His eyes warmed with admiration. "You don't have anything to worry about on that front."

Tori's face heated and she tore her gaze away. Oh, this one was a charmer, once he got past the tongue-tied stage. She picked up her mug and held it aloft. "Okay, Mr. Fast Food, tell me what you think."

He made a show of bringing his cup to his lips, elbow extended and pinkie in the air. When he lowered it, whipped cream clung to his upper lip.

He closed his eyes and swallowed. "Mmmmm. Okay, suddenly I see the attraction." He opened his eyes and gave her a stern look. "But that is not coffee. It's dessert."

"It's a treat. An adult treat." She sipped from her own cup. *Ahhh. Heavenly.* Funny how her favorite drink tasted even better in the company of someone who was experiencing it for the first time.

"So, what was so important that your boss made you come in to work on Sunday morning?"

"A new project." She grimaced. "It could either end up meaning a big promotion, or my exit from the company."

He planted his elbows on the table, the mug engulfed by his hands. Big, strong hands. Tori fought an urge to hold her own dainty one up to compare.

"Sounds important."

"Oh, it is." The espresso machine hissed as the barista prepared another order. "And it's going to be a lot of work. Just before Joan's wedding too." She couldn't stop a scowl at the mention of the Big Event.

He cocked his head. "What was that for?"

Oops. He was, after all, one of Ken's friends. "What?" She rounded her eyes and looked innocent.

"Come on, don't give me that. You made a funny face when you mentioned the wedding. Aren't you looking forward to it?"

"Oh, totally." She twisted sideways in the chair, coffee in her hand, and avoided looking into his face. "I just meant it'll be hard getting my project done and helping with the wedding at the same time."

Ryan looked unconvinced. "Hmmm."

Better change the subject quick. "Tell me about you. You mentioned a brother. Do you have more family?"

He nodded as he gulped from his cup. "My mom and dad still live in Junction City, where I grew up. Pop has a farm there, and my brother Walt and his wife bought the adjoining property a few years ago. They have a pair of rascally boys and another baby on the way. In fact, I found out today that my sister-in-law knows Joan. We all graduated from high school the same year."

"Your sister-in-law is Joan's age and she has three kids?" Tori raised her eyebrows. "She must have married young."

"Uh, yeah. She did."

He looked away. Was he embarrassed?

"I'm sorry. I didn't mean to pry." She placed a hand on his arm. Warmth from his skin tingled in her fingertips. Uh oh. She recognized that tingle. Definite attraction going on here. And she had been determined not to let that happen. She moved her hand and laid it in her lap where he couldn't see her rubbing her thumb across her fingers.

He seemed not to have noticed. "No problem. It's no secret around these parts. Walt is five years older than me. Loralee played in the band over in Mercer County, and she came to my school when their football team played ours during our senior year. Walt was there to see me play. They hooked up at halftime, and next thing they knew, Butch was on the way." He twisted his lips. "It happens."

"So Butch is how old?" She scrunched her nose, calculating. "Nine?"

"That's right. And Cody is almost eight." A smile softened his features. "They're great kids. All boy, though. Always in trouble over something or other. They remind me of Walt and me when we were growing up on the farm."

He grew up on a farm. Tori eased backward until her back was resting against the chair. Yet another big difference between them. And his parents were still together. Her smile became brittle, and she raised her cup to hide it.

Apparently not fast enough.

"What?" He cocked his head and fixed a speculative gaze on her. "You don't like farms?"

"Honestly?" She lifted her shoulders. "I have no idea. I've never spent any time on a farm."

"So what was that grimace about?"

Tori straightened, her spine stiff. "I did not grimace!"

"Yes, you did." A teasing grin twisted his lips. "It was a cute little grimace, but it was a grimace."

Stomach tickling, Tori couldn't help returning his grin. He really was nice looking, with that dark hair and those light brown eyes that didn't bother to hide his attraction to her. She relaxed and sipped her latte before answering. "I was just thinking of the differences in our backgrounds."

"Like the country mouse and the city mouse?"

She gave a small laugh. "That, and the fact that you had both your parents while I only had one."

For some reason she found it hard to meet his gaze. She stared at her fingers as she folded a napkin over and over.

"That must have been tough."

She tilted her head in a quasi-shrug. "For a while. But after Daddy left we still had Mom and our grandparents. We survived."

"Do you ever see him?"

"Not since I was nine." The napkin was as small as it could go, so she reversed the process and started unfolding it. "I have no idea if he's even still alive."

"I'm surprised you haven't searched for him."

Startled, she looked up into Ryan's face. "Why would I do that?"

His turn to shrug. "Just to know."

She had never considered looking for Daddy. He'd disappeared, deserted them, and apparently never looked back. They were still here, still in the house Gram and Grandpa had owned when he left, at least for a little while longer. He knew how to get in touch with them if he wanted to, so his fifteen-year silence spoke volumes about the depth of his concern for his daughters. Or lack of concern. Better to let him stay in whatever cave he'd crawled into.

But what if something had happened to him? What if he was dead? She could admit to herself that the thought had occurred to her more than once. That could be the reason they'd never heard from him. In fact, death was the only acceptable excuse for his continued silence, as far as she was concerned.

Tori unfolded the final crease in the napkin, but instead of smoothing it out on the table's surface, she wadded it into a ball in her fist. If he was dead, they would certainly have been informed by some authority or other.

"I don't want to know," she told Ryan. "We're better off without him."

He studied her for a moment, then gave a slight nod. "I understand."

Tori raised her gaze from the napkin. A softness in his eyes drew her; she found herself leaning toward him across the table. Ryan exuded a wholesomeness that she never saw at the office. Certainly not in Mitch, whose eyes always held secrets behind a mocking gaze. There were no secrets here, only an open honesty that hinted at reserves of strength.

"Let's don't talk about me anymore." She presented him with a dimple. "I want to know about you."

He laughed, and shook his head. "There's not much to tell. I'm—"

He didn't get to finish. The door to the restaurant opened, and a pair of boys raced inside. Two heads, both covered with mops of dark red hair, turned their way. When the boys caught sight of them, they zipped around a row of tables in their direction.

"Uncle Ryan! We came to drink fancy coffee too."

Tori's jaw went slack. Ryan's nephews? What were they doing here? She looked at him and saw that his cheeks had grown ruddy. At that moment, a pregnant woman with a thick mane of hair the same hue as the boys' followed at a more sedate pace.

"Uh, sorry to interrupt." She smiled apologetically at Ryan. "The boys just wouldn't let up pestering me."

The younger one's eyebrows drew down over his eyes. "But Mama, you said—"

The woman stopped him with a gentle shove toward the counter. "Go on, now. See what you want. Butch, help your brother read the menu." They raced off, and she raised her voice to follow them. "Nothing with caffeine." She turned back toward Tori with a grin so wide she looked like she had a coat hanger lodged in her mouth. "Hi. You probably don't know me. I used to be Loralee Planter."

Her words were weighed down with the deep Kentucky twang that seemed to strike hit-or-miss in this part of the state.

"Hello. It's nice to meet you." Tori took her hand. The skin felt rough, and she couldn't help notice the nails had been bitten, but were clean.

Ryan was staring, tight-lipped, at his sister-in-law. "I didn't know you liked The Hub."

Loralee gave an awkward laugh and patted her bulging belly. "Oh, you know. Once I get something in my mind these days, I just can't hardly stand it until I satisfy the craving."

She was an attractive girl, though the flush that colored her cheeks at the moment clashed with the red hair that hung in waves past her shoulders. She stood beside the table, hands resting on her stomach and staring at Tori with an eagerness that made her shift uncomfortably in the chair. Was she on exhibit or something? Tori threw a glance toward Ryan, who looked like he might leap to his feet and escort Loralee from the restaurant.

To cover the awkward moment of silence, Tori smiled up at the girl. "Ryan was just telling me that you're the same age as my sister Joan."

"That's right." Loralee's smile widened and she turned her body slightly away from her brother-in-law. "She might not know me, though. I went to school over in Harrodsburg. But I remember you. I carried the boys to the parade the year you were the homecoming queen. Saw you sitting up there on the back of that car, pretty as a pink petunia."

A pink petunia? Odd description. Tori stared blankly for a moment, until she remembered. She'd worn a pink dress and jacket as she rode on the back of a convertible in that parade. "Gosh, you have a good memory."

Loralee preened at the compliment. "Listen, why don't you come out to the farm with Ryan sometime?" Her face flushed. "We live in a little old trailer, but we're building a house. We can have us a lemonade while Ryan and Walt are working."

Tori glanced toward Ryan. Yes, just like she was thinking earlier—no secrets in that face. He looked like he was ready to strangle his sister-in-law. Nothing like having your relatives show up and start issuing invitations. She smothered a grin and said to Loralee, "I was just telling Ryan I've never spent much time on farms."

"Then you've just gotta come. I can show you around." Loralee looked toward Ryan's stern face and her exuberance faded. She took a backward step. "I'd better get up there and help those young 'uns find something to drink that won't send them bouncing off the walls."

She whirled and covered the short distance to the counter, where the boys were manhandling a display of wrapped biscotti under the glowering gaze of the barista.

Ryan leaned forward and spoke in a low voice. "I never thought she'd show up here."

Tori giggled. "It's okay. If my sisters knew where we were, they'd probably be here too."

An unreadable look crossed his features. He leaned forward on his elbows, his long fingers circling the mug on the table's surface. "Actually, I think they—"

"Uncle Ryan!" A high-pitched boy's voice interrupted whatever he'd been getting ready to say as a small body shot across the store like a bullet and skidded to a halt next to their table. "I'm getting a Wild Berry Bomb. Think they'll set it on fire before they give it to me?"

Ryan gave Tori a horrified look that made her laugh.

"No, they won't set it on fire," she assured him. "It's a smoothie."

Ryan looked relieved. "Tori, meet Butch, my oldest nephew."

Tori extended her hand, and the boy stared at it for a moment before giving it a solid shake. "You got pretty fingernails."

"Thank you."

His head tilted and looked at her. "Pretty face too."

"Thank you again." Tori glanced toward Ryan, whose warm eyes caught hers.

"He takes after his uncle when it comes to appreciating beauty."

Momentarily speechless, Tori wrestled with yet another flush that threatened to creep into her face. She seemed to be doing a lot of that today. To cover the moment, she picked up her mug and brought it to her lips.

"Look what I got." The younger boy approached at a gallop, waving a giant cookie in his brother's direction.

Outrage stole across Butch's features. He shouted toward his mother, who still stood at the counter, "No fair!"

"Oh, calm down," Loralee told him as she counted out money on the counter. "I got one for you too."

Butch reached out and gave Cody a shove. "So there."

The little boy's eyebrows gathered together. He planted his feet and shoved his brother back. "So there yourself."

"Here, now. You two behave." Ryan's stern voice held a note of warning.

His command went unheeded as the boys continued jostling each other. These two acted just like Allie and Joan when they were little. Tori remembered standing on the sidelines and watching her sisters' battles. She turned her head toward Ryan to tell him so.

The words never came. In the next instant, a young body knocked into her as Butch shoved his younger brother with force. Wet heat sloshed down her chest as her half-full mug was torn from her hand and emptied its contents on her blouse.

Gasping, Tori jumped out of her chair and pulled the hot, wet fabric away from her skin. Ryan, too, leaped up and took a step forward, his hands outstretched toward her. He stopped inches away from touching her chest, whirled, and scooped up the napkins on the table.

"Are you okay? Are you burned?"

For a moment Tori thought he might use the napkins to wipe off her blouse himself. She snatched them out of his hand. "I'm fine." Her voice came out a little sharper than she intended, but *ouch!* Not blisteringly hot, but definitely hot tub hot. Flapping the fabric to cool it down, she forced a smile to her lips. "It's not too bad. No harm done."

Except to her brand-new pink blouse. She blotted at the dark stain. No chance at all it would come out. The wet fabric clung to her skin, her bra clearly outlined. She turned away from Ryan. Great. Just what she wanted to do, treat him to a peep show at The Hub.

"I'm so sorry." Loralee rushed over, horror coloring her features. She turned a fierce glare on her sons and spoke through gritted teeth. "Apologize. Right. This. Minute."

Two red heads ducked toward the floor. "Sorry," a pair of voices mumbled.

A wave of compassion swept over Tori at the sight of their slumped shoulders. "Accidents happen. It's okay."

"We'll pay for your shirt," Loralee told her. "The boys will earn the money by doing chores on the farm."

They slumped further, and Tori couldn't help feeling sorry for them. She had no idea what the going rate was for farm chores, but no doubt it would take them months, if not years, to cover the cost of this blouse. She forced a smile and shook her head. "Don't worry about it. Really."

Ryan took a step toward the counter. "I'll get you another coffee."

"No, that's alright." She stopped him with a hand on his arm. "I think I'll just head on back to Lexington now."

He drew a breath to protest, but then his gaze dropped to the stained blouse that she carefully held away from her skin. His mouth snapped closed.

Loralee looked stricken. "I just hate that we ruined your date. You'll come out to the farm and let us make it up to you, won't you?"

It's not a date. If it had been, this would have gone at the top of her list of Disastrous Dates of the Decade.

She mumbled something noncommittal as she edged away from Loralee and her subdued pair of roughhousers.

Ryan followed, and jumped ahead of her to open the door. "I'm really sorry."

They stepped outside. Heat rolled off the concrete sidewalk and slapped them in the face. The wet blouse felt suddenly cool against Tori's skin in comparison. She dug in her purse for her keys and pushed the button to unlock the door as she approached her car parked on the curb.

"It wasn't your fault." She managed a quick smile. "Like you said, they're all boy."

As she reached for the handle, he put a hand on the car door and leaned against it. "Let me make it up to you by taking you to dinner Wednesday night."

Okay, now they were officially into date territory. Tori looked into his eyes and felt the stirring of attraction she'd felt back in the coffee shop. But the facts had not changed. They had nothing in common. He was raised on a farm, and she wouldn't know a chicken from a rooster. She was on a fast track in a highly competitive profession, and he worked in a hardware store. Like he said, country mouse and city mouse.

She wrinkled her nose and spoke apologetically, "I told you about my new project. I'm going to be working late."

"Well, you have to eat. If Wednesday isn't good, we could do it another night. What about Tuesday? I have class until seven thirty, so we could do a late dinner. Say around nine?"

A prickle of interest halted Tori's protest. "What kind of class?"

His slow grin sent a shaft of warmth through her. "I'll tell you at dinner Tuesday night. Where do I pick you up, at work or your apartment?"

She couldn't stop a laugh. "You don't give up, do you?"

He leaned toward her, his gaze locked onto hers. "Like I said earlier, I'm motivated."

A thrill shot through her at the hint of gravel in his voice. He seemed to have gotten past being tongue-tied in her presence and moved all the way into the realm of flirting. Well, she was no amateur in that field. She could totally handle herself there.

She tossed her head so her curls bounced, and flashed a sideways grin up at him. "Pick me up at my office at eight forty-five.

Connolly and Farrin, downtown in the Central Bank building. Sixth floor."

"Yes, ma'am." His smile deepened as he opened the door for her. Tori slid behind the wheel.

"Thanks for the latte." She glanced down at her blouse and her smile turned wry. "What I got of it."

A chuckle rumbled in his chest. "Looks to me like you got it all, one way or another."

She laughed and shut the door. He stood watching as she pulled away from the curb, his hands in the front pockets of his jeans. She watched him in the rearview mirror as she drove down Main Street. He didn't move, but stared after her until she couldn't see him anymore.

As the distance from The Hub Coffee House increased, Tori's senses returned. What was she thinking, agreeing to go out with him? Without a doubt there was an attraction between them, but that was even more reason why she should have stuck to her guns and refused. A relationship between them had only one possible outcome. When they broke it off, as they certainly would do eventually, that would make attending church with her family even more awkward than it had become in recent months. She'd fallen prey to a handsome face and a flirty invitation, and lost her resolve.

And yet, she couldn't deny the tickle of excitement when she thought ahead to Tuesday night. He was an extremely attractive guy, and he obviously liked her. It had been too long since she'd been on a date. As long as she kept him at arm's length, didn't let their relationship move beyond casual flirting, they'd be okay.

Besides, there was a new red dress hanging in her closet just waiting to make its debut. Ryan wouldn't be able to take his eyes off her.

Chapter Six

$\mathcal{R}$yan waited until he could no longer see Tori's car before he returned to the restaurant. That was one pretty woman. Sophisticated in a way that made him feel like the clod he was. But this was the first time he'd ever been alone with her, and he managed not to stumble over his words. She'd even started to open up with him a little, let down her guard when she talked about her father. He'd glimpsed something beneath the flirty surface, the hint of a serious side of Tori Sanderson in those round blue eyes. It made her appear the slightest bit vulnerable, like maybe she wasn't as self-assured as she'd always seemed.

Of course, that was before the Dynamic Duo showed up and dumped coffee all over her.

He shoved the door open with a force born from irritation. Just wait until he got his hands on Loralee.

She stood just inside, eyes wide. "Ryan, I'm sorry. I didn't aim to mess up your date."

"No?" He couldn't help spitting the word, just a little. "Tell me, Loralee, what did you think you were doing?"

She winced at his tone. "I don't know. I couldn't seem to help myself. I just wanted to see her. You know, see if she's as pretty as I remembered." She hung her head in a perfect imitation of the two boys who cowered behind her. "I'm real sorry."

"Me too," Butch whispered.

Cody nodded, his face a mask of misery.

They all three looked so miserable Ryan couldn't keep hold of his anger. He slid a stern glance to each of them before relenting. "I forgive you. Just don't let it happen again."

The boys each heaved a sigh and whirled to gallop toward a couple of soft chairs in the corner.

Loralee wrinkled her nose. "I guess she ditched you?"

"Yeah, for tonight." He grinned. "But I'm taking her to dinner Tuesday."

Her face lit, and she clapped her hands. "I knew it! I could tell by the way you two were mooning at each other that she liked you. Just wait 'til I tell Tammy you've got a date with a homecoming queen."

Ryan cast a look toward the ceiling. If there was one person with a bigger fixation on his love life than his sister-in-law, it was Tammy Adams, his mother. "Don't get Mom involved in this. It's just one date. Tori probably won't want to go out with me again after Tuesday."

"Why not?"

Ryan was saved from answering by the girl behind the counter announcing two Wild Berry Bombs and a Strawberry Stinger. He picked up the boys' drinks and delivered them while Loralee took hers to the table where he'd been sitting with Tori. When he joined her, he saw she'd cleaned up the spilled coffee mess.

"Why won't she go out with you again?" Loralee asked as he resumed his seat.

He picked up his expensive coffee and sipped. Lukewarm. "C'mon. You saw her. She's gorgeous."

"So? You're not all that ugly." Loralee grinned as she dunked her straw up and down in the slushy drink. "You two look cute together."

"I don't know. She's probably used to being taken out to expensive restaurants by men who drive BMWs." He shrugged. "I'm just a plain old boy from the country."

Loralee set her cup down with a thud. "Don't sell yourself short. You've got a lot going for you. A good job, and you're going to college. Why, I know a dozen girls who'd jump at a chance to hook up with you."

Right. Time to change the subject, or she'd be filling up his social calendar with blind dates. He took a final sip from the coffee, which didn't taste nearly as good after it had cooled, and set the mug on the table.

"I'd better get going. I've got a paper to finish before class tomorrow."

"No, wait!" Loralee straightened, a look of dismay on her face. "You can't leave yet, not before you tell me the details. Where are you taking her? What are you wearing? Are you bringing her flowers?"

Does she think I'm an idiot? He waved in the general direction of the boys. "And risk a repeat performance? Not a chance."

"Oh, come on." She grinned. "I'd leave them home next time."

Laughing, he launched himself to his feet. "Tell Walt I'll see him after work on Wednesday. I'll tell you about it then, *after* it's over."

"Bring her flowers," she called after him as he headed for the door. "It'll make a good impression."

He lifted a hand in farewell and exited the restaurant.

The smell of cinnamon and hazelnut coffee saturated the interior of Tori's car as thoroughly as the latte had saturated her clothes.

The air conditioner turned the silky wet fabric chilly, while the edges that had started to dry felt stiff. She didn't want to drive all the way back to Lexington like this. There was the box of her old clothes back at Gram's house. She could drop by there and dig something out to change into before she headed home.

But it was up in the attic, near that *other* box.

Tori's grip tightened on the steering wheel. Ryan asked why she'd never tried to find Daddy. But why should she? It wasn't her place to find him. If he wanted to see his daughters, he would have contacted them. The years had piled up, fifteen of them, without a single word.

A stoplight ahead turned red, and she rolled to a halt. A couple pushing a stroller stepped off the curb and crossed the street past her front bumper. A few years older than her. The father pushed, both hands on the stroller's handle, while the mother walked at his side. Tori's insides knotted. Had Mom and Daddy walked like this with her when she was a baby? Would this father, too, one day desert his child to go off and...

And what? What had happened in Daddy's life to make him walk away from his daughters without a backward glance? Did he just get tired of being bothered with them?

Which was so not fair. They never did anything to drive him away.

Except cry for Mom when he took us to the fair without her.

The light changed. The car rolled forward as she took her foot off the brake. She gave her head a shake, trying to dislodge the disturbing thoughts that hovered like a thick fog in her mind. That hadn't been the only time she cried, either. Her memory was sketchy, but Tori knew there were a couple of other times when Daddy had come to pick them up and she cried. And once, she'd refused to go at all. He tried to bribe her with ice cream, but she staunchly refused. She'd stood beside Mom at the front window watching Joan and Allie climb into Daddy's car, her stomach churning.

It couldn't have been easy for him, having his youngest daughter rebuff him like that.

She jerked her head upright as the thought slapped at her brain. Her deadbeat dad deserved no sympathy at all, not from her. She reached down and cranked the stereo up loud, willing the music to drown out any more ridiculous thoughts. A nine-year-old child was not to blame for her parent's failures.

Only one car sat in the driveway at Gram's house. Mom's. Tori breathed a sigh of relief as she pulled in behind it. Eric and Allie had left, and Joan's car was gone, too. Good. She didn't feel like facing her sisters and their nosy questions.

She let herself into the house and called down the stairs that led to the finished basement where Mom's and Joan's bedrooms lay.

"Mom? Are you down there?"

Mom appeared at the bottom of the stairs, surprise etched on her face. "Tori, I thought you'd gone back to Lexington." She started up the stairs, then made a face when she caught sight of Tori's blouse. "What happened?"

"Don't ask." Tori scrunched her nose. "Where is everybody?"

"Allie and Eric took the baby home, and Joan drove Mother back to her apartment." She peered into Tori's face as she ascended to the landing. "They said you left without saying goodbye."

"I didn't want to answer any questions about going for a simple cup of coffee with the guy they were obviously pushing me toward." Tori rolled her eyes expansively, which made Mom smile. "I'm going upstairs to get that box of my old clothes so I can change before I head back to my apartment."

Mom followed her down the hallway and easily reached the rope pull for the attic stairs. None of the Sanderson girls had inherited their mother's lanky height, but Joan came closest. Tori was the shortest of the three.

"Do you need help?" Mom asked.

"Um, maybe getting it down the stairs. Let me see."

Mom waited in the hallway as Tori climbed up. She rose into heat and darkness, and groped for the string that turned on the overhead light. The ringing of the telephone reached her from below.

"I hope that's not the hospital calling me in to work." Mom's voice sounded irritated. "I'd better grab it."

"Okay."

Tori looked around. Joan and Allie hadn't accomplished much after she left. In fact, it looked like they'd only gone through one more box before they gave up. There, near the stairs, was Tori's stuff. And over there—she gulped—was Daddy's box. The way they were acting, she'd half expected to find it gone, taken over to Allie's house for safekeeping.

Tori chewed at her lower lip. If anyone ever did want to find Daddy, they'd need something to work with, some sort of identification. She stared at the box, hesitant to touch it. So many memories in there, all of them bad.

Her feet moved almost of their own accord. She had to stoop as the rafters sloped toward the plywood floor. With a quick glance at the opening to make sure Mom wasn't coming, she reached out with a tentative hand and unfolded the flaps on the top of the box. Maybe Allie had taken the shoebox with her. She wouldn't have cared about those old textbooks, but she hadn't wanted to get rid of the pictures. Tori pulled back the comforter and blanket, and lifted one of the heavy books to reveal the bent corner of the shoebox.

Her heart's pounding sounded unnaturally loud in the quiet attic. Her hands shook as she freed the shoebox from its hiding place. When she did, she caught the corner of the folder beneath it, spilling a thick stack of papers into the box, old tax forms from way back in 1990. A quick glance at the names showed both her parents, Carla Hancock Sanderson and Thomas Alan Sanderson. Their names ... and their social security numbers.

Identification.

With a guilty glance toward the opening, she snatched up the form and stuffed it beneath the crushed lid of the shoebox. Then she hastily replaced the comforter and blanket, and took the shoebox to the box containing her old clothes. Working quickly, she buried the pictures in the center of folded clothes, snatched up a shirt she hadn't worn since high school, and refolded the flaps to seal the box. She finished just as Mom returned to the foot of the attic stairs.

"It was Vonda from the bowling league, wanting to tell me about her grandson's soccer game." Mom climbed the bottom few steps, her head emerging through the opening in the floor. "Is that it? Here, hand it down to me."

Tori scooted the box across the dusty plywood. "Be careful. It's not heavy, but it's awkward."

"I'll just slide it down the stairs. Ummph."

Mom jumped backward as she lost her grip on the box and it tumbled down the rickety wooden stairs. Tori held her breath, certain the flaps would come open and the contents would spill out. But they held, thank goodness.

Light glinted off Mom's glasses as she turned a grin upward. "Well, that's one way to do it."

Tori pulled the string, plunging the attic into darkness, and descended backward to the floor. While Mom put the stairs away, she ducked into the bathroom with her shirt and performed a quick clean-up job on skin that smelled like stale coffee. She emerged to find Mom trying to wrangle the box down the hallway, and rushed forward.

"Let's each grab an end."

They hefted their load through the house, out the door, and to Tori's car. The sun had started its descent in an expanse of bright blue sky, but there were still several hours of daylight left. Good, because she didn't enjoy driving the rural roads between Danville and Lexington in the dark.

"How are you going to get it in your apartment?" Mom asked when they'd stored the box in the trunk.

"Oh, I'll get a couple of friends to help." Tori looped the key ring around her finger and jingled. "Mom, can I ask you something?"

"Of course."

Tori didn't look at her. "Why do you think Daddy never tried to get in touch with us?"

She kept her gaze fixed on the grass, but saw Mom stiffen out of the corner of her eye. Since the day Daddy left, he'd become a taboo subject around the Sanderson house. Mom never discussed him, and the few times the girls had tried to ask her about him during those first lonely months, she'd looked like she was barely able to contain her anger. After a few tentative attempts early on, they'd reached an unspoken agreement not to bring up his name.

"I don't know." Mom's voice was tight. After a moment's silence she went on in a resigned tone. "But I suspect it was because he didn't want to pay child support."

That's what Allie said the last time they talked about it.

"You could have made him, you know." Tori let anger creep into her voice. "There are laws about that."

She glanced up in time to see Mom's shoulders heave with a silent laugh. "They were harder to enforce fifteen years ago. And besides"—she crossed her arms, her hands gripping her elbows—"we did okay without his help. Didn't we?"

Mom's slender neck seemed even longer than usual as her chin rose into the air. No doubt she'd faced some tough times raising three girls on her own. She'd had to swallow her pride when she moved them in with her parents so she could go to college and get her nursing degree. And she had provided the best home she could, had surrounded her girls with love. Tori felt a renewed rush of admiration for her.

She stepped forward and wrapped her arms around her mother. "We did just fine."

Mom returned her embrace, and then a soft sigh tickled the top of Tori's head. "He might also have been trying to avoid me. The last time I saw him ... Well, we didn't part on the best of terms."

"That's no excuse for deserting his children."

"Of course it isn't." Mom stepped back, her hands resting on Tori's shoulders as she searched her face. "Whatever his reason, it wasn't your fault. You know that, right?"

Tori's head dipped as she looked at the ground. Maybe it was her fault, a little. Maybe if she'd acted happier to see him when he came to pick them up. Or if she hadn't stayed with Mom that day.

Mom gripped her chin in a finger and thumb and tilted it upward until Tori was looking at her. "It wasn't your fault, Tori. You were a child. Your father's problems had nothing to do with you." She paused, then she continued in a confiding tone. "For the first few months I hoped he had gone somewhere to get himself cleaned up. But when the months became a year, and then another ..."

The sadness in her eyes tore at Tori's conscience. She should shut her mouth now, drop the subject. But this was the most information she'd ever gotten out of Mom. The chance may never come again. And besides, Daddy's absence worried her like a loose tooth she couldn't stop wiggling.

"Did you ever try to find him?"

Mom didn't answer at first, but studied Tori's face. "What brought all this up? Why all these questions now, after he's been gone so long?"

Tori glanced toward the house. "We found some of his stuff up in the attic, and I just..." She shrugged.

Mom sighed, and shook her head. "The answer is no, I never tried to find him. I wouldn't have known where to look."

"What about contacting his relatives?" Mom opened her mouth, but Tori rushed on before she could speak. "I know he was an only child and his parents were dead, but surely there was someone else he would have stayed in touch with. Cousins, aunts and uncles, that sort of thing."

A guilty expression overtook Mom's features. "You girls don't know anything about your father, and that's my fault. I'm sorry."

"No, Mom, it's not." Tori grabbed her hand and squeezed. "You couldn't be expected to talk about something that was so painful to you. I'm sorry I brought it up. Let's just drop it."

Mom shook her head. "No, you have questions and you need answers. I guess I thought you knew, but you were young when he left. And even when he was still with us, he didn't discuss his past, did he?" She bit her lip. "The truth is, your father was turned over to the courts when he was six years old by a drug addict mother who didn't want to be bothered with him. He was raised in the foster care system. He never knew who his father was, and had no memory of any relatives except his mother." She squeezed Tori's hand, her face soft with compassion. "When he was eight, the foster family he was living with at the time told him his mother had been found dead on the streets of Indianapolis."

Tori's mind reeled. What a terrible story. No wonder Daddy didn't want to talk about it when she was younger. She backed up a step to lean against her car. In the top of the tree next door, a bird began a joyful song, totally oblivious to the sad story being told a dozen feet below.

Mom's voice was soft as she continued. "It's really amazing that he was able to come out of that life and make something of himself. Even though he eventually succumbed to the same addiction as his mother."

"I know he smoked pot. Allie told us."

Mom heaved a sigh. "Oh, honey, he was doing more than that when he left. I thought if I gave him an ultimatum..." She shook her head. "But that was much later. When I first met him, he didn't even drink beer. He was working as a frame carpenter building houses. He wasn't afraid of hard work, I'll say that about him."

"He didn't go to college?" Tori nodded toward the house. "We found some old psychology textbooks up there."

A nostalgic smile curved her mouth. "Those were his. I remember the day he bought them at a garage sale. He said he'd been in enough therapy sessions that he could easily sit on the other side of the couch. Allie picked that up from him, I guess. He never read them, though."

This was the most Mom had ever talked about her ex-husband. Tori studied her mother's face, the faraway look in the eyes behind the glasses. Apparently not all her memories of Daddy were bad. He had to have had some good qualities. Otherwise, why would she have married him to begin with?

Tori knew the basics of their relationship from the stories Daddy told her when she was little, before the divorce. How he came into the drugstore where Mom worked as a clerk, looking for aspirin, but ended up finding the prettiest girl in town. He swept her off her feet and they were married a few months later. Whenever Daddy recounted that story to his fascinated little girls, a faint blush would color Mom's cheeks. It had always seemed romantic to Tori when she was little. Then after Daddy left, she'd taken it to heart as a lesson in the dangers of rushing into a relationship.

If only she had the nerve to remind Joan of that lesson.

A lone cloud moving across the bright blue sky passed in front of the sun, plunging the yard where they stood into shadow. Mom, lost in some long-ago memory, gave a slight shake and straightened. Her expression became closed, and Tori knew the moment for questions had passed. Frustrating, because she had so many more.

Reluctantly, she pushed away from the car. "Well, I'd better get home. I've got a ton of work to do tonight."

Mom hugged her, then stepped back as Tori got into the driver's seat. "Don't work too hard. You'll make yourself sick if you don't get enough sleep."

Tori started the engine and reversed out of the driveway. She thrust a hand out the window and waved. A shaft of guilt shot through her at the sight of her mother's tight smile as she waved back. Tori had stirred up some memories, and no doubt they weren't all pleasant.

But she had gotten some important information about her father, details she'd never heard. Did Allie and Joan know of Daddy's sad past? She scowled into the rearview mirror. Probably. They'd been older when Daddy left, so they probably heard scraps of information he'd let drop back when she was too young to pay attention. And after he left they'd remained faithful to the unspoken family rule to keep mum on the subject of Thomas Alan Sanderson. Or, maybe they talked to each other, but didn't discuss their memories with their baby sister. Like everything else they excluded her from.

When she left the town's last stoplight behind her, she put the car on cruise control and let the wind tangle her curls. Rolling green hills dotted with patches of yellow daffodils zoomed by on either side of the road. She should concentrate on the long night ahead of her, and coming up with a plan to finish all the work she had tonight so she could start fresh on her Maguire marketing plan in the morning. But her mind refused to cooperate. Her thoughts hovered on the box in the trunk, and the memories contained in that shoebox.

Were there pleasant surprises in there for her? She'd refused to dwell on Daddy in any positive way for so long that she'd convinced herself there was nothing good about him to remember. But that was a childish attitude. Of course there had been good times. She just needed a reminder.

But did she, really? What craziness had possessed her to pick up those photographs, when she should just leave the past alone? She did *not* have time to stir up a bunch of yucky feelings right now. She had too much to do in the next few weeks to become sidetracked.

What was it Joan and Allie had said? If we didn't forgive the people who've hurt us, the pain held us back. Tori's grip on the steering wheel tightened as she guided the car around a curve in the road. Well, she wasn't ready to forgive Daddy for the hurt he'd inflicted on Mom. Or on her. But her sisters' attitudes were understandable. They'd been older when he left; they'd had more chance to develop a relationship with him, and therefore were more ready to forgive. In fact, they were both a little like him, in their own ways. Allie's tendency to delve into the psychological reasons behind every little act obviously came from Daddy. And Joan, with her dark hair and athletic build, was physically the most like him of the three Sanderson sisters. Plus, Daddy had been quiet, contemplative, like Joan.

What had Tori inherited from him? As far as she could tell, not a single thing. And he'd left before she had an opportunity to find out.

With a suddenness that left her breathless, she wanted to know. *Needed* to know. Not just whether or not she had anything in common with the man who'd become a shadowy figure from her past, but why he left. What possible reason could he have had for deserting them? For deserting her? Maybe that box held something that could help her understand.

But first she needed enough courage to take it out of the trunk.

Chapter Seven

Ryan punched the button on the cash register and glanced at the total.

"That'll be $54.38." He slid the coil of roofing nails into a bag.

The man on the other side of the counter scowled as he handed over a credit card. "I shoulda just hired somebody. By the time I finish buying all the stuff to put that roof on, it's gonna cost me near as much."

Ryan slid the card through the register's reader. "If you find somebody who's good and cheap, let me know. I'm helping my brother build a house out toward Junction City, and I hate roofing. When we get that far, maybe I can convince him to hire the job out." He grinned. "Otherwise I might just disappear for a couple of weeks."

The man's lips twisted as he signed the receipt. "I hear you." He tossed the pen on the counter and snatched up his bag. "See you later."

Ryan nodded a farewell. "Be careful up on that roof."

As the customer threaded his way through the racks and shelves, the automatic door whooshed open. A familiar face stepped into the store. Ryan bit back a groan.

Great. She's probably coming in to tell me what a goofball I am for inviting my nephews on our coffee date.

The man with the nails nodded and mumbled a greeting to Allie as they passed. She paused just inside as the doors closed, her head turning as she searched the store. When she caught sight of him, her smile widened and she hurried forward, her blonde toddler balanced on her hip.

"Hey, Allie. You in the market for hardware?" He picked up an item from the box on the counter and held it up. "Duct tape, maybe?"

She rolled her eyes as she came forward and set the baby on the counter. "Thanks anyway. We just left the gym, and I thought I'd stop by and see how yesterday went."

Ryan tossed the duct tape back in the box. "Tori didn't tell you?"

"No." Her lips twisted with disgust. "She snuck out right after you called and didn't even tell us she was going. And she didn't answer her cell last night, either. For me *or* Joan."

Interesting. He'd assumed Tori would immediately search out her sisters and outline the harrowing details of her run-in with Butch and Cody. Maybe she didn't think it was that big a disaster after all. Ryan's mood lifted at the thought.

"So?" Allie took a tube of glass adhesive out of the baby's busy hands and moved the box out of reach. The kid let out a screech of fury, which made Ryan wince and to which Allie was apparently immune. "How did it go? Did she have a good time?"

He'd just as soon not go into the whole thing, but Allie's face wore the unmistakable expression of a master busybody. The women in his family looked just like that when they got on the trail of something they wanted to know. If Allie was anything like Loralee or Mom, she wouldn't leave until he satisfied her curiosity.

But maybe that wasn't all bad. For whatever reason, she and Joan seemed to approve of him dating their sister. Maybe he could get some advice about Tuesday night.

"Uhh, no." He scrunched his face. "Well, maybe. It was okay at the beginning. But then we had a little incident."

He recounted the humiliating story. When he got to the part where the boys baptized her in cinnamon coffee, Allie winced.

"Ouch. That's not good."

"Yeah. But it ended well. She agreed to go out to a late dinner with me Tuesday night."

Allie's eyes went round above a wide grin. "She did? That's terrific news, Ryan." She rescued a package of AA batteries just before it went into the baby's mouth. "No, sweetie, you can't eat that." The volume of her voice rose above a second shriek of protest. "So, where are you taking her?"

Ryan picked up a discarded customer receipt and rolled it absently. "I haven't decided. Any suggestions?"

"Hmmm." Allie lifted the crying child off the counter and settled her on a hip. "Something cozy and private, so you can talk. Nothing too expensive just yet, though."

Well, that was a relief. He couldn't afford anything expensive. He'd just paid his tuition for his summer term classes earlier this month, and he didn't have much left over.

"What about deSha's?" he asked. "I've only been there once, but it's quiet and nice. And it's only a block from her office."

"Perfect. As long as the weather is nice, you can walk, and you'll go right by the fountains in Triangle Park. They'll be lit up and romantic." A pleased grin settled on her features. If she'd been a redhead instead of blonde, she would have looked just like Loralee. "Now, about the dinner conversation. Tori's totally into her job, so you might want to bone up on marketing stuff before tomorrow night."

"Marketing stuff?"

She nodded. "She's got to come up with a marketing plan for a restaurant company, so she's focused on that. If you can talk to her about it, she'll feel like you're taking an interest in her work, you know?"

That made sense. And he did have a few basic marketing courses under his belt, though he'd have to pull out his notes and go over them. Not a bad piece of advice. He tossed the rolled-up receipt in the trashcan and eyed Allie suspiciously. "Does Tori know you're here?"

The blue-green eyes went round. "No, and I don't think you should tell her."

"Why not?"

The baby was working herself up into a major tantrum. Her little face turned red under the thin blonde hair as she wailed and stretched her chubby hands toward the rack of batteries now out of reach. "Because Tori has a mind of her own, and I don't want her to think she's being manipulated. Otherwise she'll drop you like you've got a contagious disease, and she'll be furious enough with me and Joan to make family gatherings a living nightmare." She flashed an apologetic smile as she struggled to keep hold of the squirming child in her arms. "I've got to get her home and put her down for a nap. But I'm glad things are progressing according to plan."

Plan? Whose plan?

She whirled to leave. As she reached the automatic doors, Ryan thought of a question.

"Hey, Allie." She turned. "Should I take her flowers?"

She grinned. "Now you're thinking! But not roses. It's too early for roses. She likes Gerbera daisies."

The baby's cries were silenced by the closing of the doors.

No roses, huh? Well, that was good. He couldn't afford roses anyway. He'd never heard of Gerbera—was that a color, like fuchsia, or what? Well, whatever, daisies had to be cheaper than roses. Surely he could afford a few daisies.

The long, wooden runway glowed like a landing strip at night, the crowd beyond the bright stage lights nothing but a blur. Tori hovered behind the curtain and watched Kate, in the wings on the opposite side, for the signal that her turn had arrived. The skirt and blouse Tori had selected was ultra-chic, ultra-professional, and the Bournes on her feet a classy accompaniment to the ensemble. Her makeup was impeccable, the shiny pink lipstick the perfect shade to complement both the pale pink silk of the blouse and the bright blue of her eyes. She looked her best, and she knew it. This trip down the runway would be a piece of cake, and then she'd become the next AE and get to wear a crown besides.

Across the stage, Kate gestured impatiently. Tori inhaled, drawing courage into her lungs, and stepped out from behind the cover of the curtains. She catwalked smoothly to the center of the stage, stopped, and executed a perfect half turn. The unseen crowd gasped with pleasure as they caught sight of her. Cameras flashed from the darkness. Exhilarated, Tori extended one elegantly clad foot and headed forward, down the runway—

And stopped. The sleek, slender Bournes had become clunky combat boots. Horror spread like a stain in her chest as she realized the skirt she'd donned was now a pair of—gasp!—striped Bermuda shorts. The pink blouse had become a horrible cocoa brown with an orange tie that didn't even match! Where had her beautiful outfit gone? A snicker from the darkness multiplied as the crowd caught sight of her humiliating ensemble. Soon their laughter filled the vast auditorium, an assault on her eardrums. Fire burned in her face as she whirled to run to the safety of the stage curtains, only to find her way blocked.

Mitch stood watching her humiliation with that smug look plastered on his face. "You are such a fraud," he said, shaking his head.

She started to protest, to say there'd been a terrible mistake, she wouldn't dare go out in public looking like this. But when she saw what he held in his hand, the words stuck in her throat. She stood, frozen, as he pulled the lid off of the cup and slung the coffee straight at—

Tori sat straight up in bed, her heart pounding. She put her hands on each side of her head and squeezed, gulping huge draughts of air. What a horrible nightmare! She peeked beneath the covers, just to assure herself that her satiny pink pajamas hadn't morphed into a fashion disaster while she slept. Reassured, she collapsed backward onto her pillow, willing her pulse to slow.

She hadn't had a dream like that in years, not since college when she used to have nightmares about showing up for class and realizing she had no clothes on. Those dreams had produced the same explosion of heart-pounding horror and deep panic. This one was perfectly explainable, though. They'd uncovered those horrible shorts in one of the boxes of Grandpa's clothes up in the attic yesterday, along with the brownie uniform and the crown. The coffee...well, the origin of that was obvious. And her anxiety over the pictures locked in the trunk of her car, not to mention the competition with Mitch for the Maguire account, was very real. Mitch's words in the dream resounded in her ear. *You are such a fraud.*

She heaved a sigh and tried to expel the lingering feelings of disquiet with the breath. It wasn't real. Just a bad dream, the result of a stressful day topped off by hours of work. What time had she finally gone to bed? Sometime after four. She turned her head toward the nightstand and opened a bleary eye to check the time—

And jerked upright for a second time. Eight fifteen! She'd overslept.

Her watch read nearly nine thirty when Tori stepped off the elevator with her handbag dangling from one shoulder and her laptop case from the other. Fran, the firm's receptionist, looked up from the computer monitor resting on the corner of her reception desk. She lifted her arm and made a show of looking at her watch.

"You're late." Her pencil-etched eyebrows rose. "Kate's called twice."

Tori stopped mid-step. "She's supposed to be on a flight to Chicago."

Fran planted both elbows on the desk and rested her chin on her palms, her acrylic nails sparkling in the fluorescent light. "Her plane was delayed. She's sitting in the Lexington airport."

Great. She'd taken her time getting dressed, counting on the fact that she'd be in the office by the time Kate landed in Chicago. If her boss had opted out of leaving a message and dialed the receptionist to find her, she must be irritated. "Why didn't she call my cell phone?"

"She tried. It went straight to voice mail."

Tori's shoulders sagged. The battery had probably died again. When was the last time she charged it? She couldn't remember. "Did she say what she wanted?"

Fran shook her head. "But the second time she asked to speak to Mitch."

Terrific. She let out a loud sigh and headed around the desk. Fran stopped her with a lifted finger. The pink acrylic, flecked with metallic sparkles, looked more like weapons than nails, a female version of Edward Scissorhands.

"You got another call too. Your sister, Allie. About fifteen minutes ago."

Probably calling to yell at her for leaving without saying goodbye yesterday. That was a call she could wait before returning. "Thanks, Fran."

She went to her cubicle and fished her cell phone out of her purse. Sure enough, the battery was completely dead. She bent over to rummage beneath the desk, where a mass of tangled wires sprouted from the power strip on the floor.

A familiar, insolent voice sounded from behind. "Looking good this morning, Sanderson."

Tori straightened in a hurry and whirled around to find Mitch staring at her backside. His expression managed to look charming and wolfish at the same time. If he wasn't so nice looking, she'd fire back an appropriately scathing response, but that little boy grin disarmed her every time. She smoothed her skirt with nervous fingers and tried to forget his taunting words in the dream.

His grin widened. "Or should I say you're looking good this *afternoon?*"

She fought her instinct to stiffen, and instead forced an unconcerned smile as she stooped—facing him, this time—to grasp the phone charger's cord. "I was up late getting some projects off my plate so I can focus on my new one." Her mouth snapped shut. She didn't owe Mitch an explanation. He was a co-worker, not her boss.

Not yet, anyway.

She banished that thought and hid any trace of worry from her tone. "I hear you've been covering for me this morning."

He wandered in and sank into the single guest chair, elbows wide, hands cupped behind his head. "Not really. Kate had some questions about that report you gave her yesterday. I couldn't answer them. You might want to check your voice mail." His face took on a carefully nonchalant expression. "So, you haven't started on your plan for the Maguire account yet?"

Tori hid a triumphant grin. He was worried. Good. The more effort he spent worrying about what she was coming up with, the less he had to come up with some brilliant plan she couldn't top. She tugged on the charger cord and stepped over the muscular legs that stretched into the center of her cubicle.

"Not yet." She plugged the charger into her cell phone and set it on the edge of her desk, then unzipped her case and slid the laptop out. "But I've got a few ideas."

Totally untrue, because she'd been too distracted thinking about Daddy and that stupid shoebox still in the trunk of her car while she worked on the other projects. But it couldn't hurt for Mitch to think she was well on the path of a dazzling campaign. She slid her laptop into the docking station and pressed the power button before giving Mitch a politely inquisitive look. "What about you? Have you started yet?"

His habitual smirk deepened. "I've got a few ideas myself."

Worry shot through Tori like a spear. What had he managed to come up with in the twenty-four hours since they'd gotten their assignment? Behind that overly confident exterior, Mitch really was a smart guy. Smarter than her? She snatched up her purse and looked away as she stored it in the desk drawer so he wouldn't see the worry in her face. It was entirely possible he'd come up with a better campaign than hers.

But she was not about to let him see even a hint of insecurity in her. If he got a whiff of her worries, he'd find a way to use it to his advantage.

She picked up her cell phone, tethered by the cord, and schooled her features into a mirror image of his confident smirk. "If you'll excuse me, I need to check my voice mail now."

He rose slowly, then stepped around the desk to stand beside her. She had to tilt her head slightly to look up at him, which set her teeth on edge. He smiled down into her face, obviously enjoying the advantage his height gave him. "Have a good day, Sanderson."

He sauntered toward his own cubicle without a backward glance. Tori found her hands had clenched into fists. What was up with him calling her by her last name all of a sudden? He had always called her either Tori, like everyone else, or occasionally Victoria when he wanted to be really unctuous. Calling her Sanderson felt like an acknowledgment of the competition between them. Almost like a challenge being issued.

She forced herself to relax her grip on the cell phone. If that's the way he wanted to play it, fine. She would give this project her best shot either way.

Even though she didn't have the faintest idea how to begin.

The symphonic ring of her cell phone jerked Tori away from her computer screen. She glanced at her watch. Almost seven. No wonder her stomach was rumbling. She'd worked nonstop all day, mostly putting out fires for Kate, who was apparently bored with the conference and chose to spend the day tormenting her employees remotely. It was only in the past two hours that the phone had finally quieted down enough to allow Tori to concentrate on her special project. The skeleton of a plan lay before her, frightening in the absence of any real creativity. Just a list of tasks that would need to be performed to produce even the most generic of presentations, but at least it was a start.

She pressed the button to answer the call without looking at the display. "Tori Sanderson."

"Why are you avoiding me?"

Allie. And she sounded supremely irritated.

"I'm not avoiding you. I'm *working*." She propped the phone on her shoulder and clicked Save with the mouse. The near-perfect silence surrounding the office outside of her cubicle was broken only by the faint hum of the air conditioner, a sound she never heard during the day before most of the staff had gone home.

"You're still at work? I figured you'd be home by now."

Tori toggled the window over to her email and breathed a sigh of relief that there were no new messages from Kate. "Not for a while yet."

A disgusted grunt sounded in her ear. "You could take a five-minute break to call your sister back. I left, like, a gazillion messages."

Tori leaned back in her chair and arched her back to stretch muscles stiff from several hours of inactivity. She'd deleted all of Allie's messages and a couple from Joan as well. There had not been a single free moment to return their calls. "I haven't taken a break to do anything, even eat."

A tempting aroma tickled her nose and stirred up an answering rumble in her empty stomach. Pepperoni. Somebody else was still here, and they had pizza. She stood and rose on her tiptoes to look over the top of her cubicle wall, but didn't spot anyone. Even Mr. Connolly's office door was closed. He must have left while she was focused on her plan.

"Then it's time you did. I've been waiting all day to hear about your date with Ryan yesterday."

Tori dropped down off her toes and scowled. "It wasn't a date. We just had coffee. We were only there about thirty minutes."

"Yeah, but would you have stayed longer if his nephew hadn't spilled coffee on you?"

Mom was a blabbermouth. Well, Tori hadn't asked her not to tell Allie and Joan, so of course she wouldn't think anything about it. "Maybe."

"So you had a good time? Up until then, I mean."

"Yes."

Tori smiled. Brief answers would drive her nosy sister nuts. She knew very well that Allie wanted details, and lots of them.

"So, what was he wearing? What did you two talk about? Are you going to see each other again?"

Tori picked up a pen and clicked the push button with her thumb as she gave each answer. "Jeans. Nothing much. And yes." Disgust flooded Allie's tone. "You're being purposefully obstinate. Wait! Did you say yes, you're going out with him again?"

Tori laughed at her sister's obvious delight. "That's right. He's taking me to dinner tomorrow night." Then she sobered. "But I don't know, Allie. I accepted in a moment of weakness, and I'm regretting it. He and I really are way too different."

"You keep saying that, but I'm not so sure. He's intelligent, like you. He's got a good sense of humor, like you. And he's definitely attractive, don't you think?"

An image of Ryan's warm smile and muscled shoulders rose in her mind. She pulled open the bottom drawer of her desk, kicked her shoes off, and propped her feet on the drawer's edge. "Oh, yeah. But..." She bit her lip. "I don't want to sound like a snob, but he works in a *hardware* store."

"So you're only dating lawyers now? Or rich guys?"

Tori heaved a sigh. "It's not that, honestly. But I don't know what kind of relationship I could have with someone who doesn't speak the same language as me, you know? I mean, he wouldn't even understand what it's like to work in an office. How could I talk to him about my job, my goals? And what about his? I mean, I just couldn't work up a lot of sympathy for someone who's major stress of the day is not being able to help a customer find the right size plumbing tool, or whatever it is they sell in those places."

A chuckle behind her sent steel into Tori's spine. She jerked upright, her stocking feet hitting the floor, and swiveled around in her seat. Mitch stood in the doorway of her cubicle, a deeper-than-normal smirk on his face and a pizza box in his hand. Heat rushed into her face. How long had he been standing there?

"I've got to go, Allie." Her voice held all the outrage she could muster as she gave Mitch the evil eye. "I've got to deal with an issue."

"But, I wan—"

She disconnected the call without waiting to hear Allie's protest and shot to her feet, glaring the whole time into Mitch's grinning face. "Were you eavesdropping on my private conversation?"

"Hey, I couldn't help it." He gestured at the cubicle opening. "No doors, you know."

Blood roared in her ears, whether from anger or embarrassment, Tori couldn't tell. "You could have announced your presence instead of standing there listening."

"Sorry." He didn't look one bit sorry with that gloating grin plastered on his face. He raised the pizza box in her direction, like a peace offering. "I was just coming over to see if you wanted some."

She didn't allow her face to lose even a touch of her anger, but she didn't stop him as he sidestepped into the room and circled the perimeter with exaggerated care to keep as much distance between them as possible. He set the box on the edge of her desk and took a backward step, hands held up in a gesture of surrender.

Tori didn't take her gaze off of him as she reached down and lifted the lid suspiciously. The spicy smell of pepperoni and tomato sauce increased, and her mouth watered painfully in response. She'd had nothing but coffee and soda all day, and her knees felt suddenly weak. Two pieces of pizza lay temptingly within reach. Okay, maybe he was a jerk, but he was a jerk who came bearing food. She managed a grudging "Thanks" as she lifted one of the slices.

He grabbed the guest chair and turned it around to straddle as she returned to her chair. He waited until she bit into the pizza before saying, "So, you've got a date with a plumber tomorrow night?"

Great. Just great.

She chewed with exaggerated care while she fixed him with an icy stare. When she swallowed, she said, "He's not a plumber. He works in a hardware store."

Mitch shrugged. "Same difference. Only a plumber makes more money."

The sound of a door opening on the far side of the office interrupted Tori's sharp retort. Someone else was also working late. Mitch gave her a look full of questions, and she shrugged in response. Then they both stood to look over the tops of the cubicle walls.

Mr. Connolly stood in the doorway of his office. "I hope you'll take some time to think about it before you make a rash decision, Phil. You're a valuable asset to the firm."

Phil Osborne's muttered reply was barely audible. He strode away from Mr. Connolly's office around the outer edge of the maze of cubicles, in their direction. Tori and Mitch remained silent as he approached, his head lowered and his shoulders slumped. He didn't look up as he passed. The defeated expression on his kind face made Tori's heart ache.

She exchanged a sad glance with Mitch as they both sank back into their chairs.

"I feel so sorry for him," she whispered. "It's not fair. He's been here longer. He's earned the position."

Mitch shook his head. "This is business. It doesn't have to be fair. Kate is a hundred times more aggressive than Osborne. She'll take this firm to the next level. The partners know that."

Tori nodded. Mitch was right. Mr. Connolly and Mr. Farrin had to choose the person they thought would be the best for the firm in the long run. It was their company, after all.

Mitch got to his feet. "I've had it for today. I'm heading out." He started for the door but surprised Tori by stepping around the desk and standing next to her chair. He placed a hand on the surface and leaned down, his face inches from hers. She caught a faint whisk of his musky aftershave. "One more thing." His voice dropped to a whisper as he held her gaze with his. "You and I speak the same language, Tori."

He was gone before she could gather her whirling thoughts enough to reply.

His footsteps faded away until the only sound she could hear was the pounding of her heart. There had been no hint of his trademark grin as Mitch uttered those astounding words. In fact, his eyes had held a note of sincerity she'd never seen in her handsome co-worker. And her pulse was stuttering like a lovesick teenager's in response.

With a slow motion, she set the pizza back in the box. She didn't think she could eat another bite.

Chapter Eight

The wipers scraped away the drizzle on Ryan's windshield as he drove down Fourth Street. The sky was a solid, gloomy gray, but the TV weatherman promised the cloud cover would break up by evening. Hopefully by the time he got out of class and headed to Lexington for his date with Tori.

Up ahead he spotted his destination, a florist shop in an old converted brick house. A white picket fence enclosed the tiny front yard, and striped green-and-white awnings covered the windows. He didn't work until ten on Tuesdays, so he still had twenty minutes. Plenty of time to pick up some flowers. He pulled into the driveway and parked in a small lot in the back.

A strand of jingling bells on the back of the door announced his presence. He paused to look around. A clash of colors and smells threatened to overload his senses. Baskets hung from the ceiling, and vines draped over shelves lined with vases. Against the wall to his right, three—no, four huge arrangements on easels were lined in a row, one with a white ribbon proclaiming *In Sympathy* in gold letters. Several other brightly colored bouquets rested on the floor beneath the spindly pole legs. Looks like they were getting ready to make a big delivery for a funeral or something. Against the back wall stood a wide, refrigerated storage case with a dozen smaller bouquets on shelves inside, the glass doors fogged as though someone had just opened them. The sweet scent of flowers permeated the room.

A woman came through a doorway beside the case, wiping her hands on a green apron. "Hello. Are you here to pick up an order?"

"Uh, no." Ryan shoved his hands in his pockets. "I wanted to get some flowers for tonight."

A smile appeared on her broad face. "Big date?"

"First date." He glanced at the bouquets in the case. "But I didn't call ahead. Was I supposed to?"

She dismissed that with a flick of her hand. "Not necessarily. I can fix something up quickly. Not red roses, since this is a first date. Did you have sometime specific in mind?"

"Daisies. There's a special color she likes. Some strange color I never heard of." He squeezed his eyes shut, trying to remember the word. Not fuchsia. "Gerber, or something like that."

The woman's stare was blank for a moment, then she covered a sudden grin with her hand. "Do you mean Gerbera?"

Ryan snapped his fingers. "That's it."

Her laughter broke forth and sent an answering wave of dismay through him. Was she laughing at him?

The laughter ended abruptly, and she patted his arm in a motherly gesture. "That's not a color, honey. It's a kind of flower. Here, let me show you."

Ryan followed her to the case and watched as she opened the door and pulled out a round glass vase stuffed with huge multicolored blooms. They looked like psychedelic daisies on steroids.

He fingered one delicate red petal. "They're giant daisies?"

"Actually, they're in the sunflower family."

Made sense. None of the blooms in this arrangement were white with yellow centers, like the daisies he knew. But the reds, yellows, and pinks were certainly more vibrant than the traditional kind. "So, how much is this bouquet?"

"Forty-nine ninety-five plus tax."

Ryan winced. Fifty bucks for flowers? He sure hadn't antici-pated that.

She saw his expression. "This is a deluxe arrangement, though. I can put together something smaller for you, if you like."

He gulped. He hated to seem like a cheapskate, but... "What can you do for around twenty-five?"

Her smile became sympathetic. "Let me see. I'll be right back."

She set the vase back on the shelf and disappeared through the doorway. Ryan examined the other flowers in the case. A couple of huge vases of roses, their deep red blooms startling and beautiful amid leafy green foliage. If this place got fifty bucks for a dozen giant daisies, how much would a dozen roses cost? His gaze slid sideways. Maybe he could afford that one, with only three flowers. No, Allie said roses were too formal for a first date, and the florist mentioned the same thing.

He closed the glass door, his fingers twitching with sudden nerves. Apparently there was a whole list of do's and don'ts asso-ciated with first dates that he knew nothing about. Where did women learn this stuff? There ought to be a class or something a guy could take.

She had only been gone a few minutes when she returned carrying a smaller version of the same bouquet. "How's this look?"

Ryan inspected it with relief. Only six flowers, but the artful arrangement looked real nice. She'd even tied a pretty red bow around the neck of the vase. "It's great. Thank you."

She grinned. "No problem. I hope she likes it."

Ryan paid her and left, carrying the vase to the car carefully in both hands. He hoped so too.

"Yes, I did include a projected inflation rate on media costs." Tori spoke calmly, a direct contrast to Kate's irritable tone.

"How much?" Her boss's question barked through the phone.

"Five percent." *The same as the last analysis you assigned me to do. And if you'd read the footnote on the graph I stayed up until 4 a.m. creating, you'd see that for yourself.*

The low hum of voices from conversations around the office rose and fell, blending with the sound of the ringing phones and fifties music coming from the next cubicle. Diana kept her radio on that station all day, and sometimes it drove Tori crazy. Sock hop tunes wouldn't be her first choice of background music to inspire professional creativity. At the moment, though, the music provided a welcome distraction to her boss's irritating cross-examination.

"The workshop I just got out of said it should be six and a half," Kate snapped.

Tori clamped her jaw shut. Why did she sound so accusing, like Tori should have known that? She wasn't the one at a conference learning all the latest trends. Apparently she was supposed to pick it up from her boss by osmosis or something.

When she could keep her tone even, she said, "Alright. I'll change it and email the updated numbers to you. Shouldn't take too long."

"Fine." Kate bit the word short. "Transfer me to Mitch."

Tori punched the buttons to send Kate's call to Mitch's extension, and hung up without announcing the transfer, a breach of office telephone etiquette. Then she wilted against the chair back and massaged her temples. She had managed to avoid Mitch all morning, and if it were up to her, she'd continue to do so. She wasn't ready to face him after that startling comment last night.

After a few moments of deep breathing had restored a semblance of calm, she straightened and reached for her computer.

The sooner she got that analysis updated and sent off, the sooner she could return to putting flesh on the skeleton of her Maguire marketing plan.

Her fingers had just touched the keyboard when someone stepped into the entrance of her cubicle. She looked up, and then blinked as her mind made the transition from business life to personal.

"Joan. What are you doing here?"

Her sister's smile stretched across her face. "I took the day off work to shop for a wedding present for Ken. I'm here to have lunch with you."

"Oh, Joan, I can't." She waved vaguely in the direction of the phone. "I'm working on a project for my boss, and I can't leave right now."

"You don't have to leave." She held up a bag she'd kept hidden behind the cubicle wall. "I picked up Subway. And look." She reached into the bag and pulled out a smaller one. "Your favorite junk food—Doritos!"

Tori glanced at the computer screen. What was the chance Kate was hanging out by her laptop, counting the minutes until the updated report arrived? Slim. And Joan rarely took a day off work.

She shoved the keyboard away. "Okay. But let's go into the small conference room." She stood and looked over the row of cubicles, where several curious heads were turned their way, probably listening to their conversation. "It has a door."

The office on the other side of Kate's had been furnished with a polished cherry conference table and six executive swivel chairs. The view was identical to Kate's, and as soon as they entered, Joan tossed the bag on the table and crossed to the window.

"Wow. Great view."

"Yeah, I know." Tori stooped to get a couple of bottles of water out of the small refrigerator in the corner. "You should see it after dark, when the lights in the fountain are on."

Joan turned. "You *shouldn't* see it after dark. Isn't this supposed to be a nine-to-five job?"

Tori answered that with a snort. "Yeah, right."

They sat side by side facing the window and Joan unwrapped their sandwiches. When she'd placed a turkey sub with all the veggies in front of Tori, she dropped her hands into her lap and bowed her head to say the blessing. The gesture took Tori by surprise, not because she was unaccustomed to saying grace before a meal with her family, but because here, in this professional environment, a prayer seemed out of place. After a moment's hesitation, she bowed her head too.

"Dear Lord, thank You for giving us this time together to enjoy one another's company. Bless our food, and the hands that prepared it. In Jesus' name, amen."

"Amen." One good thing about Joan. When she prayed, she made her point and then shut her mouth. Unlike Allie, who attempted to sneak a sermon in every time it was her turn to say the blessing.

Tori unfolded a napkin and laid it across her skirt before she picked up her sandwich. "So, what are you going to give Ken as a wedding gift?" She was proud of herself. She didn't scowl as she mentioned his name or anything.

"I have absolutely no idea." Joan squashed her overflowing sub flat-handed before picking it up. "I wish you could come with me and help me pick something out."

Tori nodded as she chewed. Shopping was her thing. Turn her loose in the mall with a credit card and she'd come up with the perfect gift every time.

She swallowed. "A watch?"

"He has one." Joan took a bite.

"Does he wear jewelry? You could get him a gold chain with a cross or a St. Christopher or something." A religious nut like Ken would probably like that.

Chewing, Joan scrunched her nose and shook her head.

Tori twisted the cap off of the water bottle and took a long drink. "I know! Get him a gold-plated stethoscope. All the other doctors will turn green with envy. He'll start a fashion trend in medical-wear."

Joan's shoulders hunched forward with her laugh, and she snatched a napkin to cover her full mouth. She gulped. "Ken is many things, but he's not a trend setter."

Tori shook her head. "I don't know, then. But I'm sure you'll come up with something."

The laughter faded from Joan's face as she opened the chips and divided them on their makeshift placemats. She didn't look at Tori as she spoke. "I wish you two got along better. He really likes you, you know."

Which implied Joan knew Tori didn't like him. Guilt stabbed at her. "I like him too." At Joan's disbelieving glance, she back-pedaled. "Well, I mean I don't *dis*like him." Joan's stare didn't waver, until it was Tori's turn to look down. "Okay, so maybe he wouldn't be my first choice to hang out with on a Saturday night. But I'm not marrying him. You are."

Joan's hand covered Tori's. Sparkles winked at her from the ring that hailed the upcoming wedding. "You're my sister. I love you both, and I want you to love each other." Tori's skin felt cool when Joan pulled her hand back. "Why don't you like him, anyway?"

Tori heaved a sigh and picked up an olive that had spilled from her sub onto the paper. She'd never made a secret of the fact that Ken's over-the-top attitude toward religion got on her nerves, but now didn't seem to be a good time to get into that issue with her sister. "I'm just worried that you're moving too fast. Marriage is such a huge risk these days, and if it fails it can be devastating for everyone. We have the perfect example in our parents." She held the olive in front of her mouth. "Do you really want to risk subjecting yourself to another divorce?"

"Of course not. If I weren't one hundred percent positive, I wouldn't have accepted Ken's proposal." Joan's smile was tender. "We love each other, Tori. Really."

Tori forestalled an answer by putting the olive in her mouth and chasing it with a swig of water. Mom had loved Daddy too, once upon a time. The expression on her face Sunday evening as she talked about him was proof of that. But Mom's fairy tale ended in tragedy.

Her sister must have read her mind. "We are not going to end up like Mom and Daddy. I promise."

Joan sounded absolutely confident. And Tori couldn't deny that the mention of Ken's name ignited a light in her sister's eyes that outshone the glow from the ring on her finger. A crack formed in the shell of Tori's resistance. Maybe she ought to make an effort to accept the inevitable and do her part to keep peace in the family. Even if it meant being nice to the religious nut.

"Well, alright." She picked up her sandwich. "I'll make an effort if he will."

Joan's smile brightened the room. "Thank you. And now, tell me about your hot date tonight."

Tori groaned. "Allie told you."

"The minute you hung up on her." Joan twisted her lips. "You really should call her back."

"I know, I know. I'll call her this afternoon." She'd meant to call Allie back yesterday and apologize for hanging up so abruptly, but after Mitch's startling comment about them speaking the same language, she'd been too distracted to think about much else. "Or maybe I'll wait until tomorrow, so I can deliver all the scoop about my date tonight."

Joan swiveled her chair around and relaxed against the leather back. "I want the scoop now. I know about the coffee mishap, but something must have gone right the other day if you agreed to go out with him again. Did sparks fly between you two?"

Tori remembered the almost electric tingle of attraction when she touched Ryan's arm. She allowed a small grin. "Maybe a few small ones. But as I told Allie—"

The door behind them opened, and Tori stopped mid-sentence as she turned to see who was interrupting them. Her stomach gave a dizzying flip-flop when Mitch thrust his head through the doorway.

"There you are, Sanderson." The familiar smirk had reappeared, along with the impersonal use of her last name.

O-kay. If that's the way he wanted to play it.

She ignored an unreasonable stab of disappointment and told him coldly, "I'm having lunch."

"I can see that." Unfazed, he opened the door wider and stepped into the room, eyeing first the sandwiches on the table, and then Joan. His smile widened as he spoke to Tori while staring at Joan with undisguised admiration. "Aren't you going to introduce us?"

The flirt. Tori used her hand to gesture toward each of them as she performed a quick introduction. "Mitch Jackson, meet my sister, Joan."

"Well, hello there." Mitch came forward to take Joan's hand, and did not release it. "I see beauty is a Sanderson family trait."

"Mitch." Joan pronounced his name with recognition as she gently disengaged herself from his grip. "You're the one who was hired about a month after Tori came to work here."

"The one and only." Mitch's smile grew smug. "I'm glad to know she talks about me outside the office."

Joan's eyes gleamed, and she spoke in a teasing tone. "Oh, yes. She told the whole family about the big project you two are working on, and how much she's going to enjoy becoming your boss."

Surprise momentarily wiped the smirk off of his face. Tori didn't bother to hide her grin. Score one for her side.

"I see beauty isn't the only thing that runs in the family." His head dipped slightly toward Joan in a silent acknowledgment before he spoke to Tori. "Our favorite ulcer dispenser is trying to reach you. She wants you to call her back as soon as you return to your desk."

Tori groaned and leaned her head against the high chair back. "I'll be so glad when she gets back to the office and has her own work to do."

"I hear you." He picked up a Dorito and popped it into his mouth before heading toward the door. "Nice to meet you," he told Joan before he slipped out.

"I hope I wasn't rude to him." Softhearted Joan sounded worried.

Tori laughed. "Even if you had been, he wouldn't have noticed. Subtle jabs are lost on Mitch. He's too focused on himself."

Joan was studying her with an odd expression. "I don't think he's only focused on himself. He seemed pretty taken with you."

An odd sense of excitement made Tori swing toward the table and start wrapping what was left of her sandwich. "You're imagining things. He's the office flirt, that's all." Obviously that's all last night's comment was to him. Flirting with a co-worker.

"Hmmm." Joan ate the last bite of her own sub and wadded the paper. "Is he a Christian?"

"Mitch?" Tori aimed a surprised look toward the closed door. "I don't know. The subject has never come up."

Joan's shoulders deflated a tiny bit, and Tori saw that she was biting the inside of her lip. Probably disappointed that her baby sister hadn't cross-examined the guy about his religious standing the minute after they met, as she certainly would have. Yet another sign of Ken Fletcher's influence on the Sanderson family. They just didn't understand that religion had no place in a professional office environment.

She tossed the rest of the chips back in the bag and folded the top. "Thanks for bringing lunch. I'd better call my boss before she has a coronary or something."

"I'm glad you could take a few minutes to eat with me."

They walked together to the elevator and Joan pushed the button. For once, the doors opened almost immediately. Joan stepped inside, turned, and put her hand across the door to prevent it from closing.

"Have fun tonight." Even, white teeth appeared as she bit her lower lip, apparently trying to decide if she should say something. "You know, Ryan is a really nice guy."

Ah. Pushing the good Christian boy over the flirty coworker.

"I know he is." Tori smiled. "Call me and let me know what you pick out for Ken's wedding present."

Joan nodded and lowered her hand. The doors started to close. "Oh!" She thrust a hand out and halted them. "I forgot to ask. Are you coming to Sunday school this week?"

Tori narrowed her eyes. "Why?"

"No reason. Just wondering." Joan gave her an innocent look. *She and Allie probably want to give me another not-so-subtle shove in Ryan's direction. Save me a seat beside him or something.*

"You should come." Joan's tone coaxed. "You haven't been in a month."

Longer, actually. She pictured Gram's fretful expression last Sunday when she arrived at the house long after church was over. Gram loved having her whole family together, crowded into the pew where she sat every Sunday morning.

Actually, this Sunday would be better than most to be away from the office. Kate was scheduled to fly back from Chicago on Sunday, so *hopefully* she'd be too busy to bother her harried employees.

"Yes, I'll be in Sunday school," she told her sister.

Joan gave a satisfied nod and dropped her hand to her side. "I'll call you tomorrow." The doors swooshed closed.

Tori stood there a moment, staring at her blurry reflection in the polished silver doors. If Joan's visit hadn't been cut short, she would have loved to turn the conversation around to Daddy so she could question Joan about Mom's revelations Sunday afternoon. Her boss's interruption had eliminated that possibility. So, what else was new? Kate made a habit of disrupting Tori's plans.

With a sigh, she headed back to her cubicle to call Kate and find out the latest crisis that would prevent her from working on her Maguire marketing plan.

Chapter Nine

The afternoon whizzed by in a flurry of rush projects and cryptic phone calls from Chicago. The only smidgen of satisfaction Tori could muster was knowing that Kate was tormenting Mitch from afar too. She caught sight of him across the office several times, and he looked as stressed as she felt. Had he made any progress on his marketing plan? She didn't have the nerve to ask him.

At eight fifteen she slipped through the deserted office and into the restroom with her makeup bag and the dress she'd brought to change into. This date with Ryan wasn't something she'd looked forward to. Not that she was dreading it, but she just couldn't afford the distraction right now. All the issues pressing in on her—her job, Joan's wedding, Daddy—gave her a claustrophobic feeling, like she couldn't breathe. The last thing she needed was to add the complication of a guy into the mix.

In the restroom, she slipped out of her suit and pulled the dress over her head. It settled around her waist with a silky whisper, and she tugged at the hem until the skirt flowed freely. Ah, there was nothing like the smell of new fabric to lift a girl's spirits. Unless, of course, it was new shoes. And she happened to have a pair of those too, adorable strappy sandals in exactly the same shade of red as the dress.

Twenty minutes later, she passed approval on the girl in the mirror. Makeup fresh. Hair perfectly arranged with every curl in place. A hint of gold in her earlobes, nothing large enough to be distracting. Gorgeous dress that made the skin on her long bare arms gleam like ivory. She twisted sideways, watching the hemline flutter gently around her calves. Perfect.

She gathered her belongings and headed for her cubicle. When she rounded the corner, she nearly plowed into someone coming in the opposite direction.

"Mitch!" Terrific. She'd thought everyone had gone home. "What are you doing here?"

"Working, what else?" His eyes grew round as his gaze swept downward. "Wow, Sanderson. You look…"

His throat moved as he swallowed whatever words he'd been about to say. Tori hid a satisfied smile. If she wondered whether she'd achieved the desired effect, she now had her answer. She'd managed to render Mitch speechless.

Wickedly, she pressed her advantage. She twisted on her sandals so the skirt fluttered attractively and tossed her curls with a wide-eyed question. "Do I look okay?"

For a moment he didn't answer. Something smoldered in the gaze he fixed on her, something that sent an answering shiver down her spine. But in the next instant, the pompous grin returned to twitch at his lips. "Kinda dressed up for a date with a plumber, aren't you?"

The elevator tone sounded at that moment. Tori turned on a heel and swept toward the reception desk as the doors slid open, Mitch following along behind.

Ryan stepped out, holding a vase of flowers. Again, she was struck by his muscular build, his wholesome good looks. His head turned, and when he caught sight of her, his face lit. A second shiver in as many minutes caused the hair on her arms to rise as he moved toward her with a powerful stride.

"You look amazing." His husky whisper reflected the admiration in his warm eyes.

"Thank you." She tore her gaze away from his and looked at the flowers, a cheerfully colorful assortment of Gerbera daisies. "How pretty."

"I hope you like them." He extended them toward her.

She lay her clothes, makeup, and purse on Fran's empty reception desk and took the vase. "They're my favorite. Thank you."

"Ahem."

Mitch stood off to one side, watching. Tori suppressed a groan. Of course, he'd want to get a glimpse of the plumber.

Ryan wore a polite expression. "Hello."

Mitch came forward, hand extended. "Hi there. Mitch Jackson. I'm Tori's"—his gaze slid to hers for an instant—"co-worker."

"Ryan Adams. Nice to meet you."

The smile Ryan gave Mitch as the two shook hands was entirely genuine. And under the regard of another guy, Mitch actually lost a touch of his smug conceit. Tori's breath caught as she looked from one man to the other, both of them extremely handsome, though in vastly different ways.

Had she ever lived through a more awkward moment?

"Well." Her voice sounded louder than she intended. Both guys looked at her. "It's late. We should be going."

"Oh, yeah." Mitch gave her a bright smile. "After all, Cinderella turns into a pumpkin when the clock strikes midnight."

Ryan's gaze warmed her skin. "Oh, I doubt that."

When Tori started to gather her stuff, he stepped forward. "Here, let me help."

She handed him the garment bag and picked up her purse. What was she going to do with the flowers, leave them in her car in the parking garage with the rest of these things? As much time as she spent at the office, she'd barely see them at all before they wilted if she took them home.

On impulse, she thrust the vase toward Mitch. "Would you mind setting these on my desk?" She turned a smile toward Ryan. "That way I can enjoy them all week."

Mitch froze for only a moment before relenting. "Sure, Sanderson. I'll be your errand boy. No problem."

"Thanks." She gave him a perky smile, picked up her makeup bag, and tucked her free hand into Ryan's arm. "Ready?"

Mitch didn't move, but stood watching them, holding the vase of colorful blooms. When the elevator doors closed and blocked him from view, Tori breathed a sigh of relief.

"Seems like a nice guy," Ryan said as the elevator plunged toward the underground parking garage.

"Mmm hmm."

Her head tilted back, Tori watched the display above the closed doors, her mind obviously elsewhere. A completely unreasonable stab of jealousy shot through Ryan. Had he picked up on some unspoken communication between the two of them up there? He'd definitely sensed a hint of rivalry in Mitch's overly firm handshake. Not that he blamed the guy. If he worked with someone as stunning as Tori, he'd be falling all over himself all day long. Of course, since 90 percent of the customers who came into the store were guys, so would they. Business would triple with Tori running the register.

"What's the grin for?" Her question startled him.

He ducked his head, embarrassed. "I was just wondering why you agreed to go out with me. Especially when I didn't exactly make a dazzling impression on Sunday."

A dimple appeared in one of her cheeks as she grinned. "That wasn't your fault. Besides, you piqued my interest by mentioning that class, remember? I want to hear about it."

"Okay, but it's not very exciting." The doors opened and he put a hand out to hold them as she exited. "Strategic Financial Management."

She stopped two steps into the parking garage and turned a surprised look on him. "Finance? I figured it was something to do with your job."

"Like what? Strategic Shelf Stocking?" He laughed. "Or maybe Change Counting 101?"

"Stop it." She gave him a playful slap on the arm. "I didn't know what it could be, which is why I was so curious." The clack-clack of her heels echoed on the concrete as he followed her across the garage to her car. "You're taking college classes?"

He nodded. "I'm getting a B.B.A. in Business at Eastern."

They reached her car, a white Toyota. She dug around in her purse for a minute, then pulled out a set of keys. "What do you plan to do when you're finished?"

He scuffed a heel on the rough cement. "I don't know. I want to own my own business someday, but I haven't settled on what kind. Maybe something to do with the agriculture industry. Or maybe retail, since that's what I know. But I have a couple of years to decide. I'm paying as I go, and I can only afford two classes per semester."

A half-smile hovered around her lips. "I had no idea."

She punched a button on her keyless remote and the trunk popped open. Ryan lifted it upward, then noticed she had gone still. Creases lined her smooth forehead as she stared inside. A box sat in the gray-lined interior.

He read the words in black marker on the side. "Tori's Stuff. I guess this came from your grandmother's attic on Sunday?"

Wordlessly, she nodded.

Judging by the look on her face, she wasn't happy to see it there. He pushed the box to the rear so he could lay the garment bag flat, then took the smaller case she held and tucked it in the corner. Maybe she'd forgotten to take the box into her apartment.

When he'd closed the trunk, he said, "I wasn't sure where you wanted to go for dinner." He nodded toward the darkened sky outside the parking garage. "It's a nice night out there if you're interested in walking over to deSha's."

With what looked like an effort, she tore her gaze away from the trunk and turned a smile on him. "That's fine. I like deSha's."

He placed a hand on her back, his touch light against the soft fabric of her dress, and gestured toward the street-level exit. They hadn't taken three steps before she stopped.

"Wait a minute." Her lips curved hesitantly. "Remember that big project I was telling you about?

"The one that might earn you a promotion."

"That's right. Well, I'm supposed to be creating a marketing plan for Maguire's Restaurant. I've only been there once."

Ryan had heard of Maguire's. It was supposed to be pretty fancy. Probably more expensive than the one he'd planned to take her to. But if he could help with her project, it might earn him brownie points. Besides, looking into those big blue eyes, what else could he do but agree with whatever she said?

"Maguire's it is. My car's this way."

Hopefully the bill for dinner wouldn't blow his budget for the whole month. He'd planned to ask her to go out with him again. And somehow she didn't look like the type to appreciate the ninety-nine-cent menu at the fast-food restaurant.

The parking lot outside Maguire's held a fair number of cars for almost nine thirty on a Tuesday night. Tori examined them with the eyes of a researcher as she walked with Ryan toward the restaurant. Most were late-model autos, shiny and expensive looking. She counted three Lexuses and four BMWs.

"Do you think I need a tie?" Ryan plucked at the collar of his button down, and tucked his shirt straighter into his belted slacks.

Tori shook her head. "I'm sure you're fine."

He swung open the polished wooden door for her, his admiring glance traveling the length of her dress. "Nobody's going to be looking at me anyway."

Warmth flooded her as she stepped through the doorway. Ryan's compliments were delivered with such sincerity, and without even a hint of the insinuating tone that turned Mitch's into near-assaults.

When the door swung closed behind them, it took Tori's eyes a minute to adjust to the subdued lighting inside the restaurant. The polished wood surfaces of carved high-back chairs reflected the softly flickering firelight from a huge hearth along the rear brick wall. A nice touch, though obviously unnecessary for heat this time of year. Silver gleamed in pools of light cast by chandeliers hovering above linen-covered tables. Most of the tables were occupied. The clink of crystal mingled with the hum of low voices as two couples seated at a table in the corner toasted with raised wineglasses.

A tall blonde in a classic black sheath dress stood behind a hostess stand. She smiled as they approached. "Welcome to Maguire's Restaurant. Will there be two of you for dinner this evening?"

Tori glanced up at Ryan. His eyes had gone round, and he gulped before nodding. "Yes, two for dinner."

The woman scratched a notation on a seating chart on the illuminated stand, picked up two menus, and smiled at them. "Right this way."

Tori paid covert attention to the customers as she followed the hostess through the main dining room to a second room beyond a well-stocked bar. Most of the diners were well dressed, the men in business clothes and the ladies in dresses or suits. She passed one table and noticed a woman wearing a ring with a diamond nearly as big as a piece of ice in the glass she lifted. A few were casually dressed, so Ryan shouldn't feel out of place.

They were given a corner table in the second dining room, which was as elegantly apportioned as the first. Most of the other tables were full of customers who spoke in low voices. At a table in the opposite corner, a lone woman wearing a black blouse and skirt leaned over a thick stack of papers, writing. As Tori watched, she raised her head and picked up a coffee cup, her eyes moving as she swept the room above the rim. The manager, maybe?

Tori lowered herself into the chair Ryan held for her and took the menu from the hostess.

"Your server will be with you in a moment."

The woman disappeared, and Tori leaned across the table to whisper at Ryan. "I thought this place would be deserted by now."

"Me too." He matched her tone. "I think I saw Stuart Saeland back there."

"The U.K. basketball player?" Tori twisted toward the door-way. "Where?"

"In the other room. He was the small giant sitting against the left wall." Ryan grinned. "Want me to get his autograph for you?"

She giggled and settled back in her chair. "No, that's okay. But Eric would probably pay good money for it."

"My brother would too." He opened the menu, and his eyes moved as he glanced down the list of items.

She saw his throat convulse with a quick, nervous-looking gulp. Apparently Ryan didn't go for fine dining often. The waiter arrived at that moment to fill their water glasses. When they both declined anything else to drink, he left, promising to return for their order in a moment.

Tori opened her menu and noted the variety of the dishes with an analytical eye. What could she find here to help her craft a unique brand for Maguire's? The menu listed a few chicken entrees, a couple of fish selections, but as she remembered, the specialty of the house seemed to be steak with signature sauces. The only other time she'd been here, she'd had sirloin with mushroom merlot reduction that was almost fork tender. Even the memory made her mouth water.

She glanced at the prices and experienced a flash of guilt. This was definitely not the cheapest place in town. Could Ryan afford it? She'd basically forced him to bring her here, and she hadn't even considered the impact of a high-priced restaurant on the budget of a hardware store clerk who was paying for college tuition. Maybe she ought to offer to pay for her own, since it counted as research and she could put it on her expense report. But how to suggest that without implying she didn't think he could afford this place? She didn't want to offend him. Better just to order something inexpensive.

He looked at her over the top of the menu. "What are you in the mood for?"

"Oh, I don't know. I don't usually like to eat much this late."

A grin curved his lips. "Except for the occasional supersize order of fries?"

She returned his smile. "Except for those."

The waiter returned, and set a basket of bread on the table between them. "Would you like an appetizer before you begin?"

"Not for me," Tori said.

Ryan shook his head. "Me either."

The waiter clasped his hands behind his back. "Have you decided on your order, or shall I give you a few more minutes?"

Tori glanced at her menu. The least expensive entree listed was chicken breast in Madeira wine sauce for twenty-two dollars. "I'm not really very hungry." She hoped the rumble in her stomach wouldn't make a liar out of her. "I think I'll have a garden salad with Italian dressing, and a bowl of French onion soup." The two added up to sixteen dollars, surely not much more than an entrée at deSha's, where Ryan had been planning to take her.

Ryan's grip on his menu relaxed. "I'll have the same, but with Ranch on the salad."

To his credit, the waiter's pleasant expression didn't change, though surely he was doing a quick mental calculation of his tip potential based on the total ticket price. "I'll bring that right out."

When he retreated toward the kitchen, Tori peeled back the white napkin covering the bread basket. The yeasty aroma that wisped into the air made her mouth water. She placed a thick slice on her bread plate and then tilted the basket toward Ryan.

"So," he said as he selected a piece, "tell me about your project. You're developing a plan to address the four P's, right?"

Tori paused in the act of tearing off a bite-sized piece of bread. "Excuse me?"

"You know." He spread butter on his bread. "The marketing process. Product, Price, Place, and Promotion."

"I know what the four P's are," she told him. "I'm just surprised you do."

He set his knife on the edge of his plate. "I took Principles of Marketing last year. But all I have is textbook knowledge. No practical experience."

Wow. The plumber, as Mitch called him, was full of surprises tonight. First he showed up with her favorite flowers. Then she found out he was attending college and paying for it as he went along. And now this. Impressed, Tori almost forgot to enjoy the soft, flavorful bread as she chewed.

She took a sip from her water glass. "Well, the Product, Price, and Place are already set, so my plan will focus on Promotion. I've got to come up with some ideas for a killer ad campaign, including branding and everything."

"So you need to study the customer demographics." He glanced around the room. "Not really a family-friendly place. Looks like a fairly well-off crowd. I wonder what the lunch crowd is like."

Tori followed his glance. He was right about the restaurant not being popular with families, at least at this time of night. There wasn't a single child in the place. "I'd be willing to bet they do a lot of business lunches. It's right off New Circle Road and only a few miles from downtown, so easy access from any business location."

Their salads arrived, with the promise of soup to come. When the waiter left, Ryan said, "Where's the new location?"

Tori picked up a gleaming silver fork and speared a crisp lettuce leaf. "Winston Street off South Limestone."

Ryan paused with his fork in front of his mouth, his brows arched. "On U.K.'s campus?" He sounded skeptical.

"Not right on campus, but nearby." Tori looked around the room. Ryan was right to look skeptical. The college crowd would feel totally out of place here. Not to mention the fact that most of them couldn't afford to walk through the front door. "I'm planning to go down there and check it out later this week, as soon as I get some breathing room."

The salad was excellent, with a blend of lettuces and just the right amount of vegetables. Tori sliced into a cherry tomato.

Enough about her job, which she'd rather forget for a while. "Tell me about growing up on a farm."

"I still can't believe you have never been on one." He shook his head, laughter coloring his words. "You really are a city girl."

She gave him a wry look. "Danville can hardly be considered a major metropolitan center of culture."

He cocked his head, a grin lighting his eyes. "It is to someone from Junction City."

"I suppose that's true." She chuckled, then assumed a superior tone. "But I have actually been on a farm, I'll have you know."

"Really?"

She nodded. "I was in third grade, and my class took a field trip to the Double Stink Pig Farm."

He tossed his fork on his plate and sat back in the chair, laughing. "That is not a farm."

"It is too," she said, indignant. "We each got to pick a pumpkin in this huge field, and they had a petting zoo with camels and sheep and even some kangaroos."

"Well, we don't raise camels or kangaroos on our farm. But we do have hogs." His lips twitched behind the rim of his glass. "Chickens and cows too. And lots of corn and tobacco." After he'd gulped a long drink of water, he set the glass down. "I'll show it to you sometime, if you want to see what a real farm is like."

Tori smiled and gave a noncommittal nod, focusing on her salad plate while trying to study him without looking at him. Was there something more behind that invitation than a chance to see a bunch of pigs? Like, maybe, an introduction to his family? Well, he was a nice guy and all, but she wasn't at all ready for that. Besides, she'd already met part of his family and been baptized with coffee in the process.

She was relieved when the waiter appeared with their soup. After he'd placed a bubbly, cheese-covered crock in front of each of them and left, Ryan changed the subject.

"So, how's the clean-up project at your grandmother's house going?"

"We've barely begun." Tori wrinkled her nose. "But it's a dirty job." An apt description for the process of trudging through an ugly past. Hopefully he would think she referred to the dust in Gram's attic.

"Your grandmother has lived in that house a long time, hasn't she?"

Tori nodded. "She and my grandpa built it, the first house on that street. It's really the only home I've ever known."

His voice grew soft. "It must be tough going through all those things from your past and deciding which to keep and which to give away."

A lump formed in her throat and threatened to choke her. "Not only that, but you know what I found Sunday afternoon?" She snapped her mouth shut. Why did she say that? She didn't intend to lay out her family's sordid history for Ryan's inspection.

"What did you find?"

His spoon poised over his own crock as he waited for her to take a spoonful of steaming soup and then wash it down with water.

"Oh, just a bunch of my father's things." She tried to make it sound casual, like it was no big deal. But her voice sounded tight, like air squeezed out through a balloon's narrow opening.

Understanding dawned on his face. "The box in your trunk?" He paused, then explained his guess. "I thought you looked troubled when you saw it."

Mom always said she wore her heart on her face. With halting words, Tori told Ryan about the shoebox full of photographs that she hadn't been able to even take out of her trunk yet, much less open and look at. He listened without interrupting, his face such a mask of sympathy that she didn't stop there, but went on to detail what she'd discovered about her father from Mom.

"Wow. It's hard to believe a man could just walk away from his family like that." She must have looked startled, because he immediately covered her hand with his. "I'm sorry. That was thoughtless of me."

"No, that's okay." She smiled to reassure him, trying to ignore the warmth from his palm as it rested on the back of her hand. "I've thought the same thing for fifteen years."

The waiter approached, and Ryan withdrew his hand. Tori placed hers in her lap where it lay, tingling faintly. When they'd both declined dessert, the man set a leather folder on the table and withdrew to a discreet distance. Tori folded her napkin as Ryan placed enough cash in the folder to cover the check and tip, and then they left the restaurant. She gave the place a final scrutinizing examination as she headed for the door, trying to soak in the ambiance. As soon as she got home she'd record her thoughts while they were still fresh. Her notes would come in handy when she started working on the branding ideas.

They chatted about nothing in particular on the drive downtown, and in a few minutes Ryan pulled into the parking garage beneath her building. He parked next to her car and climbed out. Tori waited for him to circle around to open her door. They'd come to the time of the date that caused her hands to sweat and her stomach to knot with nerves. Would he kiss her? What would she do if he did? All the reasons she'd listed to Allie for avoiding a romantic relationship with Ryan Adams still existed. And yet, she'd had a nice time with him this evening. No use denying he was an attractive man. So maybe if he tried to kiss her…

He opened her door and extended a hand to assist her out of the car. The firmness in his arm as he steadied her reminded her again of a lumberjack. There was something wholesome and outdoorsy about his strength. Tori's fingers felt small and dainty in his.

He released her the moment she stood steady on her sandals. Biting back a sigh, Tori pushed the Unlock button on her car's remote and waited for him to open it for her. The traffic noise from outside filtered into the empty parking garage.

"Thank you for the flowers, and for dinner." She smiled up at him. "And for changing your plans so I could see Maguire's. It really helped me to be there and soak up the atmosphere."

"It was my pleasure." He sounded as though he really meant it.

A thought occurred to her. Research on Maguire's new restaurant site would be much more fun with someone else along. She spoke before she could reconsider. "You mentioned that you don't have class on Wednesday nights. Do you want to go with me to check out the new location? There's a restaurant nearby that has awesome pizza."

He shifted his gaze downward, and Tori experienced a stab of discomfort. Had she offended him? She thought he'd enjoyed the evening tonight, as she had. Maybe he was an old-fashioned kind of guy who didn't like girls taking the initiative.

He gave a little nod and held her gaze. "And maybe while we're there, you could show me those pictures."

The suggestion dropped into Tori's stomach like a lump of ice. She opened her mouth to protest, but he went on in a gentle tone.

"It might help to have someone else there when you look at them, you know? Just so you're not alone."

She closed her mouth again. Ryan was right. Going through those pictures in the solitude of her apartment would be nothing but gruesome. And looking at them with Allie and Joan, listening to her sisters' commentaries on each one, would be even worse.

Her voice croaked when she asked, "What time?"

The smile that crept onto Ryan's face went a long way toward warming her cold insides. "Since I don't have class tomorrow, I'm free anytime after six, when I get off work."

She really should work tomorrow night, since nights seemed to be the only time she was able to get anything done on her project. But technically, the date would be research for her project. Sort of.

"I'll be ready to go at seven thirty." She managed a thin smile. "Why don't you pick me up at my apartment this time?"

She gave him directions, then slid into the seat. He stood watching as she backed out of the parking place and headed for the exit.

He hadn't even tried to kiss her goodnight. Her stomach was in such turmoil from the thought of going through those pictures with him tomorrow night, Tori couldn't tell if she was relieved or disappointed.

Chapter Ten

When Ryan pulled into the parking lot of Long's Hardware and Building Supply Wednesday morning, he was only mildly surprised to see Allie's car already waiting. He'd figured she would come by again this morning and try to pry the blow-by-blow details of their date out of him. But then the passenger door opened and Joan climbed out. Uh oh. He was about to be tag-teamed.

Dressed in gym shorts and running shoes, Joan approached his car while Allie got the baby out of the backseat. Ryan turned the engine off and eyed her through the window. Joan was a nice girl, easygoing and easy to talk to. But at the moment she wore the same eager expression as her older sister, and it made him want to lock the doors and run for cover. Instead, he resolutely got out of the car.

"Hey, Joan. You're out early this morning."

"Allie and I go to the gym together a couple of days a week before I go to work." She fell in step beside him as he headed for the store. "We thought we'd drop by and see how it went last night."

Okay, the gym was right down the road, so that was at least a believable excuse.

"It went fine." The doors swept open at their approach, and Allie joined them as they entered. "We had a good time." He spared a fleeting hope that they'd settle for "a good time," but there was zero possibility of that. They'd want every tiny insignificant detail.

"And?" Allie looked like she'd just been handed a shovel and told to dig diamonds out of a pile of sand. He recognized that relentless determination from the women in his own family and sucked in a resigned breath.

"I took her flowers."

"Gerbera daisies?"

He nodded, then scowled at Allie. "You could have told me that was a kind of flower and not a color." The look they both gave him bordered on pity, so he went on. "She seemed to like them."

"And you picked her up at her office, right?" Allie asked.

Sheesh, if she already knew the answer, why make him repeat it? He stooped to pick up a gum wrapper on the floor, trying to decide if he could throw them out of the store. No, probably not. His mother's lessons were too deeply ingrained to allow him to be rude, especially to women. Even if they were busybodies.

He straightened and forced a smile. "That's right. At eight forty-five, like I promised."

"Good. Tori likes punctuality." Joan nodded, encouraging him to continue.

An image of Tori coming to meet him as he stepped off the elevator rose in his mind. "She looked amazing."

"What was she wearing?" Allie shifted the baby to her other hip.

"A dress." They both waited, their expressions demanding more. "Uh, a red dress. And shoes."

"Was it sleeveless, scooped neck, hem below the knee, with a belted waist?"

"Yeah," he said, "that's the one."

Allie turned to Joan. "I was with her when she bought that dress. She looks great in it." She faced Ryan again. "Go on."

Ryan rubbed his forehead. "Uh, there was a guy there. Someone she works with. Mitch Somebody."

Joan pursed her lips. "The one I told you about," she said to Allie.

"He was still there at almost nine o'clock last night?" A line of concern creased the skin between Allie's eyes. "That's not good."

"It's not?" Ryan half turned away from them to straighten a rack of lug nuts, his thoughts tangling into a knot. He'd known there was something about that guy he didn't like.

"Don't worry." Joan placed a hand on his arm. "We're on your side."

Allie's look became fierce. "Yeah, that guy doesn't stand a chance."

My side? There were sides being taken all of a sudden?

Of course, if sides *were* being drawn, he definitely wanted Allie and Joan in his camp. They may be busybodies, but they were also insiders.

"So, you took her to deSha's, like we discussed?"

He glanced at Allie. "No, she wanted to go to Maguire's because of that big project she's working on."

Both of them looked impressed at that news, which lightened his mood a shade.

"Maguire's. Wow." Joan folded her arms, nodding with satisfaction. "Nice move, Ryan."

He started to relax when Allie gave him a stern look. "Don't get cocky. We have to plan your next move."

"Actually, the next move is already planned." Both sets of eyebrows arched. Ryan shoved his hands into his pockets. "She asked me to go with her tonight to check out the location for Maguire's new restaurant."

"She asked you?" Delight colored Joan's tone.

When he nodded, Allie raised her hand toward her sister for a high-five. He almost laughed at the glee on their faces.

"I think you two are happier than me." He didn't quite manage to filter a hint of distrust out of his tone.

Allie zeroed in on it. "We just want what's best for our sister."

His chest swelled out. "And you think I'm what's best for Tori?"

"You'll do in a pinch." Joan punched him lightly on the shoulder, grinning. Then she sobered. "Seriously, she spends too much time at work. We don't want to see her end up like that boss of hers, with her whole life revolving around her job."

"And besides, we know you're a Christian." Allie settled the baby on her other hip. "We'd rather see her with you than with someone like that Mitch guy that we don't know anything about."

The store's phone rang, and Ryan turned toward the counter, but Gary, the owner and his boss, emerged from the stock room and beat him to it.

"We'd better let you get to work," Joan said.

Allie nodded, but grabbed his arm for a parting piece of advice. "No flowers this time. You don't want to look like you're buttering her up or anything. Just be fun and relaxing."

Ryan shifted his weight, suddenly uncomfortable. Fun? Relaxing? Maybe his suggestion about those pictures wasn't such a good idea after all.

"Hey, Ryan."

He turned toward the sales counter to find Gary holding the phone toward him. "It's your mother."

Great. Gary was probably wondering if he was going to get any work done at all today, or spend the whole time on personal business.

Allie threw him a parting threat as she followed Joan out the door. "I'll call you tomorrow and find out how it went."

With an apologetic grimace at his boss, Ryan took the receiver. "Hey, Mom."

"Hi, honey. Loralee and I were just sitting here having a cup of coffee between chores and she was telling me about your date last night. How did it go?"

A low groan rumbled in his throat. "Mom, I can't talk right now. I'm at work."

Her voice became muffled as she spoke to someone in the room with her, probably covering the phone with her hand. "Says he can't talk right now." He heard Loralee in the distance, but couldn't make out her words, then Mom spoke to him again. "At least tell us if you had a good time."

"Yes, we had a good time."

"And are you going out with her again?"

He heaved an audible sigh for her benefit. "Yes, I am." He wasn't about to go into the details twice within a ten-minute period.

"Good. Well, I want you to ask her over here for lunch on Sunday so your father and I can meet her. Loralee says she's a real pretty girl."

Ryan was aware of Gary standing at the end of the counter, not exactly watching him, but obviously listening. He turned his body slightly and lowered his voice. "Mom, I am not going to bring her out there for your inspection. Besides, I happen to know she has dinner every Sunday with her own family."

"Dessert, then. I'll fix a nice peach cobbler, and your father can churn some ice cream. And I promise to leave my magnifying glass in the desk drawer."

In the background he heard Loralee say, "Tell him the boys have something to give her. A present they bought with their own money."

"Did you hear that?" Mom asked.

"I heard." The doors slid open and a customer came into the store. Ryan straightened. "I've got to go, Mom. I have a customer."

"Alright, honey. You let me know about that cobbler. Love you."

When Ryan replaced the receiver, he turned to find Gary staring openly at him, his lips twisted into a grin. "Had a date last night, didja?"

Ryan eyed his boss warily. "You're not going to cross-examine me about it, are you?"

Gary's eyes went round, and he held his hands up. "Not me." His grin deepened. "'Sides, all I have to do is stand around and listen. You got women coming out of the woodwork to do the job for me."

When Tori stepped off the elevator at seven fifty-eight Wednesday morning, Fran was just getting to her desk.

"Good morning." Tori started to sweep past.

The receptionist's keys jingled as she unlocked her desk and placed her purse in the bottom door. "How was the date?"

Tori paused. "How do you know I had a date last night?"

Tapping a sparkly tipped finger on her chin, Fran said, "Let's see. One, you brought clothes and makeup with you to work yesterday. Two, your sister told you to 'have fun' before she left." She grinned. "And three, Mitch told us yesterday afternoon."

Tori rolled her eyes. Mitch was a worse gossip than any of his female co-workers. "I should have known. No secrets in this office."

"None at all." Fran seated herself and pressed the button to turn on her computer. "So, did you have fun?"

"We had a nice time." Tori left quickly, before Fran could question her further. She'd just as soon not spread it around that she'd allowed her job to infiltrate her date by going to Maguire's last night. No sense giving Mitch anything else to needle her about. Or any ideas for market research.

She took the long way around the office so she could swing by the small break room and grab a cup of coffee. Rita always got to work before the sun came up and started a pot brewing. Tori doctored hers with diet sweetener and hazelnut-flavored creamer, and headed for her cubicle, stirring the light brown liquid with a wooden stir-stick.

When she rounded the corner to her cubicle, she jerked to a stop in the doorway. It took a moment for the sight that greeted her to register on her uncaffeinated brain.

While she stood gaping, her cube-neighbor Diana came to stand beside her, grinning widely. "You were either a very good girl," she said with a nudge, "or a very bad girl, but very good at it."

Tori felt heat gathering in her face as she looked at her desk. On the corner sat Ryan's bouquet of Gerbera daisies. But in the center stood a tall crystal vase absolutely overflowing with dozens of the rainbow-colored blooms, interspersed with colorful roses and baby's breath.

Diana's voice held a giggle. "I don't know who your date last night was with, but he sure did want to impress you."

After she left, Tori stood for a moment, staring at the flowers. They were beautiful, of course. But so many of them! There was only one person she knew who would go for such an ostentatious display. And his motive sure wasn't to please her, but to make a statement.

She crossed to her desk, tossed her purse on the chair, and searched for a card among the abundance of blossoms. The heady scent of the roses threatened to woo her into complacency, but then she plucked out the card.

"You won't see many of these on a plumber's salary."

The handwriting was unmistakably Mitch's. Her fingers itching with irritation, Tori ripped the card in two and tossed the pieces into the trash. What arrogance! She didn't think for a minute he gave her flowers to please her or impress her. No, he just wanted to one-up Ryan. And in doing so, he proved himself to be the jerk she'd known he was all along. She picked up the vase—which was nice, she had to admit—and marched out of her cubicle.

Diana looked up as she passed her doorway. "What are you doing?"

"I'm taking them to the break room, where everyone can enjoy them."

"But why?"

Tori raised her voice to be heard by everyone in the office. She had no idea if Mitch had arrived at work yet, but even if he hadn't, someone would relay her reason. "I can't stand to be in the same room with them. Roses make me sneeze."

Well, at least the first part was true.

She was transcribing her thoughts about Maguire's from last night's scribbled notes to her computer when someone stepped into her cubicle. Phil Osborne. Surprised, her fingers paused over the keyboard. She hadn't seen him since he left Mr. Connolly's office Monday night. All day yesterday he'd stayed inside his office.

"Good morning," she said.

She was struck with how kind his face was. Not even a hint of Mitch's perpetual smirk. "Do you have a minute? I'd like to ask you something."

"Of course."

He gave her a distracted smile. "In my office, if you don't mind."

Odd request. In the two years since she joined Connolly and Farrin, she hadn't exchanged more than five words at a time privately with Phil. Oh, they'd been in plenty of meetings together, so Tori felt that they had a good professional relationship, but she couldn't remember ever going into his office.

"Sure, Phil."

She rose and followed him to his office, identical in size and furnishings to Kate's but on the opposite side of the building, and so without windows. The walls boasted several nice paintings, and a happy-looking family smiled at her from a row of framed photographs lining the top of his credenza. An attractive table lamp rested on the corner of his desk, shedding a warm light into the room that gave the place a much homier feel than the harsh fluorescent lighting overhead. Tori felt herself relaxing as she sat in the chair he gestured toward. Instead of sitting on the other side of the desk, Phil took the second guest chair and turned it to face her.

"I wanted to congratulate you on your promotion opportunity." He spoke in a low voice with a glance toward the open doorway. "Becoming an AE so soon after joining the company will be quite a feather in your cap."

Tori shifted in her seat. Should she say anything about Kate being promoted over him? Like maybe an expression of sympathy for the unfairness? No, definitely not. "Thank you, but the job isn't exactly mine yet."

"True, but I'm sure you'll do a fine job on the Maguire campaign. You've got talent and enthusiasm." He rested an arm on the edge of his desk. "Kate recognized that in you when she hired you, and she's got an eye for talent."

"She hired Mitch too."

He dipped his head in a silent assent. Tori noticed, a little smugly, that Phil didn't comment on Mitch's talent or enthusiasm.

A pen lay on the desk blotter, and he picked it up and began waving it absently between his thumb and forefinger. "I wondered if you'd be willing to help me out with a client."

Interesting. Phil handled most of the firm's lower-revenue accounts, small business owners with matching marketing budgets. He had his own employees who helped him with those accounts. Since Tori had joined the company, she could count on two hands the number of times an AE had requested the assistance of a research analyst who worked for another AE.

As though he could hear her thoughts, he said, "I know it's an unusual request, but I'm a little under the gun. I've got a personal appointment Friday morning I'd prefer not to cancel. Samantha is off work that day, and I need to keep Randy heads-down on another project."

Heads-down on *a project*? Well, Tori was heads-down on a half-dozen projects. Everyone had more work than they knew how to handle lately, and Tori had the added responsibility of the Maguire plan.

But she liked Phil. She couldn't help remembering the dejected slump of his shoulders as he left Mr. Connolly's office Monday evening. In fact, a touch of sadness still hovered around him, evident in the smile that didn't quite make it all the way to his eyes.

"What do you need me to do?"

"You'll probably enjoy it," he told her. "I need someone to oversee a commercial shoot for the Nolan's Ark account Friday morning."

Tori straightened to attention. A commercial shoot? "Nolan's Ark is a pet store, right?"

"That's right." He tossed the pen on the desk and picked up a folder. "Everything is arranged. Artistic Video will do the filming, and they've already been briefed on what we want. Ed Nolan tells me he's memorized the script." He shook his head, a slow grin lifting one corner of his mouth. "I'm afraid he'll be horrible on-camera, but he's insistent."

"I've never done a commercial shoot, Phil."

"All you have to do is show up as the official representative of Connolly and Farrin. Just stand around and watch. Of course, if you get any great ideas, you'll be free to express them."

He extended the folder. Excitement stole over her as she realized what Phil was handing her. This wasn't a researcher's job. It was the responsibility of an AE to oversee something as important as filming a television commercial. Phil was giving her the opportunity to gain some experience in the job to which she aspired.

Mitch would choke when he found out.

Trying to contain her excitement, Tori took the folder. "Thank you, Phil. I really appreciate your vote of confidence. I won't let you down."

The grin spread to the other side of his mouth. "I'm sure you'll do a fine job, Tori. That's why I picked you."

They stood, Tori eager to get back to her desk and read his notes on the account. As she turned to go, her gaze fell on a small, framed plaque on the corner of his desk. She skimmed the calligraphed script.

"Choose for yourselves this day whom you will serve... But as for me and my household, we will serve the Lord. Joshua 24:15."

Tori stole a glance at him. So Phil was a Christian. Funny, but the news didn't surprise her at all. He didn't spout Jesus-talk at every turn, but his manner had always been one of quiet integrity. He instilled trust. Unlike Kate, who instilled stress.

Thoughtful, Tori headed back to her cubicle.

Chapter Eleven

is watch read a few minutes past seven thirty when Ryan knocked on Tori's door. He'd circled the apartment complex a few times, looking for her building and trying not to feel intimidated. Between the tree-shaded grounds, golf course-quality lawn, and crystal clear ponds complete with ducks floating peacefully on the quiet waters, the place looked more like a country club than an apartment complex. He plucked at the collar of his polo shirt. Maybe he should have dressed a little better.

The door opened, and Tori stood smiling at him. Ryan's pulse did something weird as he looked down into those round blue eyes. Whatever made a gorgeous girl like her agree to go out with him?

"Come on in." She stepped back. "I'm almost ready to go."

Ryan entered an apartment that was surprisingly sparse in the way of furnishings. And spotlessly clean. A square sofa was centered along the back wall facing an entertainment center, a traditionally styled coffee table between them. A dinette set filled the other side of the room near a serving window that led into the kitchen. A few framed black-and-white pictures decorated the walls, and in one corner stood a tall vase with artistic-looking stick-things protruding from the top. The room lacked the clutter of knickknacks that filled the homes of most of the women he knew. Instead, he felt like he'd stepped into a professionally decorated waiting room.

"This is a great place." He nodded toward the patio doors to indicate not only her apartment, but the entire complex.

"Thanks. I like it here." Tori gestured toward the sofa as she headed down a hallway. "Make yourself at home. I'll only be a minute."

When she disappeared into a room at the end of the hall, Ryan crossed to the entertainment center to examine the shelves of DVDs. Chick flicks, mostly, with a few adventure movies. And what looked like a complete collection of James Bond. On the top were a couple of photos, one of Joanie, Allie's baby, and the other of Tori and her sisters in front of a Christmas tree. Ryan studied their smiling faces. Tori and Allie were both blonde, while Joan's brown hair and athletic build made her look like she might be from a different family entirely. Until he looked closer, and then he caught the resemblance in the shape of their eyes and their identical smiles.

Tori returned carrying a small purse.

"You must like James Bond." He pointed toward the DVDs.

She smiled. "I like the earlier ones best."

"Should I try to talk with a Scottish accent to impress you, then?" He spoke in his best imitation of Sean Connery.

She cocked her head to the side, curls bouncing as she giggled. "Not bad, but I can still hear Kentucky in your voice. Shall we go?"

He stepped outside into the breezeway. "Where are your pictures?"

Her nose wrinkled with distaste. "Still in my car." She locked the door and turned to face him. "Are you sure you want to see them? I wouldn't want to bore you with a bunch of old baby pictures of Allie and Joan and me, and a guy you never even met."

"You, bore me?" He laughed as he guided her to the parking lot. "I don't think that's possible."

With a loud sigh, she veered toward her car where it sat under a long awning with numbered spaces. When they stood before the trunk, she caught her lower lip between even white teeth as she pulled out her keys. She looked so reluctant, Ryan felt a little guilty.

The trunk popped, but he put a hand out to stop her from opening it. "If you'd prefer not to go through them, it's okay."

Her lips, shining from a fresh coat of lipstick she must have applied in her bedroom, formed a sad smile. "I don't want to, but I sort of do, you know? And you were right—I don't want to look at them by myself."

"Okay."

He lifted the trunk and watched her draw a fortifying breath before she opened the flaps of the box inside and took out a smaller one, the edges creased and wrinkled. She held it in both hands at arm's length, as though it contained something distasteful. For her, he realized, it did.

Gently, he took the box from her hands. She shot him a grateful look, then crossed the parking lot at his side. He shortened his strides to match hers. For some reason she seemed especially small and vulnerable this evening.

She was quiet on the ride across town. When they neared the sprawling campus of the University of Kentucky, she straightened in her seat and gazed keenly outside.

"Could you turn down here?" She pointed out a side street, and Ryan followed her directions to a large, deserted building with darkened windows.

He pulled over to the side of the street and put the car in Park. "This is where Maguire's new restaurant is going to be? I didn't even know this building was back here."

She leaned forward to look through the windshield. "I checked the property records this afternoon. It's had three different owners in the past ten years."

"Restaurants?"

She nodded. "Independent owners, all of them. The last was an Indian restaurant that didn't even make it six months."

Ryan examined the building with a critical eye. It looked nice enough, a squarish structure with a covered entry. It was cleaner than some of the ones surrounding it. "Then why do the Maguire people want to open a restaurant here?"

"The others were start-ups." She gave a brief shrug. "I guess they figure they've established a reputation in town. People have heard of them, and like them."

"Makes sense." With a few enhancements, like a new front door and some different lighting, this building could be dressed up to support the atmosphere they saw last night. "At least there's plenty of parking." He pointed out the large lot to the right.

"That's good, I guess." She didn't look convinced.

He narrowed his eyes and looked at her troubled face. "You don't think this is a good decision for them, do you?"

Her lips tightened, and she didn't answer right away. "I'm not sure. Do me a favor, would you? Drive around and let me look at the area."

Ryan complied, driving slowly down a series of one-way streets, past several other restaurants in a five-block radius. Tori studied them intently. He tried to look at them with the same analytical view, but to him they just looked like a bunch of restaurants. A couple of fast-food places, a health food restaurant, a café with neon lights in the front window that boasted Caribbean food and draft beer. Finally he pulled into the parking lot for the pizza restaurant that was their destination, a block north of the building in question.

"So, what do you think?" he asked when he'd put the car in Park and turned off the engine.

She wore a thoughtful expression. "I think maybe I need to add another one of those Ps to my marketing plan."

"Place?"

She nodded, then turned a grateful smile on him. "Thank you for driving me around."

"My pleasure." He dipped his head, then reached into the backseat for the box of photos. "And now, you can introduce me to your father."

Her smile melted into a resigned frown. "And I was having such a good time too."

"C'mon." He opened the door. "It won't be that bad."

Before he closed his door, he heard her grumble, "That's what you think."

An apron-clad server led them up a set of worn wooden stairs to the upper dining room. The heels of Tori's sandals clacked as she crossed the floor to a table for four, bypassing several picnic tables in the center of the room. The spicy odors of oregano and basil mingled with the yeasty scent of beer from the wide bar downstairs. A window in the back wall gave them a perfect view of the cooks in the kitchen.

Ryan held out a chair next to the wall for her, and when she was seated, he surprised her by sliding into the one next to her instead of across the table.

"So you can tell me what I'm looking at." His grin as he set the box on the table almost took away the knots that tightened in her stomach every time she looked at it.

Tori glanced around the room. Theirs was one of only three occupied tables. She'd been here dozens of times when she was a student at U.K., and the place was usually packed. Apparently summers weren't as busy.

"Did you know this is where Allie and Eric met?" She pointed down the stairs. "Right downstairs at that bar. Apparently he was with a group of his rowdy buddies, and he got so drunk she ended up having to drive him home."

Ryan laughed. "He sure has changed a lot since then. Now he's a responsible, churchgoing husband and father."

Husband and father, yes, but Eric never went to church until last fall, when he got sucked into the Ken Fletcher revival movement. Now he was at church every time the doors opened, along with Allie and Joan. He was still a great guy, but personally, Tori liked him just fine before. But since Ryan was one of Ken's friends, she couldn't really say anything about that. And besides, she'd promised Joan she would try to like her fiancé. So she kept her tone pleasant as she said, "Yes, he sure has."

The server came for their order, then brought their soft drinks. When she'd disappeared down the stairs, Ryan put a hand on the shoebox and gave her a look.

"Are you ready?"

Tori raised her chin. "As ready as I'll ever be."

"Okay." He lifted the lid and lifted out a piece of paper. "What's this?"

"Oh, that." Tori took it from his hand and set it on the table. "It's nothing. Just an old form I found."

He nodded and reached into the box again. A smile lit his face. "Hey, look at you."

He held the family portrait she'd seen in the attic, the one where Daddy stood behind Mom. "I think I was about two months old in that one."

"You were a cute baby. Sort of like Joanie, with that white-blonde hair."

Tori glanced at her infant self. "Only I was chubbier." She reached into the box and pulled out another one. She flipped it over, and her breath caught in her throat. A wedding picture. Mom's dress was a floor-length strapless sheath, no train, but with a lace overlay. Perfect for her tall, slim figure. Beside her stood Daddy in a suit and tie.

"Wow, look how young Carla was." Ryan studied the photo. "How old was she when they married?"

"Twenty-two," Tori replied absently. "Two years younger than I am now."

"I never noticed how much Allie looks like her." He glanced up at her face. "And you too, a little. But Joan looks a lot like your father."

Tori nodded, her gaze fixed on the photo. Joan's eyes stared up at her from Daddy's face. Funny, she'd never noticed how gaunt he was, how his cheeks sank in. Where Joan's body was lean and athletic, his was too thin. He didn't look like that later on, did he? With hesitant fingers, she reached into the box and sifted through the photos until she found the one of Daddy washing his car. Not chubby by any means, but he was more filled out then, several years after marrying Mom.

"Hey, look at that. A 1978 Buick Skylark."

That made Tori chuckle. Guys always noticed the cars. "I thought we were looking at pictures of my father."

"And you. I want to see one of you as a little girl." He grinned as he reached into the box. "If your mother is anything like mine, there might be some embarrassing ones, like of you taking your first bath."

She slapped playfully at his hand. "These are pictures Mom packed away of Daddy, so there won't be any of me by myself in there. Those are all in the photo albums at home."

"Just my luck." He pulled out a couple of snapshots and flipped through them, then held one up. "Who's this?"

Tori's heart wrenched as she looked at the photo he held. "That's Allie with my grandpa and Daddy." The two men sat side by side on the sofa that still graced the living room of the family home, an adolescent Allie wedged between them. She couldn't take her gaze from Grandpa's kind face. A prickle began in the back of her eyes. If she wasn't careful, she would embarrass herself and blubber.

She sifted quickly through the stack she held in her hand. Many of these were familiar, though she hadn't seen them since she was a young child. Mom had obviously cleaned out the photo albums after the divorce.

She came across a family shot she remembered. She was dressed like a fairy princess, complete with cardboard wings and a glittery wand. Allie wore a pirate's eye patch, and Joan had cat whiskers drawn on her face. "Here's one of me." She held the old Polaroid up for Ryan to see. "I think I was about seven. I still remember that Halloween costume. We went trick-or-treating at Gram and Grandpa's house, and Gram snapped this."

Ryan's eyes narrowed as he looked at the photo. "Your father doesn't look thrilled to be there."

He didn't. In fact, he looked bored. In the photo, Allie and Joan stood on either side of Daddy, while Tori hugged Mom's legs with one hand and held her wand in the other. A noticeable gap stretched between her parents. Between young Tori and her father.

"I think I was kind of a mama's girl." She stared at her arm wrapped around her mother.

"Kids that age are," Ryan said. "Butch wouldn't let Loralee out of his sight until about last year."

Tori tore her gaze away from the photograph. "Were you?"

"Honestly?" He lowered his voice and leaned close. "I still am. She cooks better than Pop does."

Tori joined his laughter, her somber mood broken by his lighthearted manner. When he leaned forward to take another photo from the box, he placed an arm casually across the back of her chair. She hid a smile. Tonight he would kiss her goodnight, for sure.

They went through the pictures quickly, and finished by the time their pizza arrived. As the server set a Garden Special in front of them, Tori shuffled all the photos into a semblance of order and stored them back in the box. She started to replace the lid, and Ryan picked up the folded paper.

"Don't forget this." He unfolded it, glanced at it, and looked up at her. "A tax form?"

She took it from him, avoiding his eyes. "Yeah, after we talked the other day I snitched it from the attic. I figured if I ever wanted to try to find him, I'd need his social security number."

He placed it inside the box. "That would probably help, but I don't think you need it."

"I don't?"

He shook his head. "A customer in the store last year was talking about tracking down his old high school buddies on the Internet. Apparently all you need is a name and a state where they used to live."

"Really?"

His shoulders lifted in a shrug. "I've never done it, but that's what he said."

Could it be that easy? Now that she thought about it, Tori felt a little foolish that she'd never even looked to see if she could trace Daddy. She was a market research analyst. She, of all people, knew how easy it was to search public records on the Internet. Just today she'd pulled up property values and sales history with a few mouse clicks.

"Mmm, this looks great." Ryan lifted a slice of pizza onto a small plate and swept the hanging strings of hot cheese with a finger before setting it in front of her. "I'm starving."

A moment ago, Tori's stomach had churned with dread at the thought of looking at pictures of Daddy. Now the task was accomplished, and it hadn't turned out nearly as bad as she expected. She pried a napkin out of the holder and handed it to him with a smile. "Me too."

A trace of humidity hung in the warm night air as Tori walked beside Ryan from his car to her apartment. The fountain in the duck pond had been turned off for the night, and the silence around the complex was broken only by a host of crickets serenading them from somewhere in the shrubbery that lined the sidewalk. Ryan carried the box of photos tucked under one arm.

As she walked, Tori hooked her hand through his other arm, enjoying the strength she felt in him. "I had a really nice time tonight."

His glance held a smile. "Even going through these pictures?"

She wrinkled her nose, then admitted, "It wasn't as bad as I thought it would be. Even though..."

Her words trailed off as they mounted the steps in the breezeway that led to her door.

"Even though what?"

Tori released his arm and took her time opening her purse, feeling inside for her keys. The anxiety that had wrenched her stomach into knots every time she thought of those photos in the past few days was gone, chased away by the act of looking at them. But an uneasiness had taken its place. Her fingers touched metal.

"I don't think I really had much of a relationship with my father." She spoke slowly as she extracted her key chain. "Looking at those pictures, it's Allie and Joan who were always with Daddy, while I hung back with Mom. And that's how I remember it too."

"Well, they were older." Ryan's voice was gentle. "They had more time with him before he left. And maybe the last few years he was becoming distant. I mean, a guy doesn't just decide to leave his family on an impulse. Maybe he went through a period where he separated himself emotionally."

That made sense, especially since most of her memories of Daddy before the divorce were of him sitting in front of the television, present in body but his attention focused elsewhere. Was he stoned during those times? Had he begun to slip into his addictive lifestyle then?

She nodded without looking up. "You're probably right. I . . . feel sort of bad. Like my sisters had a relationship with a man I never had a chance to know."

"That was his loss." The admiration shining in Ryan's eyes softened the sharp edges of her discomfort.

"Thank you." She pitched her tone low, inviting him to come closer as she stood very still and gazed deeply into his eyes. Now would be a good time for him to kiss her. She knew he wanted to, could feel the attraction vibrating between them almost like a magnetic force.

The feeling broke when he leaned away and thrust the box toward her. "I had a good time tonight too."

Fighting a shaft of disappointment, Tori took the shoebox from him. "Thanks for driving me around." She unlocked the door and pushed it open.

"Glad to help." He stepped back, his eyes fixed on her face. "Hey, I was wondering if you'd like to come out to my parents' place Sunday afternoon. Butch and Cody have something for you."

Ah, the meet-the-parents trip. A bit soon, since he hadn't even kissed her yet.

She tilted her head and gave him a look of mock distrust. "It doesn't involve coffee, does it?"

He grinned like a little boy. "I have no idea. But if they come at you with anything liquid, I promise to throw myself in front of you like a human shield." His grin deepened. "Besides, I can show you the difference between a real farm and a tourist attraction."

"I'd like that." Tori realized she spoke the truth. She really wanted to see Ryan in his home environment, to see how different his home was from hers.

He spoke as he backed down the stairs. "Great. I'll pick you up at your grandmother's house around two."

"See you then."

Tori stepped into her apartment and closed the door. She leaned against it for a moment, reviewing the evening. Ryan was an interesting man. Uncomplicated, unlike most guys she'd dated since college. A what-you-see-is-what-you-get kind of guy. Definitely different from Mitch.

Chapter Twelve

"Long's Hardware." Ryan propped the phone on his shoulder so his hands were free to tear open a box of plastic bags as he talked.

"It's Allie. How'd it go last night?"

He'd expected to see her car in the parking lot when he came to work this morning, so her call wasn't a surprise. "Fine. We had a good time."

"And?"

"And what?"

"Details, Ryan! I want details!"

He grinned as he positioned the bags beneath the counter, ready for use with the next customer. "Okay. We had the Garden Special with extra cheese. She sprinkled Parmesan on hers. I used crushed red pepper."

Her disgusted grunt made him laugh. "Did she have a good time? What did you talk about? Are you going out again?"

No way he was going to mention the photographs. "You know, Allie, at some point you're going to have to let go and trust me to handle things on my own."

"I know, but we're not there yet. Answer the questions."

He blew a loud sigh in her ear. "We both had a good time. We talked about her project and my father's farm. And yes."

A pause. "Yes? You mean she agreed to go out with you *again?*"

She sounded so surprised he wondered if he should take offense. "You sound shocked."

"Well, frankly, I am. Three times in a row is something of a record for Tori. Where are you taking her this time?"

"We're going out to the farm Sunday afternoon. My nephews are going to give her a present or something, to apologize for the coffee incident, and my mom's fixing dessert." The door slid open and a customer entered. Ryan straightened and held the phone to his right ear.

"That's great news, Ryan! I can't believe she agreed to meet your family. Just wait 'til I tell Joan."

The delight in her voice was enough to bring a smile to his face. No doubt she'd call Joan as soon as they hung up.

He shifted the phone to his other ear. "Listen, I've got a customer. I'll talk to you later, okay?"

"Okay, but one more thing. Her favorite dessert is lemon meringue pie. Feed her lemon meringue pie and she'll love you forever."

"I thought you said if I feed her mocha-flavored coffee she'd love me forever."

"Yes, but you didn't feed that to her," Allie said dryly. "You dumped it on her."

Good point. "Okay, thanks for the tip."

He shook his head as he disconnected the call. Mom's cobbler was her specialty, but maybe she wouldn't mind making a pie instead.

At seven o'clock Friday morning, Tori pulled into the parking lot of the strip mall that housed Nolan's Ark. She glanced at the three vehicles parked near the pet store. Thankfully, she didn't recognize any of them. She'd been half afraid Mitch would show up this morning to horn in on the commercial shoot. All day yesterday she'd kept quiet about this assignment, and as far as she could tell, Phil hadn't said a word to anyone about asking her to help out. That suited her fine. If Mitch heard about it, he would elbow his way in for sure. And if Kate had caught wind of it, she might have put the kibosh on Tori's involvement. Why Tori thought so, she couldn't really pinpoint, except Kate seemed like the kind of person who didn't voluntarily share her employees. She probably hogged the crayon box when she was in kindergarten too.

Tori parked next to a small white van with the Artistic Video logo on the door. The freelance company was one of several that Connolly and Farrin hired to handle the commercial filming for their clients, but Tori had never met them. She glanced into the rearview mirror to assure herself that her makeup was okay, then got out of the car and smoothed a crease in her skirt. Phil said all she had to do was show up and watch. Surely she could handle that without looking like an amateur.

She paused for a moment to allow her nerves to settle and examined the exterior of the store. A window looked in on a display box where a litter of cuddly kittens played. She watched them for a moment, smiling when a gray-and-white striped one pounced on the fuzzy tail of another.

The door was locked, but she caught the eye of a man inside who hurried over to let her in.

"Are you Miss Sanderson?" A film of sweat glistened on his forehead as he ushered her inside and locked the door behind her.

Tori expected to step into cool air, but the store's interior was almost as warm as outside, only stuffier. The smell that hit her was a mixture of wood shavings and wet fur. Ugh. With an effort, she didn't wrinkle her nose as she answered. "Yes. And you're Mr. Nolan?"

"Call me Ed." He led her toward the back of the store. On the far left, a wall of kennels housed a dozen or more dogs. Ed raised his voice to be heard over their yapping and barking. "Can you believe it? The air conditioner went out yesterday, and the repairman can't come until later this morning. And let me tell you, those lights are hot!"

The sales counter was situated at the rear of the store, and the two people whose T-shirts identified them as the Artistic Video team had already set up the lights and two silver-lined umbrellas. A severe-faced woman caught sight of Tori and advanced with an outstretched hand.

"Susan Murphy." Her grip was so firm as to be almost painful. "I'm the director. And this is Hal."

The cameraman lifted his eye from a camera mounted on a tripod long enough to nod in Tori's direction.

"Tori Sanderson, from Connolly and Farrin." She retrieved her hand and, by sheer willpower, didn't massage it to rub out the sting.

"We're almost ready," Susan told her. "Just give us a minute to get the lighting right and we'll get started."

"Okay, let me know if you need me to help." Tori had no idea what assistance she could possibly offer, since she knew absolutely nothing, but as her company's representative, she felt the offer was expected. Thank goodness Susan and Hal seemed to know what they were doing.

Ed Nolan had gone to stand at the edge of the counter to study a typewritten page. He picked up a red handkerchief and mopped at his forehead and the back of his neck as he read. Judging from the way the paper trembled in his hand, his sweating wasn't entirely due to the heat inside the store.

Not wanting to get in anyone's way, Tori stood to one side, near a wall of large aquariums. Heat radiated from the spotlights angled into each one. A movement inside the nearest drew her attention. She glanced down and then recoiled, her skin crawling with revulsion. A large gray lizard scurried across the sand-covered floor of its glass home. Yuck. She crossed quickly to the other side of the store and stood near another rack of aquariums, these filled with schools of brightly colored fish. She didn't have time to care for any kind of pet, but if she had to choose, fish seemed to be the least labor intensive. And they didn't mistake the carpet for a toilet, either.

A little girl rounded the fishy wall. Tori watched the curly-haired child skip across the floor toward Ed, a wiggling ball of white fuzz clutched in her arms. "Daddy, Miss Muffett is hungry. Can I give her a treat?"

Daddy. Tori looked at the girl more closely. Around five, maybe, with a strong resemblance to Ed in her high, rounded forehead and thick dark hair.

"Hmm?" Ed looked up from his paper, distracted. "Not now, Zoe. Daddy's getting ready to film the commercial. Remember we talked about how you have to stay quiet this morning?"

"I remember, but Miss Muffett is hungry."

Ed waved a hand absently as though shooing the girl away. "Alright, but only one. And break it up for her." He went back to his perusal of the paper.

The little girl shot a look toward the ceiling in a gesture that would have made a teenager proud. "I know the rules, Dad."

She went to the opposite end of the counter to retrieve a treat from a cookie jar shaped like a dog, then headed back in the direction she came from. As she passed, Tori saw that the fuzz ball she held was the world's tiniest dog. Two black eyes peered out from a cuddly, teddy bear face. In fact, this creature was more the size of a guinea pig. Now, that might be a dog Tori could handle. Unlike that monster of Ken's. Tori watched as the girl went into another section of the store and disappeared behind a waist-high barrier where, presumably, she would feed Miss Muffett her treat.

"Are you ready, Ed?"

Ed jerked upright at Susan's voice. "I think I've got it."

Tori watched as Susan directed Ed to stand at the edge of the counter. From the angle of the camera, she guessed that would include a good shot of the colorful fish aquariums and, on the counter beside Ed, some hamsters in a plastic cage with bright yellow tubes running throughout. The pegboard behind the counter held a mishmash of items, and looked...well, messy. Not the best shot, in Tori's opinion, but she didn't want to offend the experts, so she kept her mouth shut. Susan adjusted Ed's stance and positioned his arms so that one rested casually on the counter. Then she backed up to stand beside Hal, who watched through the camera. Tori saw him press a switch, and Susan said, "And, we're rolling."

Ed swallowed, and managed to look stiff in spite of his carefully casual stance. He stared at the camera and cleared his throat. *"At Nolan's Ark, we understand that your pet is a special member of your family."* His voice trailed off, and he froze for a long moment, then slumped. "Uh, I've forgotten what comes next."

Tori turned to Susan. "I could hold cue cards for him."

The woman's lips tightened. "You could, if we had any. But we were told he'd have the script memorized."

Tori would have made some cue cards herself, if she'd known. *Next time,* she promised herself. In the meantime, she crossed to the opposite end of the counter and grabbed Ed's script. *"We've been in the pet business for more than ten years,"* she read.

Ed's face cleared. "That's right. *We've been in the pet business for more than ten years, and we know about your pet's needs."*

He stopped and looked at Susan. "Should I start again from the beginning?"

Tori watched as Hal pressed a button on his camera, then straightened. Susan's smile was thin. "Yes, let's try it again from the top."

Ed stretched his neck and ran a finger around his collar. "Okay."

Susan waited for Hal's nod, and then told Ed, "We're rolling."

The man's expression became wooden, his stare fixed. *"At Nolan's Ark, we understand that your pet is a special member of your family. We've been in the pet business for more than ten years, and we know about your pet's needs."* A pause. A gulp. *"We..."* He shifted his weight from one foot to the other. *"Whatever you need..."* His shoulders slumped as he shook his head, his gaze sliding from the camera to Tori. "I'm sorry. I thought I had it."

Susan didn't bother to hide her heavy sigh. Tori felt sorry for the man, who's face became a darker shade of red with every second that ticked by. Not all of his flush was due to the heat, though Tori was starting to feel a little sticky herself.

She glanced at the paper. "You do have it. That was the next line. *Whatever you need, you'll find it at Nolan's Ark.*"

He put a hand on his forehead. "I thought so. I'm sorry. I shouldn't have stopped."

"Tell you what." Susan took the script from Tori and handed it to Ed. "Let's run through it a couple of times with you reading from the script. We're going to do some panning of the store, and we can use that as a voice-over. Then maybe we can get just a few shots of you doing one line at a time. Sound good?"

Instant relief flooded Ed's face. "I can do that."

That sounded like a good plan to Tori. And maybe going over it once out loud would help him remember his lines.

Susan turned to face the camera, and crossed her eyes where Ed couldn't see. Tori had to duck her head to hide a grin. The director returned to her place slightly behind Hal and spoke with a patience Tori wouldn't have credited the stern-faced woman with.

"Alright, Ed, go ahead, read it all the way through."

Ed nodded. He stared at the paper, his lips moving.

"Out loud, Ed." Susan's voice held the first hint of irritation.

"Oh!" Ed's head jerked upward. "I was waiting for you to say, 'We're rolling.'"

Tori turned away, laughter threatening to bubble through the lips she pressed tightly together. Poor Ed. He really was trying, but his nerves were getting the best of him.

The muscles in Susan's jaws bunched as she clenched her jaw. "We are rolling, Ed."

"Alright." Ed drew in a deep breath and began to read from the paper. *"At-Nolan's-Ark-we-understand-that-your-pet-is-a-special-member-of-your-family-we've-been-in-the-pet-business—"*

"Stop!"

From where she stood, Tori could see the director's hands grasp each other tightly behind her back. "Ed, the purpose of this take is to get a good reading of the script so we can use your voice while the audience looks at the interior of your store. So it's important that your voice sound natural. It's coming out a little stilted."

Ed hung his head. "I'm not a very good reader. That's why I was trying to memorize it."

"I see." The knuckles on her clasped hands turned white. "Let's try it again without the script, then. I can give you verbal cues, and as long as you stand in one place, we can edit my voice out back at the studio."

The red handkerchief appeared, and Ed wiped frantically at his forehead. "Okay."

He'd barely begun his recitation when one of the puppies in the kennels along the far wall let out a yap, which was quickly answered by a bark from the opposite end of the line. In the next instant, every puppy in the place had joined in.

Hal clicked off the camera and lifted his head. "There's no way I'm going to be able to filter out that noise."

The director didn't bother to hide a very loud and dramatic sigh. "Ed, can you do anything to shut them up?"

Tori covered her grin with a hand. Did all commercial shoots have this many problems, or was she just lucky enough to get a weird one on her first assignment?

Ed looked around blankly for a moment, as though he hadn't noticed the Bark Fest. "They must want attention. I usually let them out of their kennels to play while I'm getting the store ready to open."

Tori heard a low giggle coming from the other side of the wall of fish, where Zoe and Miss Muffett played. "Can your daughter keep them busy for a few minutes?"

Ed's expression cleared. "Yes! But she can't safely reach the upper kennels. If you could…"

Great. And get dog hair and puppy stench all over her clothes? But the protest died on her lips at the pleading look on Susan's face. She pasted on a resigned smile. "Sure."

"Here. Take these." Ed snatched the cookie jar off the counter and thrust it into her hands. "They're puppy approved. Just break them up for the smaller breeds."

Smaller breeds? Meaning there were larger breeds? An image of Ken's giant mongrel loomed in Tori's mind as she cautiously made her way to the back corner of the store to find Zoe. She eyed the double row of kennels warily, but none of the dogs appeared to be saddle-ready.

She found Zoe inside an eight-foot-square area cordoned off by a waist-high wall. A sign on the wall read "Pet Play Area." Two folding chairs sat empty in one corner while Zoe crouched on the floor, giggling as she tossed a stuffed toy for Miss Muffett.

The little dog hopped across the floor after the toy, which was as big as she. The girl looked up as Tori approached.

"Hi. You're name's Zoe, right?"

A strand of dark hair that had come loose from high pigtails waved as the child nodded.

"Your daddy told me to come help you get some more puppies out to play with." She held up the cookie jar. "We're supposed to give them treats to keep them quiet."

As though to emphasize the point, the dogs' barking grew louder. Tori glimpsed Susan through the aquariums, her grim expression magnified to fierce proportions by the water.

"We can get them all?" Delight lit Zoe's face as she leaped to her feet.

"Well..." Tori glanced around the play area. "Do you think they'll fit in here?"

"Sure they will." The girl opened the half-door and eased out, gently keeping Miss Muffett from escaping with her foot. Tori set the cookie jar on the floor and followed her to the kennels.

The chorus of barking increased to a frantic pace as Zoe opened the bottom kennel and lifted out a wiener dog puppy. A pink tongue appeared and bathed the child's face, which sent an answering flutter of revulsion to Tori's stomach. Gram and Grandpa had a dog when she was living at home, and she used to let that one lick her in the mouth. Until Allie pointed out that dogs used their tongues as toilet paper.

"You get those," Zoe instructed, pointing to the kennel on top of the wiener dog's.

Tori eyed the much larger kennel's occupants. Two puppies, each one easily three times the size of the little one Zoe had taken to the play area. German Shepherd, the sign mounted on the front of the wire crate read. Both puppies shoved noses through the grating, their long, thin tails wagging behind them as they tried to see which could out-bark the other. Tori lifted the spring-loaded handle on the kennel and eased a hand inside. Her fingers touched fuzzy puppy fur.

"Okay, just stay calm," she told one while she tried to get a grip on the other one, who was using her fingers as a teething ring. "I'll come right back for—oops!"

Just as she lifted one puppy out, the other, determined not to be left behind, leaped out of the kennel toward her. She snatched it out of the air with a scooping motion, wedging it to her body with her free hand and arm. The wiggling creature dangled with its front paws scrabbling at her skirt and its hind claws digging into the skin of her neck.

"Aack! Help!"

She whirled to find Zoe rushing toward her, arms outstretched. "You're supposed to use two hands," the little girl chided as she rescued the animal.

"I was trying. That one is a kamikaze puppy."

Zoe cocked her head, a question on her face. "No, her name is Shaylee."

The child marched to the pen and opened the door a crack to wedge her way in without letting the two inmates escape. Tori tried to ignore the stinging in her neck as she followed, holding tight to the other puppy. Giant ears stood at attention on top of a narrow face like satellites, the poor thing. This baby was going to have to do a lot of growing to justify ears that big. Tori's hand encircled the soft fur of its chest, and felt a wild heartbeat pounding against her palm.

"Here, I'll take her."

Zoe stood inside the pen, arms outstretched. The tiniest hint of reluctance surprised Tori as she handed the puppy into the little girl's arms. Then she felt the stinging scratch on her neck, which had become a long welt.

"Ouch."

Zoe tilted her head up to inspect it. "You'll be okay. Just wash it with soap when you get home."

The voice of experience, apparently. Tori nodded, and then followed the child to the next set of kennels. In a few minutes they'd unloaded twelve puppies in sizes varying from Miss Muffett's sister to an adolescent yellow lab that Tori didn't want to carry, so Zoe led with a firm grip on the collar. When they put the last animal in the playpen, Zoe climbed over the wall and descended into the mass of fur and wiggling puppy bodies.

Except for an occasional happy yap, silence reigned. The smell of puppy fur and dog breath clung to Tori's clothes. She brushed at a suspicious spot on her blouse, and tried not to think what it might be. In the other end of the store she heard the drone of Ed's voice, then Susan's, then Ed's again, saying, *"All our animals receive the highest level of care, and are guaranteed to be healthy and happy. Because here at Nolan's Ark, pets are not just our business. They're our family."* At least they were getting it done.

She started to turn away, and looked into the play area in time to see Zoe break a treat into pieces and feed the two Shepherd puppies. Miss Muffett and another fluff-ball jockeyed for position in her lap while the yellow lab licked her neck from behind. The child's delighted giggle rang musically in the store.

Tori stopped, an idea clicking into place. If the point of the commercial was to project a family appeal, wouldn't it be better to show some family fun instead of panning across the kennels with the puppies staring through wires like a bunch of inmates while Ed's dull voice droned in the background? Of course, she knew nothing about commercials, but Phil did say if she had any ideas...

She hurried over to the filming site and plucked Susan's sleeve. "I want to show you something."

At first she thought the director would refuse, but then the woman heaved a loud sigh and followed. Apparently she didn't want to argue with the official representative from Connolly and Farrin. Tori led her quietly to the edge of the pet play area, where an ecstatic Zoe lay sprawled on the floor, covered in playful puppies.

Tori didn't have to say a word. Susan watched for only a few seconds before a wide grin transformed her features. "Hal," she called, "how quickly can you get a light set up back here?"

As the cameraman moved one of the umbrellas, Tori stood out of the way with Ed Nolan and explained. "Since you're talking about pets being part of the family, I thought it would be a good idea to show pets interacting with a child. They'll probably use the original voiceover idea, and some clips of you talking as well as some clips of the rest of the store. But Zoe was having so much fun with the puppies, it seemed like a good idea to capture that fun on camera."

Ed's eyes fixed on his giggling daughter. "She'll steal the show from her old man."

"I hope it's okay," she said. "If you'd rather not, we can always go back to the original plan. Or if you like the idea but don't want to use Zoe, we could even schedule another shoot and hire a child actor."

"And rob her of her chance to be a star?" He shook his head, laughing. "No way."

"And, uh, you know what else you might consider?" Tori didn't look at him, but watched Hal fiddle with the camera's angle as she spoke. Phil had mentioned that Ed insisted on doing this commercial himself, so she didn't want to offend him by suggesting too many changes. "Instead of standing there behind the counter with your arms at your sides, maybe you could be interacting with the animals too. You know, hold a kitten or something. It might help you appear less…" She bit her lip and cast around for a word that wouldn't give offense.

"Awkward?"

"I was going to say *nervous*. Plus, I think it will help keep people focused on the animals, which is the whole reason for advertising, right?"

"That's a good idea." His grin widened. "See, this is why I hired your firm. I needed an expert to tell me what works and what doesn't." He rubbed his hands together. "This is going to be a great commercial. I can hardly wait to see it on TV."

Tori folded her arms and gave a satisfied nod. She'd received a battle wound and she smelled like a cross between a doghouse and a locker room, but if the client was happy, her first commercial shoot was a success.

Tori took the time to go home for the second shower of the day before heading to work. It was almost lunchtime when she parked her car in the garage. Her cell phone rang as she stepped into the elevator. She pressed the button for the sixth floor before sliding the cover up to answer the call.

"Hello?"

"Kate Bowman here." Tori straightened to attention, and immediately felt ridiculous. Her boss couldn't see her all the way from Chicago.

"Hello, Kate. How's the last day of the conference going?"

As always, niceties were lost on Kate.

"Where are you?" Undisguised irritation made her voice snap like a whip. "Mitch told me your desk has been empty all morning. You didn't tell me you were taking the day off."

Tori fought a wave of irritation, whether at her nosy co-worker or her demanding boss, she wasn't sure. "That's because I've been working. Phil asked me to fill in for him at a taping this morning."

In the silence that met her, Tori worried that she'd gotten Phil in trouble. But surely he didn't expect her to keep secrets from her boss, especially when she had been doing legitimate work for one of the firm's clients.

"I see."

The weight of those two words made Tori wince. She decided the wisest course of action was to change the subject. "Did you need something?"

"I wanted to let you know that the Maguire people will be in the office on Monday."

Tori snapped to attention a second time, just as the doors opened on the sixth floor. She wasn't ready to present anything. She barely had any ideas at all. "What's the purpose of the meeting? They're not expecting to see preliminary ideas, are they? Because I haven't got anything good enough for the client's eyes, yet."

"You haven't come up with *anything*?"

Tori sucked in an outraged breath, fighting against an angry retort. *Maybe if you'd stop calling and emailing every ten minutes, I would.*

The doors started to close, and Tori slipped between them. She emerged in the lobby of Connolly and Farin, where Fran sat behind her desk, tapping on her computer keyboard. Tori waited until she could speak calmly. "I'll work on it. Do we have an agenda for the meeting?"

"Rita's working it up. No presentations. Just a meet-and-greet. Their request, so they can get a look at the firm and the team who's working on their account."

The team. Yeah. What an interesting idea, letting your employees work as a team instead of pitting them against each other.

"I see."

"Nine o'clock. Make sure you're not late."

The line went dead. Tori scowled at the phone as she rounded Fran's desk and headed for her cubicle. As expected, her computer hadn't even finished powering on before Mitch sauntered in and draped himself across her guest chair.

"Well, well, well. Look who finally decided to show up for work."

Tori ignored the jab. The smirky Mitch had returned. One thing about the guy, he was anything but predictable. He had more moods than a menopausal woman.

She planted her elbows on her desk and stared at him over steepled fingers. "I didn't realize you were the official keeper of the time clock. Is that a self-appointed task, or did you receive a special assignment from Kate to keep an eye on my hours?"

"Hey, don't be like that. I'm just kidding around." He leaned forward. "Actually, I've been waiting for you to get here so I could propose a sort of truce."

"Go on."

"I'm sure we'll both be working tomorrow." He raised his eyebrows for verification, and Tori gave a single nod. Saturdays off were a thing of the distant past. "So I was thinking we might as well perform a little field research. What say tomorrow night you and I head over to Maguire's Restaurant for dinner?"

Tori narrowed her eyes. Was he proposing a business outing between co-workers, or asking her for a date? With Mitch it was hard to tell. Probably the former, but something in the way he wasn't breathing while he waited for her answer told her he wasn't as indifferent as he might seem.

Her reply was forestalled by an interruption. Phil rounded the corner and entered the cubicle, a wide smile on his face. He paused for a moment when he caught sight of Mitch, but then came toward Tori with outstretched hands.

"You are terrific."

Pleased, Tori stood and allowed him to take her hands. "I am?"

"Ed Nolan called and left a message on my voicemail singing your praises. I've tried for weeks to talk him out of the monologue idea, but he wouldn't listen to me. But you?" Phil squeezed her hands. "He thinks you're a creative genius, and he says his daughter is so excited she's changing her career goal from veterinarian to movie star."

Tori laughed. "As long as it's her and not Ed who wants to become an actor."

Phil grimaced. "Was he that bad?"

"Awful."

"I was afraid of that. I'm so glad you were there to handle things, Tori. Thank you. I'll make sure Kate knows how big a help you were."

He gave her hands a final squeeze, then left the cubicle. Tori settled back in her seat, aware that Mitch was staring at her with barely concealed curiosity.

She shrugged. "Phil needed help filming a commercial for one of his accounts this morning, so I filled in."

"You went out on a commercial shoot?"

"That's right."

The smirk had disappeared completely, replaced by undisguised envy. "How did you wrangle that?"

"I didn't wrangle anything. He asked for help. I said yes."

That he didn't believe her was apparent. He watched her suspiciously, then rose and edged toward the exit. When he stepped out of her cubicle, Tori stopped him.

"Oh, Mitch?" She gave him a bright smile. "About that dinner tomorrow night. Great idea. What time do you want to go?"

Judging from his expression, he regretted asking her. She half expected him to back out. Instead, a shadow of his former smugness returned as he said, "Let's plan to head over around seven."

When he was gone, Tori sat back with a sigh of satisfaction. Any day she managed to get one over on Mitch was a good day.

Chapter Thirteen

The office was blessedly quiet all day Saturday. The few people unfortunate enough to be working kept to themselves—even Mitch, Tori was pleased to note. The phone was satisfyingly silent. Kate's cell phone battery must have died or something.

Drawing on her notes and her memories of the atmosphere at Maguire's, Tori came up with a few rough advertising ideas that she thought held real promise. She also assembled some ideas for an approach to the question of Place for her marketing plan. By early afternoon, she'd made enough progress that she felt justified in taking a break to do some research for Joan.

She pulled up her favorite search engine. The screen displayed a multicolored logo, the cursor flashing in the search box. Fingers poised over the keyboard, Tori hesitated. *Wedding gifts for groom.* Her brain sent the signal to her fingers. But her heart supplied a different phrase.

Find a person.

The words appeared on the screen as though put there by someone else. She stared, her finger hovering over the mouse key. In her ears her heartbeat sounded like somebody held a microphone to her chest and cranked the volume. Seeing the request on the monitor flooded her with dread. If she'd come far enough in her decision process to actually type the words that might lead to her finding Daddy, what did that mean was happening inside her? Was she really ready to confront him, to ask him the question that hurt so much she could barely phrase it to herself?

Why did you leave me?

Her finger plunged downward. The mouse clicked.

A list of URLs appeared—52,100,000 of them, according to the statistics at the top of the page. A frantic laugh burst through her lips. Apparently lots of people had someone they'd like to find. She scanned the ones at the top. Find a Person. Free Person Search. Find a Missing Friend. Well, it didn't matter which she chose, did it? She clicked the first link.

A simple-looking search box opened up, along with a few instructions. All she had to do was enter a name and, if she had it, an old address. They didn't even ask for a social security number.

Her throat tightened as she typed *Thomas Alan Sanderson.* No hesitation before clicking the search button this time. When the results flashed up on the screen, for a moment Tori sat there, stunned. This site listed over a hundred Thomas Sandersons from all over the country. And the amount of data it gave was pretty amazing. Besides the name, the page displayed aliases, age, the cities and states where that particular Thomas Sanderson was known to have lived, and—most amazing of all—a list of possible known relatives. The entries appeared to be in no discernible order, so she paged down, looking for a sixty-one-year-old Thomas.

A name in the relative column of number twenty-nine snagged her eye before she even noticed the man's age. The pounding of her heart stuttered when she saw her own mother's name. *Carla Hancock Sanderson (age 55).* She'd found him!

But right below Mom's name was another. *Patricia Ann Parker (age 38).*

Blood buzzed through her head. Who was Patricia Ann Parker? She was listed below Mom, in the relative column. But

Daddy had no relatives. Had he remarried? If so, he'd married a much younger woman. Allie was twenty-nine. That meant this woman was closer to his daughter's age than his! Did Mom know? Tori remembered Mom's expression on Sunday. No, she didn't think so.

And look at that list of addresses. Apparently he'd moved around quite a bit after he left Danville. In fact, Danville wasn't even included in the list, but five other cities were, including Phoenix, Las Vegas, Dayton, Columbus, and... Tori gulped. The last city listed was Cincinnati. Did that mean Cincinnati was his most recent address? Was he, even now, living only ninety minutes from here?

A button beneath her father's name invited her to *View Details*. Tori tried to wet her lips with a dry tongue. Did she want details? Yes, she certainly did, but this site couldn't tell her what she wanted to know. The details she wanted all had to do with *Why,* but this search engine could only tell her *Where.*

And what if it turned out he lived in Cincinnati? How could he be so close to them and not let them know? Anger flickered at the edges of her thoughts. Ninety minutes was nothing. He could have driven down for Joan's band concerts. Or to see Tori cheer at basketball games. Heck, Allie got her license a year after he left. If they'd known he was so close, they could have driven up to visit him.

The mouse button took the brunt of her anger. She clicked *View Details* with force. The display revealed a menu of choices, each one with an associated price tag. This was where the website made its money. The first option was an expanded version of the report she'd just seen, only with full addresses and phone numbers. For ten bucks she could get that address in Cincinnati. But the second option provided even more information for only five additional dollars. Tori scanned the list. People search. Property search. Marriage search. Divorce search. Her pulse faltered as she read the next item on the list.

Death search.

With a savage gesture, Tori closed out the browser window and then clasped her fingers in her other hand as though they'd been burned. No. That was one detail she couldn't handle knowing.

The walls of her cubicle seemed to press in on her. She couldn't sit here in front of this computer one more minute. Where could she go? Home? No. Danville? Her stomach formed a knot at the thought of facing Joan and Allie with the news that their father had lived only ninety miles away for who-knew-how-long. Where, then?

She jerked open the drawer and picked up her purse, hating the way her hand trembled as she draped the strap over her shoulder. The mall. Perfect. She'd go shopping for something to wear to Monday's meeting. They didn't call it retail therapy for nothing.

The slamming of the drawer echoed through the nearly empty office as Tori exited her cubicle at almost a run. She took the long way around to the elevator so she could stop by and tell Mitch she'd meet him at Maguire's at seven.

Mitch beat Tori to the restaurant. She parked her car next to his and wound her way through the nearly full parking lot. As she approached the door, a well-dressed couple exited, and the gentleman politely held the door open for her to enter. She stepped into the crowded waiting area and stopped, blinking in the subdued light.

A familiar voice sounded in her ear. "Wow, Sanderson, you look great."

Tori rounded. Mitch stood so close she had to tilt her head to look him in the face. His crooked smile held the hint of a leer that brought an uncomfortable warmth to her cheeks. Her afternoon at the mall had proven profitable, yielding not only a new suit for Monday's meeting but a stunning new Italian silk satin dress. Hardly everyday attire, but she justified the expense with the assurance that she could wear it tonight to go out with Mitch, and again the next time Ryan asked her to dinner, and a third time at Joan's rehearsal dinner. But judging from the way Mitch's gaze lingered, maybe the draping neckline should be a little higher for an evening with a co-worker.

"Thank you." She couldn't help flashing a dimple at him, even as she turned sideways and unobtrusively hitched up the silky fabric on her shoulder to disrupt his view.

"The hostess said it'll be a few minutes while they get our table ready."

Tori glanced at the black-clad pair of girls behind the hostess stand. Neither was the blonde from Tuesday night. Beyond them, every table in the restaurant was full, and the dining room was noisier tonight. Once again, firelight flickered from gas logs in the far wall, adding a nice ambiance to the room. Romantic. Tori cast an uncomfortable sideways glance at Mitch. He was watching her with a stare so direct it might almost be interpreted as impertinent. But then again, that was Mitch.

"Mr. Jackson?" One of the hostesses smiled in their direction. "We have your table ready."

Tori trailed the girl through the first dining room into the second, aware that Mitch followed close enough so she could hear his breath. The diners seated at the tables they passed formed a more diverse crowd tonight. No jeans, but she saw a few casually dressed couples interspersed with the elaborate dresses. There was even a family in the corner, a boy about ten years old and a girl a few years younger. They sat with an older couple who Tori guessed were their grandparents. She hid a grin at the idea of Gram and Grandpa bringing the Sanderson sisters to a restaurant like this when they were that age. Her grandparents hadn't been poor, but she doubted if Gram had ever been in a restaurant more expensive than Cracker Barrel. She would have been outraged at the menu prices here.

Tori's foot stumbled when the hostess led them to the same table she had occupied with Ryan on Tuesday night. *O-kay.* That felt a little weird. Mitch reached out a hand to steady her, his touch electric on her bare arm. She straightened away from him and shot him a quick smile of thanks.

"Steady there, Sanderson. Don't want you falling off those ridiculous high heels you're wearing."

"Ridiculous?" She allowed a chill to creep into her tone as she slid into the chair he held out for her. Someone needed to give the guy lessons in dating etiquette. And maybe a lesson on recognizing quality footwear.

"I meant ridiculously high." His soft voice purred in her ear as he settled the chair beneath the table. "But I guess a four-inch heel makes a big difference when you're only five feet tall."

"I'm five-two, thank you very much."

She took the menu from the hostess and opened it, even though she'd memorized it a few days before. Tonight she intended to eat without worrying about the price. This was honest-to-goodness field research, and Connolly and Farrin would pick up the bill.

"Kind of a snazzy place." Mitch's eyes moved as he scanned the room. "Surprising for a restaurant in a strip mall, don't you think?"

Tori followed his gaze. Candles flickered on every table, the light reflecting warmly off of silver and crystal. Was Mitch starting to have the same suspicions about Maguire's new location as she? If not, she didn't want to give him any leads. In fact, she'd prefer not to discuss any of her ideas with him. She shrugged and went back to her examination of the menu.

His grin deepened. "Ah. I get it." He picked up his own menu and opened the leather folder. "Not giving anything away, are we?"

"That's right."

The waiter approached, and Tori bit back a groan when she recognized the same man as on her last visit. What would he think of her, coming to the same restaurant with two different guys within a few days of each other? She sank a little behind her menu as he filled their glasses with ice water.

"Can I bring you something from the bar?"

"We'll have a bottle of Shiraz," Mitch said instantly.

Tori hesitated. The firm would reimburse them for wine without even a question. Liquor flowed freely in the marketing community. The large conference room at the office even boasted a well-stocked bar for client meetings that ran late. But after Mom's revelations about Daddy, the thought had occurred to Tori more than once that addictive tendencies seemed to recur in families. Apparently her paternal grandmother was an addict, as was her father. She'd rather not take a risk with something like that.

"I'll just stick with water," she told the waiter.

Mitch's eyebrows arched. The waiter, who didn't appear to remember her, thank goodness, picked up the wine glass from the setting in front of her and disappeared in the direction of the bar. They kept their attention focused on their menus until he returned with the wine.

When the waiter left again, Mitch raised his glass toward her in a silent toast, sipped, and then asked, "So, how are you coming along on your presentation?"

"Fine. You?"

"Good. Great, in fact." He sipped again, then set the glass down. "I've got some good ideas, I think."

Tori's grip on the menu tightened. If he was trying to make her nervous, it wouldn't work. Well, not much. "Good for you."

He leaned forward and dropped his tone suggestively. "Tell you what. I'll show you mine, if you'll show me yours."

Heat flared into Tori's face. "That's inappropriate, Mitch."

"What's the matter, Sanderson?" He straightened and picked up his glass. "I'm talking about our presentations."

His eyes held hers over the rim of his glass as he drank deeply of the rich, red liquid. The ever-present smirk was starting to get on Tori's nerves. He really would be handsome if he could manage to lose it every so often. Then maybe she could tell what he was actually thinking behind that mocking expression.

"I'm sure that's what you mean, Mitch." She smiled as sweetly as she could manage. "When I'm your boss, I'm all for a free exchange of ideas. Until then, I don't care to discuss mine.'"

A slow grin slid across his lips. He drank again, then leaned forward and spoke in a low voice. "When I'm *your* boss, you'll have to be nicer to me, won't you?"

"Be careful, Mitch." She didn't bother to tone down her irritation. "Someone who didn't know better might mistake your joking for harassment."

"What a good thing you know better, huh, Sanderson?"

The waiter arrived, and Tori welcomed the interruption. The conversation was getting just a little too close to some sort of ill-defined boundary for her. The attraction she had for Mitch was rapidly fading and turning into something that wouldn't be comfortable in the office. Maybe she'd been wrong to come here. Or maybe coming here with a co-worker was fine, but she definitely shouldn't have worn this dress. She lifted her menu to form a shield and hitched the neckline high.

What was it he had said about speaking the same language? Yeah, right. She and Mitch *sooo* didn't.

The evening accomplished one important thing—any secret attraction she'd felt for Mitch was completely eradicated. They might work in the same field, and he might be handsome and intelligent and experienced in her profession, but if there was one thing Tori couldn't stand, it was a mean drunk. The longer the evening went on and the emptier that wine bottle became, the more cutting Mitch's comments got. He never became sloppy, but he criticized everything—their clients, Kate, the partners, even the coworkers he spent all day flirting with. Every comment was delivered in the style that had become Mitch's trademark, complimentary and nasty in equal parts, until Tori wanted to scream at him to *just shut up!*

She wrestled the bill away from him, left a sizable tip, and marched toward the exit, relief making her step light. The sooner this evening ended, the better. A long night curled up with her laptop and six months' worth of traffic pattern data to analyze sounded almost heavenly compared to another ten minutes in Mitch's tipsy presence.

He followed her across the parking lot, his long stride confident. Not even a wobble that would surely have made the restaurant staff wonder if he was okay to drive. Amazing, since he'd almost finished that whole bottle of wine by himself. It must be true that people built up a tolerance to alcohol. He'd apparently been working on immunity for years.

"Are you okay to drive?" she asked as they approached their cars.

"Of course I am." His eyebrows waggled and he leaned toward her. "Unless you want to take me home."

"Tempting, but no." The smile she gave him was chilly, but he seemed not to notice. "But I can call you a taxi if you like."

He scoffed. "What for? I'm fine."

"Okay, if you say so."

She opened her purse and held it up to catch the glow from the streetlight so she could see inside for her keys. In the next instant, she found herself pressed against her car door, Mitch's face inches from hers. On either side of her head was one of Mitch's arms, elbows locked, his hands resting on the car window.

"What are you doing, Mitch?"

"Well, I was hoping for a goodnight kiss."

His eight-inch height advantage seemed to double as he loomed over her. Though he wasn't nearly as muscular as Ryan, a jolt of fear shot through Tori as she realized her coworker was no weakling. And she, most definitely, was. He could probably overpower her without breaking a sweat.

"I don't think that's a good idea."

"Oh, but I do, Tori."

His whisper smelled strongly of alcohol, tainted with a hint of garlic. Her stomach gave a queasy lurch. She wasn't afraid of the Mitch she knew from work, but alcohol made people do crazy things. She had to get control of the situation, quickly, and get out of here.

"You have ten seconds to back off." She poured steel into her tone. "Or else."

He leaned closer, his alcoholic breath nearly smothering her. "Or else, what?"

"I have two knees, Mitch, and I know how to use them."

Surprised, he jerked backward, his palms held toward her. "Gee, Sanderson, no need to get hostile."

Relieved, she pressed a button on her remote by feel and heard a click as the doors unlocked. Without another word, she opened her door just wide enough to slip inside. Mitch backed up to lean against the hood of his car as she started her engine, shifted into gear, and pulled away. Only when he was no longer visible in her rearview mirror did she relax her clutch on the steering wheel.

What a terrible night. At least she'd solved one question in her mind. A relationship with Mitch away from the office was not an option. It would probably take a while for her to feel comfortable working with him *in* the office after tonight.

And what about when this competition was over, and one of them became the other's boss?

With a sinking feeling, Tori headed for home. Maybe she should check the want ads again before she started working on that analysis.

Chapter Fourteen

When Ryan entered the church building on Sunday morning, it was with a slow footstep. He'd driven through the rows in the parking lot looking for a white Toyota, but it wasn't there. Maybe Tori was working again. Or maybe she was avoiding church because she didn't want to see him. And maybe that was for the best.

Every time he'd started to call her since their date Wednesday night, something stopped him. First, he told himself he didn't want to appear too eager. She'd agreed to go out to the farm on Sunday, and that was soon enough to see her again. Second, what could he talk about? He couldn't ask her out again for the simple fact that he had blown his food budget for the entire month on their two dates. He wouldn't starve, not with Mom loading him up with leftover roast beef or chicken every time he stopped by the house, but he couldn't very well ask Tori over to the cracker box he lived in for a dinner of his parents' leftovers.

But there was a deeper reason his hand froze every time he reached for the phone. The time he'd spent with her had confirmed what he'd known all along—Tori Sanderson and he lived in different worlds, no matter what her sisters and his sister-in-law said. She drove a nicer car. Lived in a much nicer place. Worked in a stylish office with professional men who had paychecks to match their egos. What did he have to offer?

The church building bustled with activity this morning. Ryan sidestepped a laughing pair of preteen girls running up the stairs as he made his way to the basement, where most of the Sunday school rooms were. He nodded hello to Mrs. Bowers and Mrs. Penegor, on their way to the nursery with toddlers in tow. When he turned the corner toward his classroom, he heard his name.

"Ryan, wait up."

No mistaking that voice. His stomach did a weird flip-flop as he turned to see Tori hurrying to catch up with him. The smile on her face lit the windowless hallway like a beacon, and as she neared, he looked into small pieces of summer sky framed by her delicate lashes.

His resolve evaporated like mist in the sunshine of her smile. Maybe she wouldn't mind leftover chicken so much.

She hurried up to him, looking so happy to see him for one crazy moment Ryan thought she might kiss him on the cheek in a friendly greeting. She stopped just short of that, but her hand on his arm sent an army of goose bumps marching over his skin.

"I tried to catch you in the parking lot, but I guess you didn't hear me."

"N–no. Sorry." He gulped. "I was hoping you'd be here this morning."

"Well, I should be working instead of listening to Mr. Carmichael's *captivating* Sunday school lesson." The grimace she gave him managed to be expressive and cute at the same time. "But I couldn't face another day in that office. Besides, I've got plenty of work I can do from the comfort of my apartment later tonight."

"I'm afraid you're out of luck if you were counting on one of Mr. Carmichael's lessons." He put a hand on her back while they walked toward their room. "His mother has been sick, so he's spending a lot of weekends down in Knoxville."

"That's too bad." She grinned. "About his mother, I mean. Not about the lesson. So, who's teaching in his place?"

"Joan didn't mention it?" They approached the door. "Ken."

"Oh. Well, he certainly knows the Bible."

Did he imagine it, or did she roll her eyes? Just what was it Tori had against her future brother-in-law? Ken was a great guy, caring and intelligent. Ryan liked hanging out with him in hopes that some of his solid faith would rub off. Maybe this afternoon he'd ask her about it.

But at that moment, they entered the room and Tori was swept into her sister's hug. Joan guided her to an empty pair of chairs. Ryan took the seat next to Tori, then looked up to the head of the table. Gordy Reynolds sat in the teacher's place, his Bible and a Sunday school booklet opened in front of him. Ryan scanned the room and found Ken seated on the other side of Joan.

"Hey, man, what are you doing up there?" he asked Gordy.

Gordy sat taller in the chair. "I'm the substitute teacher, dude."

Of everyone in the class, Gordy was the last person Ryan thought would agree to step into Mr. Carmichael's place. Not that his faith wasn't sincere, but Gordy wasn't exactly studious. He was better with a basketball than a Bible. Around the room, Ryan saw his own skepticism reflected on every face.

Beside him, Tori's eyes widened with disbelief. "You?"

"Me." Gordy's lips twisted into a sheepish grin. "Go figure, huh?"

Tori gave a small laugh. "Yeah. Go figure."

Ryan caught Ken's eye and asked an unspoken question by lifting his eyebrows. Ken responded with a very slight shrug. His glance rested on Tori for a second, then his attention slid to Gordy. Ryan turned back around. For the first time, he noticed Gordy's hair was sculpted spikier than normal, like he'd spent extra time on it. And his shirt wasn't wrinkled, either.

Gordy got up out of the chair. "Okay, everybody, let's get started." He closed the door and paced back to his place at the head of the table, but didn't sit down. "Ken's gonna pray, then I'll teach."

Just before Ryan bowed his head, he caught a glimpse of Gordy's hands clutching the back of the chair. They trembled. Poor guy was nervous.

Ken's prayer was short, and then Ryan turned toward Gordy. He'd made a mistake in the seating arrangements. Looking in this direction, Tori sat behind him. If he'd taken the other chair, he'd have her in his line of sight as he watched Gordy.

Gordy picked up the booklet on the table in front of him. "Somebody want to look up the Bible verse? It's John 13:12-17." His glance scanned the room, and settled on Ryan. "What about you, dude?"

Ryan shrugged. "Sure." He leaned forward and picked up one of the Bibles scattered across the center of the table. The passage in John relayed Jesus' words to His disciples right after He finished washing their feet. He read it, then closed the Bible.

"That's the one." Gordy opened the booklet Mr. Carmichael usually taught from, glanced at it, and closed it again. He held it up for their inspection. "Now, the lesson in this book is good, but before we talk about washing dirty feet, I wanted to say something else. I've been thinking about this ever since Ken twisted my arm to teach today." The class chuckled, and Gordy grinned in Ken's direction. "Jesus said He set an example for us, and we're supposed to do what He did." His gaze fell on Ryan. "No offense, dude, but I've smelled your feet after an hour on the basketball court, and they're rank."

Behind him, Tori's giggle joined with several others. Ryan scowled at Gordy. *Great. Announce to the woman I'm trying to impress that I have stinky feet.*

Gordy stepped away from the chair and paced a couple of steps to the side. "Now, I started thinking about that. Does Jesus really want me to get down on my knees and scrub the toe jam out of somebody's stinking dogs?"

"I think He does," said Brittany Daniels, who was seated across from Ken. "Y'all remember I told you about a foot washing I went to in Lexington a few months ago."

"Yeah, but that's supposed to stand for serving others. It's, like, a symbol, you know?" Gordy held the Sunday school booklet aloft, shaking it for emphasis. "We're gonna talk in a minute about how Jesus was telling us we were supposed to be servants. But first I want to tell you something I thought about. When I read that piece in the Bible, I couldn't stop thinking about Jesus saying He set us an example. I mean, that's large, you know? That's like, *Whoa, Dude. How am I supposed to do all the stuff You did,* you know?" He looked around the table, his gaze coming to rest on Ryan. "So I got to thinking, what Jesus was telling us to do is like playing Guitar Hero."

Ryan ducked his head to hide his smile, and risked a glance at Tori. She was looking at their substitute teacher as though she couldn't decide whether to laugh or scoff. Behind Tori, Joan let out an audible groan. But Ken nodded and said encouragingly, "Go on."

Gordy set the booklet on the table and held out his hands, palms up. "Now, I know it's weird, but stay with me on this. When I'm on lead guitar and I play a song for the first time, I pretty much stink. Since we're in church, let's say I'm playing 'Living on a Prayer' by Bon Jovi." He grinned, and pretended to hold a guitar, feet spread apart. "I know the song, but I've never *played* it, you know? So at first I bomb big time. I get booed off the stage. But I'm just learning. I'm watching the screen, watching the music, trying to act out what I'm seeing and hearing. And the more I practice, the better I get."

As he spoke, his hands strummed his air guitar, his weight shifting from one bent knee to the other. Then he threw back his head and broke into song, the Bon Jovi lyrics bouncing off the classroom walls.

Laughing along with everyone else, Ryan caught Tori's gaze. Amusement made her eyes twinkle.

Gordy dropped his fictitious guitar and stood behind his chair. "I think that's what Jesus is saying here. We're the ones with the arms and legs and hands and feet. We're the ones holding the guitar. But He's the one who wrote the song. Unless we're watching for Him to tell us what chords to play, we can stand up there and strum all we want, but we're gonna crash and burn." He lunged forward and grabbed his Bible. "And this is like our video screen. It's got all the notes of His song already laid out. We've just got to read them, and then act them out."

He stopped and sent a stupid grin around the table. "So, what do you think?"

Brittany shook her head. "I almost hate to say it, but that makes sense."

"It sure does." Ken applauded, and a few people joined in. "Not bad, Gordy."

"Thank you." Gordy took an elaborate bow before finally sitting in his chair. "Okay, now, here's what the Sunday school lesson book had to say about the whole example thing." He opened the book and started reading aloud.

Tori leaned forward, and Ryan tilted his head to hear her whisper. "That actually did make sense."

Ryan laughed quietly and whispered back, "Scary, isn't it? The Gospel according to Guitar Hero."

Her breath tickled his ear. "Mr. Carmichael would have a fit."

They exchanged a smile, and she settled back in her seat. Behind her, Joan was watching them with satisfaction etched on her face. She crossed her arms and gave Ryan a nod.

The delicious aroma of Gram's crock pot rump roast filled the house when Tori came through the front door.

"Oh, yum." She stopped just inside, eyes closed, nose held high. "I just want to stand here and breathe for a couple of hours."

Joan slipped in behind her. "Well, close the door first, because you're letting out the a/c along with the good smells."

Tori did as she was told. Just before the door clicked shut, she noticed Ken striding across the front lawn toward his house. "Is he going to change clothes?"

"Yes." Joan's voice floated up from her downstairs bedroom.

Tori followed her and flopped onto her sister's bed while Joan slipped out of her church clothes and into a pair of jeans.

"Are you wearing that to meet Ryan's parents?" Joan nodded toward Tori's summer dress before she slipped her arms and head into a T-shirt.

"No, I have a change of clothes in the car." She kicked her shoes off and stretched her legs out on the bed. "Joan, Ryan told me Ken has been filling in for Mr. Carmichael recently."

"Mmm hmm." Joan's head emerged from the collar of her shirt.

"Why didn't he do it today?"

Her sister paused in the act of finger-combing her hair. "The truth?"

"Of course."

"I told him you'd probably be here this morning, and he didn't want to teach in front of you."

Tori sat straight up. "Why not?"

Joan dropped to the mattress beside her. "Because you think he's a fanatic, and he didn't want to perpetuate the idea." She put a hand on Tori's arm. "He really wants you to like him."

So now she was some sort of anti-religious witch? Tori drew her mouth into a pout. "He doesn't have to walk on eggshells around me. Now I feel like a jerk."

"Don't. Just be yourself." Joan's grin grew shrewd. "It seems to be working well with Ryan."

Tori looked away. "I don't know what you mean."

Her evasion earned her a punch on the arm. "Gimme a break. You two have a Thing going, don't you? Why else would he want to introduce you to his parents?"

She raised her nose. "I'll have you know, I'm not going to the farm to meet his parents. I'm going to meet his pigs."

For a fraction of a second, Joan's stare held disbelief. Then she dissolved into laughter. "No way."

"Yes way. He told me he's going to show me a real farm." She grinned. "But I know the parents are part of it."

"And you're okay with that?"

Tori plucked a fuzzy from Joan's blanket off her dress and didn't answer. She didn't know exactly what she felt about Ryan. They'd had a good time together Tuesday and Wednesday. Looking at the pictures of Daddy had been so much easier with him beside her, and he'd seemed to understand her hesitancy even though he came from a normal family. And there was no doubt she was attracted to him physically. But she'd also been attracted to Mitch until last night's disastrous "research trip."

Joan nudged her with a shoulder. "Still not sure, huh?"

"No, I'm not."

"Has he kissed you yet?"

Tori shook her head.

Joan's smile was loaded with secret knowledge. "When he does, you'll know."

Tori rolled her eyes. "Oh, puh-lease. I've kissed guys before who turned out to be real jerks, and liked it." She arched her eyebrows. "And so have you. Remember Clyde Cummins?"

Bringing up Joan's first crush was a dirty trick, but Tori didn't hesitate. What were sisters for, anyway?

"Aaah!" Joan threw herself backward into the pillows. "I can't believe you're throwing Clyde in my face. I was in seventh grade! Nobody has good boy-sense in seventh grade."

Tori laughed. "You sure didn't."

"Well, I have no defense for the Clyde crush. All I can say is kissing him and any other guy I may have kissed in my past just gave me a basis for comparison."

"Even Roger?" Tori hesitated to bring up Joan's longtime boyfriend who dumped her last year. The whole family had been really worried about Joan when Roger broke her heart by marrying a co-worker not long after the breakup.

But there was no sadness in Joan's face as she gave a decisive nod. "Even Roger." She snatched up a tube-shaped decorative pillow and hugged it, sighing happily. "You know what the song says. The only way to tell if a guy really loves you is in his kiss."

Tori asked dryly, "You're not going to go jump up and start playing air guitar, are you?"

Laughter bubbled from Joan's throat. "That was hysterical. Leave it to Gordy. I'm glad you were there to witness the spectacle."

"You know what?" Tori settled back into the pillows and tilted her head sideways to lean on her sister's shoulder. "Me too."

It felt good, just hanging out with Joan. Now would be a good time to discuss what she'd discovered about Daddy living in Cincinnati, but Tori hesitated. Why spoil the moment by dredging up a painful subject? All she wanted right now was some good sister-time in the family home, since she wouldn't have the opportunity much longer. Joan had always been the quietest of the Sanderson sisters, the most laid back and relaxed. And whether Tori liked to admit it or not, in the past year since Joan met Ken, she'd become more than laid back. Peace seemed to radiate from her. In the midst of the chaos Tori's life had become lately, it was good to have someone like Joan.

Tori's thoughts slipped out before her verbal filter could snap into place. "I hope someday I meet someone who does for me what Ken does for you."

"What do you mean?"

"You know. You're so happy and ... well, peaceful."

Joan's head tilted sideways to rest on Tori's. "Ken does make me happy, but he's not the source of my peace."

Here it came. She should have known better than to give Joan an opening. Next she'd be talking about Jesus. Tori fore-stalled the sermon with a quick question.

"So, what did you end up getting him for a wedding present?"

"Not a thing." An exaggerated sigh blew through the curls on the top of Tori's head. "I went in every store in the mall and saw lots of stuff he would like. But I want *the perfect* gift to cel-ebrate our marriage, and I couldn't find it."

Tori straightened so Joan could see her teasing smile. "I'm telling you, a gold-plated stethoscope is your answer."

"You're a big help."

A door slammed above them, and Allie's voice drifted down the stairs, answered by Mom's. The rest of the family had arrived.

Joan launched herself off the bed. "Come on, let's go help Gram with dinner."

Tori stood. "You do that. I've got dibs on Joanie."

"Not if I get to her first!"

Joan leaped for the door. Tori left her shoes lying on the floor and raced after her sister.

A few minutes before two, Tori was putting the finishing touches on her makeup in the bathroom when she heard the doorbell. She smiled at her reflection. He was right on time.

"Tori?" Joan's muffled voice came through the door. "Ryan's here.'" Tori whipped open the door, and enjoyed watching her sister's eyebrows climb up her brow. "Wow. Those pigs are going to be really impressed."

Tori twisted sideways to the mirror and admired the appliquéd lace strip that ran from her waist down the straight leg. "Do you like them? They're D&G, and the blouse is DNKY."

"Ah. You're arming yourself with the whole alphabet of designers." A smile hovered behind Joan's mock-serious expression. "Let me clue you in on something, little sister. Pigs don't give a flip about the label. And I doubt if Ryan knows the difference, either."

"That doesn't matter. I know." With a final check to be sure everything was in place, Tori tossed her curls as she marched past Joan. "Life's too short to dress frumpy. Clothes are an investment in your self-image."

He might not know the difference between Levis and D&G, but Ryan certainly seemed to appreciate her appearance. When Tori stepped into the living room, his eyes gleamed. "You look great."

She flashed a dimple. "Thank you."

He gestured toward the door. "Shall we go?"

"See you later," she told her family.

As she opened the front door, she glanced back. Allie and Joan immediately snapped to attention, guilt plastered over their faces. To her surprise, Ryan wore a similar expression. Was something up between the three of them? She narrowed her eyes and let her gaze slide from one too-innocent expression to another.

"Bye." Allie waggled her fingers in the air and whirled to leave the room, Joan close on her heels.

Tori allowed herself to be led through the door. When Ryan pulled it shut behind her, she stopped on the front stoop. "Are you passing secret messages to my sisters?"

"Who, me? No!"

Before she had a chance to question him further, she heard her name called from next door.

"Tori. Do you have a minute?" Ken stood in his front yard. "I need to ask a favor."

She looked at Ryan, who shrugged. "Sure, Ken."

He shot a quick glance toward the front window of Gram's house, then gestured for them to come. "I don't want Joan to see us talking."

They crossed the grass to where he stood at the corner of his house. A wild barking started in the backyard. Tori glanced toward the fence, where Trigger, Ken's gynormous canine, was running back and forth, barking like crazy. She shuddered. At least the creature was contained. That mongrel outweighed her by twenty pounds, and if it raised up on its hind legs, it stood at least a foot taller than she did. She spared a kind thought for Miss Muffett, who had the sense to be the perfect size for a household pet.

"Trigger, lay off," Ken shouted at the dog.

The barking stopped, but Trigger continued to race back and forth, whining. Tori kept a wary eye in that direction while Ken talked.

"I need some help with the honeymoon, and I think you're the best person to do it." He glanced again toward the house.

"Me?" Tori managed to keep the scowl off her face, but she wasn't sure she filtered the disdain out of her voice. "I don't know a thing about building houses in foreign countries, or whatever it is you two are planning to do in Taiwan."

"It's Thailand, and it's a church building we'll be helping with."

"Whatever." She pretended not to notice Ryan's curious stare.

Ken shoved one hand in a pocket. "Actually, it's not about that. Before we head up to Udon Thani where the church is located, I'm taking her to Ao Nang in the south of Thailand. I've rented a luxury villa on the shores of the Indian Ocean."

Surprised, Tori looked closer at him. "Really?"

He nodded. "We're both passionate about the mission part of this trip, but…" He shrugged. "I want our honeymoon to be something special for her. We're staying at Ao Nang for a week, then we'll go work on the church for a couple of weeks. It's a nice place, palm trees everywhere, our own garden and a private pool. Jacuzzi overlooking the ocean. Perfect place for a honeymoon."

"But how are you going to arrange it all without her knowing?" Tori shook her head, details zipping through her mind.

"I've got that covered. I told her since she's so busy handling all the details of the wedding, I'd handle the trip. She's never seen the airline reservations, so she doesn't know the real dates. Our contact at the church in Thailand is in on it, so in his emails to us he just moves everything up a week. And I talked to her boss months ago, so he knows she's going to be gone an extra week, and says he'll handle the store."

"Man, you've thought of everything." Ryan sounded impressed. In fact, Tori was impressed too.

Ken glanced toward the house. "I hope she doesn't suspect."

If Joan suspected at all, she would have confided to her baby sister, especially since she was so eager for Tori to think well of Ken. "I'm sure she doesn't."

His shoulders relaxed. "Good. Anyway, she thinks all we're going to do is the building project so she's going to pack for that. She won't find out until we get on the plane. But I don't want her to get over there and not be able to enjoy herself. Do you think you could get a bag together with the things she'll need for a beach vacation and a few nice dinners out?"

Tori looked at him suspiciously. "Why me? Both Mom and Allie are here more often than I am. They could get her stuff without her noticing."

Ken kicked at the grass. "Allie can't keep a secret, and your mother is so busy I hated to ask her."

The part about Allie was true. She blabbed everything she knew, especially really good stuff like this. But Mom would have been happy to do it. Tori suspected his reason had less to do with Mom's busy schedule and more to do with trying to impress the only member of the family he knew didn't like him very much.

Well, if that was the case, it was working. How could she not be impressed with such a romantic gesture?

"Clothes *are* my specialty." She inclined her head. "Okay, I'll help."

"Great!"

Ryan pointed toward the backyard. "Look what your dog's doing."

Tori turned to see Trigger gnawing at the latch to the chain link fence's gate. It was an old-fashioned one, with a horseshoe-shaped piece of metal that slid down over a post to hold the gate shut. As they watched, Trigger got hold of the latch and flicked his head upward. In the next instant, he was through the open gate and galloping toward them. Toward *her*.

"Ack! Keep that creature away from me." Heart pounding, she grabbed Ryan by the arm and stepped behind him, angling his body between her and the approaching menace. Unfazed, Trigger bounded in a circle around Ryan, a long string of slime dangling from one corner of his mouth.

"Trigger, come." Ken's stern command went unnoticed.

Laughing, Ryan thrust an arm back to create a shield and Tori cowered behind him. Ken lunged for Trigger's collar, but missed when the dog leaped away. Obviously having a great time, Trigger bowed close to the ground, his hind end high in the air, and let out a loud bark, his eyes fixed on Tori.

Laughter colored Ryan's voice. "I think he's after you."

"It's not funny." Tori watched Ken make another grab, this one successful. She released her grip on Ryan's arm and willed her heartbeat to return to normal. "Every time that dog sees me, he tries to knock me down. He loves to torment me."

"He's not trying to torment you." Ken winced as he hauled the gigantic creature toward the backyard. "Honestly, he likes you. He wants to be your friend."

"My friends do not drool." Tori watched as Ken put the dog away. A sting of compassion pricked her as she noticed the creature's drooping head. It obviously knew it was in trouble.

"Are you afraid of him?" Ryan asked.

"Of course not." She drew herself up, but when Ryan's stare didn't waver, she conceded, "Maybe a little. But who wouldn't be afraid? He's bigger than I am and every time he sees me he acts like he's a bowling ball and I'm the head pin."

"Dogs are smart. He probably knows you don't like him and he's trying to win you over."

Not unlike his owner, in fact. Tori scowled. "I'd rather he just keep his distance."

But she felt a tiny bit sorry for the creature. Trigger sat quietly as Ken scolded, staring mournfully at her through the chain link.

She turned her back on them. "Are you ready to go?"

Ryan nodded and called, "See you later, Ken."

"Okay. And thanks, Tori."

She waved and walked beside Ryan to the car, mentally listing the things Joan would need on the surprise portion of her honeymoon. Maybe Allie was right. Maybe Ken wasn't a bad choice for Joan after all. A guy who went to such lengths to surprise his bride with a romantic honeymoon couldn't be all bad.

Chapter Fifteen

*R*yan drove past The Hub Coffee House and glanced at the location of the disastrous first meeting between Tori and members of his family. He'd sat the boys down yesterday after working with Walt on the house, and threatened their lives if they misbehaved today. Their promises to make a good impression seemed genuine, and they were eager to present her with a gift to make up for the coffee fiasco. Mom had seemed a little put out with his request for lemon meringue pie instead of cobbler, but she'd agreed without too much of a fuss. Apparently she'd been cleaning the already spotless house for days in anticipation of today's visit. Pop just shook his head and remained silent, an amused grin on his face.

"Joan is going to be so surprised," Tori said. "I'm sure she doesn't have a clue that Ken has anything planned at all."

Ryan drove with one hand at the top of the wheel, the other resting casually on the armrest between them. "He's a pretty amazing guy."

"Mm hmm."

Something in her tone pricked his attention. He cast a quick sideways glance at her. "You don't like him much, do you?"

"Oh, it's not that," she said quickly. Then her head tilted slightly. "Well, okay. He wouldn't have been my first choice for Joan."

"Why not? Ken's a great guy."

"I'm sure he is." The pause stretched out before she continued. "Frankly, he's a little too religious for my tastes."

That took him by surprise. He raised his eyebrows. "He's no more religious than Joan."

"Ah, but that's a recent occurrence." She kept her eyes forward, watching through the window as they passed the last of the buildings in Danville. "Until Ken, Joan wasn't ultra-religious either. He's changed her. In fact, my whole family has changed since he showed up, spouting prayers with every other breath."

Bitterness edged her voice. Ryan hadn't realized she felt that way Ken's openness about his beliefs was one of the things Ryan admired deeply.

"I don't think of Ken as religious so much as..." He cocked his head and searched for a word. "Genuine. His faith isn't just something he gives lip service to. He lives it. It's part of who he is. I wish I was more like him in that respect."

Ryan shifted in his seat and stared at the road ahead of them. In the past year, Ryan had been watching Ken closely, trying to emulate the care he showed for the needy boys they played ball with every week. He'd even started reading a short daily devotional Ken recommended. How could anyone not admire a man who walked the talk as openly as Ken did?

Tori straightened in the seat and changed the subject. "I want to see where you live. Can we drive by?"

"We already passed it." Thank goodness. After seeing her apartment complex, she'd think he lived in a dump. "Besides, it's not much to look at. Just a couple of rooms up over a dentist's office."

"Where is it?"

"Down near the hospital, on the second floor above Dr. Patrick's office."

"I know just where that is. He was my dentist." She flashed a smile full of white teeth at him.

The sun shone overhead, a great day for a trip out to the country. Tori fell silent, her head turned toward the window as she watched the countryside speed by outside the car. They glided over the country roads Ryan had driven all his life, even back before he was old enough to drive legally, when Walt used to let him drive the old junker to school so he could sleep in the backseat a few extra minutes. If Mom had ever caught them, Ryan figured he'd still be grounded today.

A gigantic metal mailbox, the sides crumpled and rusted from years of teenagers playing mailbox baseball, stood sentry at the entrance to the farm. Ryan had urged Pop to replace the old thing, but Pop said it was no use; every year a new set of boys started driving and set out to prove their daring by hanging out of a speeding car swinging a baseball bat. A new one would act as a beacon, drawing them to a shiny target. Ryan figured he was probably right.

"Is this it?" Tori leaned forward to look through the windshield as they turned onto the packed dirt driveway carved through the center of a thick stand of trees that served as a three-season privacy screen.

"This is it. The next driveway down that way," Ryan pointed, "leads to my brother's farm."

"Where you're helping him build a house."

"That's right. We can head over there after a while, if you want to see it."

Her eyes sparkled with interest. "I'd like that."

The house sat back a quarter of a mile from the road, behind a field of neatly planted rows of tobacco. The treeline fringed the property on both sides, though only thinly between Pop's farm and Walt's. Ryan pointed out a glimpse of his brother's trailer, just visible at the far end of the field.

"So your father is a tobacco farmer?"

Ryan cocked his head. "Not so much anymore. He still has these two front fields, but he's switched mostly to cattle, along with some other livestock. The tobacco industry isn't what it was when he was growing up. Pop was smart enough to see the decline coming and started branching out to try new things when I was a kid. By the time I became a teenager, the livestock was bringing in more than the tobacco."

"I'd think raising animals would be a lot better than tobacco."

He screwed his face up into a mock scowl. "That's because you've never had to crawl out of bed at four in the morning to help milk the cows before school."

Her eyes widened. "Don't they have machines for that?"

"Yeah, but they don't run themselves." He laughed. "And my dad believed in teaching his kids the hands-on approach."

Ryan parked in the grassy area in front of the picket fence that surrounded the small area of yard Mom had claimed as hers. A rainbow of flowers bloomed in glorious display in neatly weeded beds all over the place. Nestled among the blossoms were concrete statues of fairies or angels or birdbaths, and a variety of other objects that struck Mom's eye over the years. In one corner a herd of butterflies rested atop spindly spikes, their opalescent plastic wings shining with reflected sunlight. Ryan opened Tori's door and led her to the gate, watching her eyes sweep the yard as they walked up to the gate.

"How pretty," she remarked. "Gram would love this yard."

Something stirred the tall ornamental grass in a flower bed on the right. In the next instant, a streak of white and black bounded into view.

"Shep, Mom'll skin you alive if she catches you rolling in her flowers," Ryan told the dog as it raced toward them.

Beside him, Tori stiffened for a moment as the animal approached. "Is he friendly?"

"Shep? Oh, yeah." Ryan dropped to his haunches and rubbed the dog's shaggy neck fur with vigor. "He's a little high strung, but he's a good old dog. Aren't you, boy?"

Tori leaned over and held her hand out for Shep to sniff, and the animal obliged. When he accepted her with a brief lick, her tension left and she petted his head. "Now, see, this dog is a perfectly acceptable size. Nothing remotely horse-like about him. What kind is he?"

Ryan stood and rubbed his hands on his jeans. "Border collie, mostly. He helps Dad with the cattle."

The front door of the farmhouse opened before they reached it, and the two redheaded menaces flew out. Jostling for position, Butch and Cody tumbled down the walkway, a whirlwind of flying arms and legs. For a moment Ryan thought the pair would bowl them both over. Beside him, Tori halted and braced for impact. But the two miscreants screeched to a halt a foot in front of them.

Butch stepped up and elbowed Cody out of the way to stand in the center of the walk. "Miss Tori, we got you a present."

For a moment Cody's outraged expression spoke of violence to come, but then he caught sight of Ryan's glare over the top of Tori's bright head. With a final grimace at his brother, he straightened and made a wide path around Butch to stand at Tori's side. He shyly took her hand and told her, "I helped pay for it."

Ryan's lungs deflated with relief. Violence averted. Apparently the boys had taken his lecture to heart and were going to behave.

Tori smiled at each of them in turn. "Thank you. But you didn't have to get me a present."

Butch nodded, his face solemn. "Yes, we did."

"Mama made us," Cody added.

She looked at Ryan, fighting a smile. "Well, I can hardly wait to see what it is."

Her right hand clutched by Cody, she extended her left toward Butch. Ryan jumped ahead to open the door as the boys pulled her into the house. For a moment, he paused before following them inside. When was the last time he'd brought a girl home to meet his family? Not since high school, when Mom insisted he bring his prom date by so she could take pictures of them all dressed up. Funny. Here he was, a grown man, and he felt as nervous as he had that night. Maybe more.

Tori stepped into a small living room so crowded there appeared to be barely enough space to turn around. At second glance, she realized the impression was overemphasized because of all the *stuff* that took up every available space. Not a single inch of the room's perimeter had been left bare, and every tabletop proudly displayed a collection of knickknacks. She spied a cluster of Precious Moment figurines crowding the shelves of a display case in one corner, and an assortment of what looked like porcelain bells covering a lace-covered tabletop next to it. The walls held more stuff than a Cracker Barrel: china plates mounted in metal frames, a collection of thimbles, family photos, elaborate needlework, even a couple of decorative crisscrossed swords. At least, she hoped they were decorative. The two little boys who clasped her hands shouldn't be allowed within five miles of a real weapon.

Two women stood in the center of the room, greeting her with broad smiles. The familiar one, Ryan's sister-in-law Loralee, stepped forward and grabbed her in a friendly hug. Surprised, Tori released the boys' hands and returned the embrace, a little awkwardly over Loralee's large baby bump.

"It's so good to see you again." The redhead's voice gushed with pleasure. "Though we had to practically take a cattle prod to Ryan to get him to ask you. We were beginning to think he was ashamed of us or something."

Tori caught a quick glimpse of Ryan's mortified face before he schooled his features.

"No, it was totally my fault," she told Loralee. "I've been so busy at work lately I barely have time to visit my own family. And trust me, my sisters let me hear about it too."

A flicker of gratitude warmed Ryan's eyes as he stepped forward and gently rescued her from Loralee's enthusiastic grasp with a hand on her arm. He gestured toward the other woman. "Tori, this is my mother, Tammy Adams."

She was younger than Tori expected. She must have been pretty young when she had Ryan's brother, much younger than Mom when she gave birth to Allie. Tammy's face was smooth, with creases only around her eyes. Curly hair, prematurely more gray than brown, flowed across her shoulders, a few of the front strands caught back in a barrette at the base of her skull. The hand that grasped Tori's was strong, and rougher than most of the men at the office. She peered at Tori with eyes the exact color of Ryan's.

"It's nice to meet you, Mrs. Adams." Tori tried not to squirm under the gaze that searched her face. She was being evaluated, and experienced an irrational bout of insecurity. What would Ryan's family think of her? And why did it matter, all of a sudden?

After a moment that seemed to stretch to awkward lengths, a smile curled the edges of her lips. "We don't stand on ceremony here. Everybody calls me Tammy."

Tori released the breath she'd unconsciously been holding.

"Everybody except Ryan and me, else she'd skin us alive."

The tall man who had been standing behind Loralee and Tammy stepped forward and put his arm around Loralee's shoulders. The grin he directed toward her looked so familiar that Tori glanced at Ryan for a comparison. No doubt who this was.

"You've got to be Ryan's brother." Tori held out a hand, which he pressed more than shook.

"I guess I've *got* to be, whether I want to or not." He delivered his good-natured jibe with a chuckle aimed in Ryan's direction.

A movement in the corner drew her attention. A man she hadn't noticed rose from a recliner. Without a doubt, Ryan's father. With a keen gaze that Tori would bet didn't miss much, he studied her features in the two steps that brought him to his wife's side. If Ryan had inherited his mother's light brown eyes, everything else came from his dad. The strong nose, the firm chin, the warm smile. And especially his muscular build, the unconscious confidence with which he moved. Warmth engulfed Tori's hand, and his friendly blue eyes put her immediately at ease.

"The name's Walter, but you can call me Pop like everybody else."

"Thank you." Tori let her smile circle the room. "It's nice to meet you all."

"Lookie here, Miss Tori."

The older boy, Butch, dove through the empty space between Loralee and Walt, and came back with a brightly wrapped package. He thrust it into her hands, all of his oversized teeth visible in an eager display. "This is your present. Open it."

Cody leaped into the tiny space in the center of the adults and bounced up and down. "Yeah, open it."

Loralee issued a stern command. "Boys, y'all better settle down, y'hear? Let Miss Tori catch her breath a minute."

Tammy put her hands on Cody's shoulders and pulled him close for a hug that also served to still the bouncing. "That's right. She hasn't even had a chance to sit down yet."

The room was so small there wasn't room for everyone to have a chair, but apparently they were used to it. Pop returned to his recliner, and Tammy perched on the arm. Ryan led Tori to the couch, and Loralee settled beside them on the third cushion. The boys and Walt all three dropped onto the floor in the doorway that led into another room, where Tori glimpsed a dining room table. They all stared at her, obviously waiting for her to open the present. Ryan looked completely at ease, and even more handsome than usual leaning back with one arm draped across the sofa behind her and the other resting casually along the padded arm. How easy it would be to lean backward and settle into the inviting space beneath his arm. Instead, Tori sat on the edge of the cushion, knees together, the gift in her lap.

Loralee tapped the box with a finger. "Sorry it's in Christmas wrap. I thought I had some other paper, but…" She shrugged.

"No, this is great." Tori held the box up and admired the Santa Claus paper and shiny red bow. "Christmas in June."

"Well, ain't you gonna open it?" Cody asked.

"Right now?"

He and Butch nodded eagerly. She turned the box on its end to find the seam, and slipped a fingernail beneath the folded paper. Despite her care, green paper came away with the tape. She unfolded that end, and turned to the other.

Pop's voice cut the silence. "Good Lord, she opens presents like a girl."

His good-natured teasing eased her tension-tight muscles. Tori grinned up at him. "I was trying to be ladylike."

His lips twitched. "Honey, that's just a waste of good manners. We're plain old country folks here."

"Well, in that case, this is how we do it at my house on Christmas morning."

She grabbed the edge and jerked. The paper gave a satisfying *rrrrriippp,* and both boys laughed with high-pitched voices as she uncovered a generic white box. When the paper was off, she wadded it into a ball and tossed it sideways into Ryan's lap with a playful glance. She lifted the lid, fairly certain she knew what lay inside. Yes, a new pink shirt to replace the one they'd ruined. She lifted it out and held it up in front of her. Cotton instead of silk, and cheaply made. Not something she'd be able to wear to work, but the gesture was what mattered. This shirt probably cost them at least fifteen dollars, an enormous amount for a couple of boys.

"Oh, how pretty!" She gave the pair her deepest dimple grin. "And it's pink, my favorite color."

"Is it the right size?" Loralee asked.

Tori checked the tag. Small. "It's perfect."

Cody preened, and Butch knee-walked across the floor to kneel in front of her. "It's the same as the one the other day, ain't it?"

"*Isn't* it," Ryan corrected.

The boy rolled his eyes. "Isn't it?"

"It's not exactly the same," Tori told him. His face fell, until she continued. "This one is better, because it came from you."

He sank back onto his feet, a grin splitting his face.

Tammy stood and dusted her hands across the thighs of her jeans. "Who feels like a piece of pie?"

Two boys both jumped up to thrust their hands high into the air.

"Me!"

"Me too!"

Loralee scooted her rear toward the front of the cushion and grabbed the sofa arm to heft herself up. "I'll help."

"Me too." Tori stood and turned to offer a hand to the pregnant redhead, who gave her a grateful smile.

Tori followed Tammy and Loralee from the room, aware of Ryan's eyes fixed on her as she left. They wound around a table in a dining room nearly as crowded as the living room, and into a kitchen not much bigger. The appliances looked old, almost as old as Gram's, but everything sparkled with cleanliness and the faint odor of bleach mingled with the scent of coffee and the sweet smell of something sugary and recently baked. On the counter rested two pies with fluffy meringue piled high and beautifully browned.

"Oh, those are gorgeous," Tori said.

Pride illuminated Tammy's face. "Thank you. Sometimes my meringues don't come out at all, but this time they did."

"Don't listen to her." Loralee's lips twisted. "Her meringues never flop. She's the best cook in the county."

Tammy didn't deny it. She slid open a drawer and pulled out a big knife and a pie server. "Loralee, you want to get those plates down? And Tori, you'll find some napkins over there by the refrigerator."

Tori went to the counter as directed, the last of her uneasiness dissolving as she pitched in to help. She felt just like she did at home in Gram's kitchen with her family.

When Tammy sliced into a pie and lifted out the first piece, Tori exclaimed, "It's lemon! That's my absolute favorite dessert."

Tammy didn't say anything, but her smile took on a satisfied curve as she sliced a second piece. Tori and Lora-lee delivered pieces of pie and mugs of coffee to the men in the living room. The boys, who apparently couldn't be trusted not to make a mess, were seated at opposite ends of the dining room table with hardly any protest. Settling on the sofa beside Ryan, Tori devoured the gigantic slice of pie Tammy cut for her. She'd never tell Gram in a million years, but it was the best lemon meringue pie she had ever tasted.

When she'd scraped the last crumb from the plate, she leaned back with a loud sigh. "I feel like a Thanksgiving turkey, stuffed to the gills. That was amazing, Tammy. Better than any I've ever had, and I'm something of a connoisseur of lemon meringue pie."

"I told you she was the best cook in the county." Loralee swallowed her last bite and leaned back beside Tori. She balanced the plate on her pregnant belly, exactly the same way Allie used to do.

"She is." Pop gave Tammy a familiar pat on the knee.

Tammy inclined her head in acceptance of the compliments being showered on her. Then she fixed her eye on Ryan. "I make a pretty good peach cobbler too."

Her look was full of hidden meaning. Tori glanced at Ryan, curious, but he didn't explain. Instead, he hefted himself to his feet and held a hand out toward her.

"Come on. I promised you an introduction to some pigs."

Tori shook her head. "Let me help clean up first."

"No, we can handle that." Loralee took the empty plate from her hands. "You go walk off that pie."

Tori opened her mouth to protest, but Tammy stopped her. "Next time you come, we'll put you to work. But you're our guest this time."

Ryan stood in front of her, his hand inviting.

"Well, okay. If you're sure." When she took his hand, a delicious tingle tickled her palm. From the way he held her eyes, he felt the sensation too. Nor did he release her when she stood, but held on as he guided her to the door. Tori knew his family watched them leave and probably whispered about their clasped hands the minute the door closed behind them. Funny, but she didn't care. She was too busy enjoying the feeling of her hand engulfed in Ryan's.

Outside, he led her around the house to the back. The dog, Shep, bounded out of the flower bed where he'd been napping earlier and joined them briefly, then raced ahead and leaped over the white picket fence with seemingly little effort.

Amazed, Tori pointed after the animal with her free hand. "Did you see that? He cleared that fence with six inches to spare."

Ryan nodded. "I told you he was mostly border collie. We figure the rest of him is terrier or something that jumps. That dog bounces like a kangaroo."

He led her through a gate. Beyond the fence lay two barns, one on either side of a dirt path like the driveway that led from the street to the house. The barn on the right was painted white, with wide doors. The one on the left was a double-decker structure with a steep, pitched roof. Openings punctuated the wide, flat planks, the inside lined with racks.

"A tobacco barn." Tori glanced at him to see if he was impressed that she recognized it.

Ryan nodded, and pointed toward a slatted structure beyond. "There's the corn crib."

"What's in there?" She pointed toward the white barn.

"Equipment. Tractors and the like."

Tori's nose detected the first hint of their destination before she saw it. "Eewww. What is that disgusting smell?"

The grin he turned toward her was as teasing as his father's had been earlier. "That, my dear Miss Sanderson, is the aroma of a real pigpen."

The closer they drew to the edge of the barn, the stronger the stench became. Her nostrils twitched in protest at the mixture of ammonia and…something totally disgusting. The smell really did defy description.

"Your pigs must stink more than most. I'm sure I would remember a smell like this." Tori's step slowed. Did she really have to go closer to that foul stench?

He laughed and tugged her forward. "You visited a petting zoo! They probably gave those pigs a bath every morning before the tourists arrived. And besides, what was the name of the place?"

She heaved a heavy outward breath through her nostrils, trying to blow the smell away. "The Double Stink Pig Farm."

"I rest my case."

They rounded the barn and Tori got her first sight of the pigpen, an unimpressive building of wooden slats surrounded by a wire fence. The small barnyard boasted a gigantic puddle of thick, black mud in the center. In one corner, resting in the shade of the building, a huge pig lay on her side, surrounded with piglets. Most were gray, like their mother, but one little piglet was pink, like Wilbur in *Charlotte's Web.*

"Oh, look. They're adorable!" Taking care to inhale through her mouth, Tori approached the wire. "Will they let me touch them?"

Ryan's laughter echoed off the side of the barn. "Why would you want to touch those stinky things?"

"Because they're so cute. I'm sure the smell is coming from their mother, not them."

She squeezed his hand and turned to face him. The sun shone brightly above, and she squinted as she looked up at him. Heat from their clasped hands radiated up her arm as she shifted her fingers to intertwine with his.

The air between them grew heavy, expectant. A tickle fluttered in Tori's belly. He was going to kiss her. Right here, in front of the pigs. Not exactly the most romantic of locations, but she felt herself drawn toward his warm brown eyes, his soft lips. If Joan was right, one kiss and she'd know if this was just another attraction or something more. She tilted her head and rose slightly on her toes...

"Miss Tori, Miss Tori, Grandpop said we could show you how we jump in the haystack. You wanna see?"

Disappointment doused the flutter in her stomach as Ryan pulled away. The boys ran to them, and Cody came to a stop with a giant leap to land flat-footed in front of her.

Laughing, Tori ruffled his mop of red hair. "Sure I do. I'll bet you're a great jumper."

Butch pointed behind her. "Uh oh. He's doing it again."

Tori turned in time to see Shep wiggle beneath the wire fence on the opposite side of the pigs' small barnyard.

Ryan's voice was stern as he called, "Shep! You know better than that. Come on out of there." He looked down at Tori, shaking his head. "That dog loves to tease the pigs. But one day that big old sow is going to catch him, and he'll be sorry."

The dog ignored Ryan's command. It ran toward the mama pig, barking in a high-pitched, excited yap. The piglets squealed and scattered as the gigantic sow got to her feet faster than Tori would have thought she could move. She let out an ear-splitting scream of fury. No delicate little oinks from this angry pig. Shep's barking grew more rapid as he raced forward and darted around the sow, obviously enjoying himself as the piglets fled before him. Ryan continued to yell for the dog to come out, and the boys' delighted peals of laughter joined the sound of Shep's joyous taunts. Then the sow charged. Shep's barking stopped, and dirt kicked up from his back paws as he turned and raced for the fence.

"Now you've done it, you dumb dog," Ryan yelled. "You better hope she doesn't catch you."

Tori couldn't hold back her laughter as the dog, obviously having the time of his life, charged across the barnyard and right through the center of the black mud hole, the furious sow close behind. Where Shep's hind claws had kicked up puffs of dirt a moment before, now chunks of mud flew as he dug in for purchase in the thick ooze.

In the next minute, Tori's laughter stopped abruptly. Wet, slimy mud flew through the air and landed with a sodden splat—right on her! Gasping, she looked down at her clothes. Big splotches of the oozy black stuff dotted her designer clothing.

Beside her, the boys' laughter rose to hysterical levels, while Ryan, clearly horrified, stood with his mouth gaping. Out of the corner of her eye, Tori saw Shep clear the mud hole, take a giant leap toward the fence, and scrabble over the top while the angry pig screamed and snorted from below. Tori dropped Ryan's hand and flicked at the biggest chunk of wet mud to knock it off the front of her jeans.

Ryan's shirt had taken some of the splatter too, but the majority of the muck had hit her.

"Tori, I'm so sorry."

Forcing a brave smile, she told him, "It's okay. It's just mud. Once it dries, I'm sure it'll come right out."

He blanched, and Cody piped up with a giggle in his voice. "That ain't just mud, Miss Tori. It's got poop in it."

Tori's breath stuck in her lungs. Poop? Her stomach gave a lurch as she turned a horrified stare toward Ryan. "Do you mean to tell me I have *pig poop* on my three hundred dollar jeans?"

The boys dropped to the ground and rolled, gales of laughter filling the air. Disbelief creased Ryan's forehead as he took another look at her jeans.

"You paid three hundred dollars for a pair of *jeans*?"

O-kay, that was so not the correct response!

"They're D&G," she snapped, twisting sideways to point toward the leather patch on the waistband. From the blank look he gave her, he didn't know what that meant. "Dolce & Gabbana," she ground out through gritted teeth. "They're made in Italy."

Ryan folded his arms, apparently oblivious to the fact that he was smearing splotches of muddy pig poop on his shirt. "Well, hopefully Italian jeans can handle a washing as well as the cheap domestic kind. Let's go get you cleaned up." He held a hand toward the house. "Shall we?"

Tori hesitated. A moment before she'd been hoping he would kiss her, and now she was covered in disgusting filth. So much for her "dress to impress" strategy. The only one she was likely to impress in this condition was the dog, who apparently *liked* the smell of pig poop. Not only was Ryan not impressed, the disbelief hovering in his eyes as his gaze dropped repeatedly to her jeans held a faint note of disapproval.

Ouch. That stung.

Tori forced a smile. "Well, there is one consolation."

"What's that?"

She plucked at her splattered blouse with a thumb and forefinger. "At least I have a clean shirt to change into this time."

His laugh echoed off the wooden barns as they headed for the house.

Chapter Sixteen

The apartment seemed unusually quiet. Tori tried watching a DVD, but even Daniel Craig as James Bond failed to hold her attention, so she turned it off. Music used to draw her in for hours when she was in school, but tonight the stereo couldn't distract her. She curled up in the corner of her sofa, her uneasy thoughts back on the farm she'd visited this afternoon.

Being splattered with manure was revolting, of course, but why did she act like such a prima donna about the stupid jeans? In fact, what in the world had possessed her to wear D&Gs to a farm, anyway? A lame attempt to impress Ryan's family, when they obviously didn't know the difference between her pricey clothes and the ones they bought at Walmart. And what's more, they wouldn't care if they did know. Except, maybe, they'd think she was insane for spending so much money on an article of clothing, like Ryan did.

At the memory of the disapproval she'd seen on his face, she launched herself off the sofa and paced to the patio doors. He had no right to disapprove of her! She had a good job and could afford to buy whatever clothes she wanted. Just because he had to scrimp and save, that didn't mean everybody else did too. When he finished his degree and got a better job, his attitude would change.

She stopped in the act of pulling the cord to close the vertical blinds. No, actually, Ryan's attitude toward money probably wouldn't change much, no matter how big his paycheck grew. He had worked hard all his life to earn his way. She couldn't see him ever dumping a ton of money on something he'd consider frivolous, and his reaction today proved he thought her expensive clothes were frivolous. Now Mitch, on the other hand, probably had as much money in his wardrobe as Tori.

With a jerk, she shut the blinds. She did *not* want to be compared to Mitch. Ryan was so much more fun, so much easier to be with. So much more … genuine. She grimaced at the word he'd used earlier to describe Ken.

Ryan's family was nice too. She liked them, liked being around them. Even Loralee, with her thick hillbilly drawl, was friendlier than most of the people Tori worked with. And Walt, who was building a house for her and their children with his own hands. And Tammy, who loved flowers and baking, and who loaned her a pair of baggy sweatpants to wear home. And Pop … Tori's eyes misted as she remembered the familiar way Pop's arm circled his wife as she perched on the arm of his chair, and the way he'd teased Tori about opening her gift like a girl. Pop would have welcomed her if she'd been wearing rags.

A tear slipped from the corner of her eye. Why couldn't her father have been like Pop?

She brushed the tear away, but another quickly took its place. They'd been there, waiting to spill over since yesterday afternoon when she searched for Daddy's name on the Internet. She wouldn't give in to them, to *him*. Wouldn't allow him to break her control. Why should she, when he didn't even care enough to call and let them know he was alive?

If he *was* alive.

Her throat tight, Tori started forward, then stopped, uncertain, in the center of the room. Why did the thought of Daddy being dead send her into such a panic? His absence wouldn't be any more painful than it already was. There wouldn't be any difference at all. She wrapped her arms around her middle and hugged. So how come she'd avoided telling Joan and Allie what she found on the Internet yesterday? How come she'd refused to even think about finding out more? What was she afraid of? She sucked in a quick breath. She was *not* afraid. He's the one who ought to be afraid. Of her, showing up on his front porch and demanding to know why he'd deserted his daughters. Deserted her.

Spine stiff with sudden determination, she marched across the room to the dinette table, where she'd set up her laptop. A few quick commands brought up the search box she'd seen yesterday, the one with Daddy's name. And Mom's. And Patricia Ann Parker's. She clicked the *View Details* button, and the screen displayed the payment options she'd seen before. Moving quickly, before she could change her mind, Tori dug a credit card out of her purse and paid the fifteen dollars to get the expanded report.

The first screen that opened included full addresses in Phoenix, Las Vegas, Dayton, Columbus, and—she gulped—Cincinnati. He'd lived in apartments most places, but the Cincinnati address looked like a house, with no apartment number listed. Snatching a pen and a piece of paper from her purse, she jotted down the address. At the top of the screen, a series of buttons offered the additional searches she'd paid for. She clicked the button to perform a marriage search, and entered Daddy's name.

A ton of Thomas Sandersons came up, as before. Tori scanned the column labeled *Bride's Name* and quickly found Mom. The date of their marriage and the county was correct. Nothing new there. She looked for another marriage record for Daddy, but didn't see one. Patricia Ann Parker was nowhere on the list.

Interesting.

The row of search buttons at the top of the screen drew her eye. *People Search* and *Marriage Search* she'd done. *Property Search* and *Divorce Search* didn't interest her. But the other one ...

Her mouth dry, Tori's finger slid across the touchpad. The mouse arrow glided across the screen and came to rest on the button labeled *Death Search*. Steeling herself, she clicked.

Another list appeared on the screen, with columns labeled Name, Age, Year Born, Birth Date. *Gulp.* The last column held Death Date. A quick glance revealed the entries were sorted in order of that column, with the most recent dates on top. Tori's breath caught in her lungs as, fearfully, she scanned the list of all the Thomas Sandersons who had died.

Her eyes snagged on one.

Thomas Alan Sanderson. Sixty years old. Born January 14, 1949.

Died March 2, 2009.

The screen disappeared in a blur of tears. The pain in her chest was vivid and sharp, as though someone had plunged a knife directly into her heart. Tori lowered her head to the keyboard and wept.

Chapter Seventeen

At eight fifty-four Monday morning, Kate led a man and woman down the hallway outside of Tori's cubicle. She glanced over her shoulder and caught Tori's eye with a nod toward the conference room.

Fingers trembling with nerves, Tori opened her top drawer, pulled out a pressed powder compact, and glanced in the small mirror. Her eyes were still a little puffy from where she'd cried herself to sleep, but at least the imprint of the keys from her laptop's keyboard had finally faded from her cheek. The news washed over her again—Daddy was dead!—and fresh tears threatened. By sheer willpower she forced them not to appear. No red eyes for her first meeting with the clients. With a quick dab of powder on the swollen skin beneath her eyes, she snapped the compact shut and headed for the meeting.

Kate stepped out of the conference room as she approached. "Go tell Rita to let Dan and Stephen know the clients are here, and ask her to bring in some coffee."

Tori nodded, and glanced into the room where the couple stood by the window, looking down into Triangle Park. "They really aren't expecting us to pitch any ideas, right? I don't have anything ready to show them."

Her boss's smile was cold. "Maybe if you concentrated on your own work instead of Phil Osborne's, you'd have something to show for your time last week."

The room dimmed around her as angry blood rushed to heat Tori's face. She clamped her teeth together to keep from snapping a response as Kate turned away and stepped into the room. Not a single hour had passed last week without a phone call or email from Kate, demanding numbers or updates that easily could have waited until she returned to the office. That woman was a micromanaging maniac! Tori ought to quit, that's what she ought to do. Just walk in there and say the words. "I quit!" Watch Kate's mouth drop open. If she had another job, she'd do it in a heartbeat.

Mitch arrived at that moment, a notebook in his hand. He'd ignored her so far this morning. The memory of their encounter in Maguire's parking lot lay uncomfortably between them as he edged past her into the conference room. He didn't meet her eye, but mumbled, "'Morning, Sanderson."

While she walked around the cubicle maze toward Rita's desk, Tori gulped deep breaths of air and tried to force herself to calm down. Puffy eyes, Kate, Mitch, and a pair of clients for whom she was totally unprepared. This was shaping up to be the worst morning of her life.

"I assure you, Ms. Sanderson and Mr. Jackson are two of our brightest analysts. They'll come up with a campaign that will knock your socks off."

The smile Kate flashed around the conference table held so much confidence that Tori almost didn't recognize her boss as the same woman who'd insulted her an hour before. Mr. Connolly and Mr. Farrin had both put in an appearance early on, and then excused themselves, assuring the Maguires they were in capable hands.

Mrs. Maguire, whom Tori immediately recognized as the woman she'd assumed was the restaurant's manager when she and Ryan were there, nodded as she sipped from a white coffee mug. When she lowered it, a new lipstick mark decorated the rim. "I know they're certainly on the ball. I'm impressed that you've already visited the restaurant." Her gaze settled on Tori, and she gave a small nod. "You've been in twice, even."

Mitch shot her a narrow-eyed glance, but Tori ignored him. Instead, she focused on Mrs. Maguire, impressed. How many customers had dined in the restaurant in the past week? "You're very observant of your customers."

She smiled. "That's my business."

Mr. Maguire leaned forward, his fingers entwined before him on the table's surface. "So, you two will put together some ideas and then run them by us, right? How soon will we be able to get a look at what you've come up with?"

Kate answered. "We'll have something ready for you to look at on July fourteenth. You can come back—"

"That's too long. I'd like to see something next week."

Beneath the table, Tori squeezed her hands into fists. She didn't even have a solid idea yet, and it took time to work up sketches and graphic representations suitable for a client's eyes.

Kate's smile didn't change. "I assure you, this timetable is already accelerated. Some of our campaigns take months to create. We're moving quickly on yours because we value you as a new client of Connolly and Farrin."

"Look, we've never hired an advertising agency before." Mr. Maguire flattened his palms on the table. "You're probably used to having people sit back and wait for you. But we don't work like that. We're used to doing things ourselves, not turning them over to someone else to do for us."

Tori glanced at Mrs. Maguire. She was apparently content to remain silent and let her husband speak for her, but her slight nod made it clear the two were in complete agreement. She picked up her mug for another sip, her eyes moving as she looked from her husband to Kate.

"If this is the first time you've hired a marketing firm," Kate told him, "you may not be familiar with the process involved in creating a highly effective campaign."

The man's lips pursed. "You're right. We don't understand. And maybe we can't have a finished product next week, but I want to see where you're heading. That way, I can give my input before you get too far down a path I don't like. Is that too much to ask?"

Kate paused for only a moment. "Of course not. We'll show you what we have next Monday." She held up a finger. "With the understanding that the ideas will be conceptual, not final."

"Done." Maguire sat back, a pleased smile on his face.

Great. I hope she gives me time to work something up.

Mrs. Maguire spoke. "Do you have any questions for us?" She gave Mitch an inquisitive look.

He shook his head and indicated the notes he'd taken from their conversation thus far in the meeting. "I think we've got an idea of your expectations." His expression became overly polite as he turned toward Tori. "What about you, Ms. Sanderson?"

Tori mirrored Mitch's polite smile, then allowed her expression to warm as she looked at Mrs. Maguire. "I did have one question. What interested you in the new location?"

Mr. Maguire held up a hand and ticked off fingers as he answered. "It comes with a lot of the equipment we'd have to buy new elsewhere. It's empty, so we can move in quickly. It has plenty of parking. The rent is cheap compared to some of the other places we looked at. And the owner is willing to sell sometime next year, if our business supports the investment."

She sat up straight. "So you did consider other locations?"

He nodded. "A few. But this building is perfect. It has everything we're looking for."

Tori started to ask what other locations they'd considered, but Kate's expression had hardened. Aware of her boss's eyes fixed on her, Tori smiled and told Mr. Maguire, "Thanks. I was just wondering."

"Well." Kate rolled her chair back and stood. "If you have no more questions for us, I think that does it. We'll expect you at nine next Monday."

Everyone got out of their chairs. Mr. Maguire extended a hand across the table to Mitch. "If you have any questions for us in the meantime, give us a call. We don't mind."

"Thank you, sir. I look forward to showing you my ideas. I think you'll be pleased."

The brown-noser. Tori noticed that Mitch's habitual smirk was absent, replaced by a confidence he projected toward the clients. He'd been calmly professional through the whole meeting, exuding competence. No wonder Mr. Maguire directed most of his questions toward Mitch instead of her. With a sinking heart, she realized Mitch looked like an account executive. Whereas she probably looked like an inexperienced analyst pretending to be an executive, even dressed in the new suit she'd bought just for this meeting. For the first time, new clothes weren't giving her the confidence she needed. What was up with that?

Now the meeting was breaking up, and Tori hadn't asked for permission to conduct the research she wanted to do. Nor did she want to say anything that might tip Mitch off to the direction her ideas were heading.

As she shook Mrs. Maguire's hand, she was given an opening.

"I'd like to use the ladies' room before we leave, if you don't mind," the woman said in a low voice. "Can you tell me where it is?"

"I'll show you," Tori said quickly. "It's on the way out."

Mr. Maguire nodded a farewell to Kate and Mitch, and fell in beside them as Tori led the way around the cubicles toward the elevators and the restrooms beyond. She didn't speak until she was sure they wouldn't be overheard.

"I'd like to do some customer analysis work this week, if it's okay with you."

Mrs. Maguire's expression became curious. "What kind of analysis?"

Tori kept her tone casual. "Oh, just some exit interviews to identify customer demographics and preferences, things like that. It will help me better understand your customer base, so I can craft an ad campaign to communicate a message that appeals to them."

Mr. Maguire frowned. "But we want to get new customers. That's the whole point of advertising, right?"

"Oh, we will," Tori assured him. "Still, we need to know why your existing customers choose Maguire's over the other dining choices they have. If we can understand that, we'll find something we can use to attract others."

He nodded slowly. "That makes sense."

"It's usually best if we provide an incentive to answer a few questions. Would you be willing to give away some desserts?"

"You mean like giving them a coupon for a dessert on their next visit?" Mrs. Maguire asked.

"Exactly."

The two exchanged a glance, and then they nodded. "We could do that."

Tori smiled. "Terrific. I'll create a coupon and have some researchers there this week."

They arrived at the restrooms then. Tori promised to be in touch within a day or two, and left to return to her cubicle by way of the breakroom. While she stirred creamer into a Styrofoam cup of coffee, Kate entered.

"There you are." She tossed her head in the direction of the conference room. "What was all that about?"

Tori tossed the stir stick into the trash. "All what about?"

Kate crossed her arms and tapped a finger. "The questions about the new location. Where were you going with that?"

Tori glanced toward the doorway and lowered her voice, just in case Mitch was hovering around somewhere. "I went by the new restaurant a few days ago, and I'm not convinced it's a good location for them."

"Why not?"

"It's right off campus, for one, and their prices are too high for most college students. Plus, I don't think their menu will appeal to that age group. Three previous restaurants have failed there."

"I'm sure they know that."

Tori leaned against the counter and sipped from her cup. "Yes, but do they know why, so they don't make the same mistakes? I think they need an in-depth analysis before they sign that lease."

"Tori, you're thinking like a research analyst, not an account executive." Tori drew breath to protest, but Kate forestalled her with a raised hand. "I know what you're going to say, and I don't disagree that research is an important part of any campaign. But in this case we haven't been asked to weigh in on the location. You heard the man. They're calling the shots. They don't want us making decisions for them. Nor are they paying us enough to justify a full-scale analysis on their location decision."

"But if we can prevent—"

A high-heeled shoe tapped the floor impatiently. "They've hired us to create an ad campaign. Period. And that's what we will deliver." Kate took a step further into the room and lowered her voice. "If the Maguires have to find another location, that will delay their campaign. But Connolly and Farrin needs the revenue from this account on the books this quarter. So give the client what they've asked for, and let it go."

Tori pressed her lips together to stop from arguing further. Apparently she was supposed to just stand back and let a client make what might be a costly mistake. What kind of sense did that make? When she could speak without sounding like a sulky child, she asked, "Is it okay if I hire a research firm to conduct some exit interviews this week?"

"What for?"

She lifted a shoulder. "Demographics."

Kate studied her with shrewd eyes. "I don't think you need that. There's plenty of data available already. Just come up with something creative to show the clients on Monday." She turned and left the breakroom.

Tori dumped her barely touched coffee in the sink. Plenty of data available? Yeah, but it was generic data. She needed data specific to Maguire's. If Kate wouldn't let her hire a marketing research firm, then she'd do it herself.

"Please say yes, Allie. I need you!"

Tori covered the phone with her hand and spoke as quietly as she could. For once, she was glad for Diana's fifties music in the next cubicle. "Rock Around the Clock" provided the perfect sound screen for her conversation.

"I don't know, Tori." Uncertainty doubled Allie's syllables. "I can't see myself as one of those people who stand in the middle of the mall with a clipboard and accost people as they leave Dillards."

"You wouldn't be in the mall. You'd be outside Maguire's accosting people as they leave the restaurant."

"Oh, pardon me. Sorry, but that's not my idea of a good time."

"You mean you won't help your baby sister?" Tori pulled a pout, which was totally wasted since her sister couldn't see her. "And after I hosted a makeup party for you last year and everything."

"Don't you have people who get paid to do this stuff?"

"Usually we hire a research firm." Tori glanced in the direction of Kate's closed office door. "But I don't have any budget for that. Besides, I just need some quick-and-dirty statistics to check my suspicions. Come on. You can bring Joanie with you. People will want to stop and talk to you because she's so cute."

"Yeah, like I want to lug her around in the hot sun all day. What about Gram? She doesn't have anything to do. Maybe she could bring some of her friends too."

An image flashed into Tori's mind: *The van from the assisted living center pulls up to the curb outside Maguire's. The door opens. Out files a group of geriatric researchers with clipboards swinging from their walkers. An hour later, they collapse from heat exhaustion. Connolly and Farrin is sued for cruelty to old people.*

"You don't want your daughter in the hot sun, but you'll subject your grandmother to it? Nice, Allie." She added a note of pleading. "Please? It'll be fun. A sister thing. We can make Joan come help."

There was a pause. "When do you need to have it done?"

Tori became hopeful at the hint of capitulation in her sister's voice. "I can handle the Wednesday and Thursday lunch hours by myself. But I really need help Friday night, because that's their busiest night."

"Tell you what. I'll do it, and I'll even call Joan and make her do it. But there's one condition."

"Anything. Just name it."

"We're spending the night at your place for a Sanderson sister sleepover. And you have to supply all the goodies."

"Done." Relieved, Tori collapsed against the back of the chair. "Thanks, Allie. I'll owe you big-time for this."

"Oh, trust me. I know. I'm counting on it." A cry sounded in the background. "Darn! That kid's nap gets shorter every day. Gotta go. Love you!"

"Love you t—"

The line had gone dead. She replaced the receiver and stared at it for a long moment. Maybe Friday night she'd tell her sisters about . . . she swallowed. She couldn't even finish the sentence in her own mind. How could she ever manage to say it out loud and watch their faces crumble?

Well, one good thing about drowning in work. It didn't leave time to dwell on painful thoughts.

The only thing that surprised Ryan when he looked up to find Joan coming into the store Monday afternoon was the time. She'd waited until almost lunchtime. He'd fully expected to find Allie camped in the parking lot when he got to work that morning, armed with a spotlight and rubber hose, ready to beat information out of him. He'd rather face Joan any day.

She caught sight of him and veered toward the shelf where he worked restocking light bulbs. "There you are. I just made our daily bank deposit and thought I'd stop by to see how it went yesterday."

He made a show of looking behind her. "Is Allie sick?"

She laughed. "No, but she had some things to get done this morning."

He straightened a row of 60-watt packages and added three more to fill out the shelf. "I figured she'd want to yell at me for the latest social disaster. Which I assume you two heard about."

Her face scrunched with sympathy. "Yeah, we were both there when Tori got home so she told us about the, uh, mud incident. But other than that, how'd it go? What did your family think of her?"

"They loved her, of course. Who wouldn't?" He didn't look at her, but moved to the energy efficient bulbs. "She seemed to like them too."

"Oh, she did. She told us."

"Well, that's good."

He was aware of Joan studying him as he worked, waiting for more. Allie would have had him by the collar, threatening his life if he didn't provide a minute-by-minute account of the afternoon.

"So what's next? Are you going out again?"

He knelt to straighten the packages on the lower shelf before answering. "I don't know."

"But why not?" Joan put a hand on his shoulder. "Is something wrong, Ryan?"

Yeah, something was wrong. He'd thought about nothing else all last night, when he should have been working on the paper he had due in class tomorrow. And he still hadn't sorted out his thoughts completely. Not enough to articulate them well. But one inescapable truth refused to be ignored. No matter how attracted he was to her, Tori Sanderson and he were wrong for each other. They had absolutely nothing in common.

He stood and looked over the shelf behind them, toward the cash register where Gary stood chatting with a customer. "I don't have a lot of money, Joan. I can't afford to take a girl out several times a week."

"So take her somewhere that doesn't cost much. Go to the dollar movies. Or on a picnic. Or drive out to the horse park to see the horses."

This was *Tori*'s sister? Was she serious? "Tori Sanderson wouldn't set foot in the dollar movies. She expects to be wined and dined in style." He bent his head closer to hers and lowered his voice. "Do you know how much she paid for those jeans she was wearing yesterday? Even if I *had* that kind of money, I wouldn't spend it on a pair of jeans, no matter where they came from."

Joan's lips twisted sideways. "She is a little extravagant when it comes to clothes."

"A little?" Ryan's laugh blasted through the store. Gary glanced their way, and then returned to his conversation. "She makes Paris Hilton look like a coupon-clipper."

"But that's all surface stuff, Ryan. It's how she covers up what's inside."

He folded his arms. "Really? And what would that be?"

"I wish I knew." Joan's expression grew soft. "Maybe you can help her figure it out."

Ryan started to protest, but then he remembered the box of pictures. She had been so hesitant to look at them. Fearful, even. But after they started, she'd relaxed and even smiled as she recounted some of her memories. She'd opened up.

But the idea of him helping someone like Tori? Ridiculous.

He shook his head. "Honestly, I think you and Allie would be better off putting your matchmaking skills to use somewhere else. Tori and I are just too different."

Joan smiled. "Sometimes those are the best matches." She backed up. "I'd better let you work. Just do me a favor and pray about it. If God wants you two to get together, He'll let you know. And if not…" She shrugged. "Allie and I will just have to start over."

He couldn't help laughing. Allie would be furious to have her plans thwarted, even by the Almighty.

Chapter Eighteen

The lunch crowd at Maguire's on Wednesday and Thursday didn't hold any surprises for Tori. Mostly well-dressed business people, more than a few of them entertaining clients or conducting informal meetings over a nice meal. Polite, but many of them weren't overly interested in answering her questions, free dessert or not.

Her spirits low, she returned to the office Thursday afternoon. On the one hand, she did have a couple of ideas for her ad campaign. But the specter of those three failed businesses cast a shadow over her enthusiasm for the project. Between that and the distant but intense ache over the discovery that Daddy ... but she kept that thought tucked in the back of her mind, where it belonged. Nor would she think about the pictures she and Ryan had looked at.

And why hadn't Ryan called her since he dropped her off Sunday afternoon, clutching her smelly clothes in a plastic bag? She could have talked to him, told him about her discovery. A couple of times she'd thought about calling him, but then she remembered the look of shock in his eyes when he found out the price of her jeans. He thought she was foolish. Heck, he might even be right. The thought depressed her even further.

She followed a car into the parking lot and pulled into an empty space beside it. When the driver stood, she recognized

Phil Osborne. He caught sight of her, gave a nod of acknowledgment, and stood waiting by his rear bumper while she gathered her purse and exited her car. His car displayed one of those gold fish emblems on the back, just like the one on Allie's.

He gave her a wide smile as she approached. "Hey there. Late lunch today?"

Phil had been friendly all week, which Tori appreciated since Kate's manner toward her was decidedly chilly. Not that Tori minded, particularly, since it meant she'd been relatively free from her boss's constant demands. Still, she couldn't help notice that Mitch had spent an abnormal amount of time in Kate's office this week.

Tori held up the folder containing her questionnaire and coupons. "Actually, I've been doing some research over at Maguire's."

They fell in step together. "How's that coming?"

She shrugged, then admitted, "Not as well as I'd hoped."

"Anything I can do to help?" They arrived at the stairwell, and he opened the door for her.

She paused before stepping through. Phil and Kate were about as different as two people could be. Imagine what it would be like to work for someone who actually tried to help you with your job, instead of throwing you into fierce competition with your co-worker.

What was it Mitch had said? Kate would take the firm to the next level, and the partners knew it. When she was made partner, the whole attitude of the firm would change. What would happen to Phil then? He'd seemed so distraught the night he came out of Mr. Connolly's office after learning of Kate's impending promotion.

Tori eyed him. "Can I ask you a personal question?"

He seemed surprised. "Sure."

"Are you okay with this partner situation?"

"Ah." He let the door close and turned his back to it, his gaze scanning the parking lot absently. "I admit I wasn't happy when Stephen told me of his and Dan's decision. There are sure to be some changes when Kate becomes a full partner." His smile became wistful. "But after spending a lot of time thinking and praying about it"—he glanced at her as he said the word—"I've realized it was a logical move for this firm. Kate's a strong marketing professional."

"So are you." Tori didn't know why she felt the need to defend him, but she did.

He smiled. "Thank you. But there's a difference between us. Our priorities are different, and I'm not willing to change mine." He held up a hand and unfolded a finger as he listed them. "God first. My family second. My job third."

The pictures in his office, prominently displayed, supported his statement. The framed Bible verse, the row of smiling family members. Tori had noticed several shots of a young woman who looked a lot like Phil. His daughter, she'd assumed.

Lucky girl, to have a father who actually lists her as a priority.

Unexpected tears filled her eyes. She turned away quickly, but not before Phil noticed.

"Tori? Is something wrong?"

The note of concern in his voice conjured even more tears to blur her vision. To her embarrassment, they overflowed to slide down her cheeks. She dashed them quickly away and sniffed.

"Nothing. I—" A sob choked her. She drew a shuddering breath and risked a glance at him. His eyes held such compassion that words tumbled out before she could stop them. "I haven't seen my father since I was nine. I just found out that he ... died last year."

A car pulled into the concrete garage and approached slowly, looking for an empty parking space. Great. Someone else to see her unprofessional behavior. Tori wiped away another couple of tears with her fingers.

"Here." Phil put an arm around her and steered her away, back toward their cars. "My wife keeps a package of Kleenex in the glove compartment."

"No, I've got one here." Sniffing, she opened her purse and rummaged in it as they walked. "Somewhere."

They arrived at Phil's car before she could find anything to wipe her eyes with. She managed to get herself under control as he retrieved the tissues, and by the time he pressed the small package into her hands, the tears had stopped flowing. How absolutely mortifying, to cry in front of an executive from the office.

"I'm sorry." She swabbed at her damp cheeks and avoided looking at his face. "I didn't mean to get all emotional."

"Please don't worry about that." He leaned against his car door, and she heard a smile in his voice. "I have a daughter about your age. I'm used to displays of emotion."

"I know. I saw her picture in your office. That's what made me—" Drat! There came more tears, just when she thought she had them under control. She covered her eyes with the tissue to catch them before they fell. "I was just thinking how lucky she is to have a father who cares about her."

From the corner of her eye, she saw him put a hand in his pants pocket. "I'm sorry for your loss, Tori. It's hard to lose a parent, even one you don't know well. Maybe it's even harder then."

She gulped in a breath of air to stop another sob. That's one of the thoughts she'd been trying so hard to ignore all week. It *was* harder, because now, it was too late to confront Daddy with her questions. Too late to find out why he'd left her.

"Listen," she managed to choke out, "I'm going to sit in my car for a few minutes and get myself under control. You can go on upstairs. Thanks for this." She held up the tissue, damp and covered with mascara smudges.

Phil hesitated, but then straightened. "Okay. Take all the time you need. If anyone asks where you are, I'll tell them you weren't feeling well."

That was the understatement of the year. "Thanks."

He started to walk away, then stopped. "I'll be praying for you, Tori."

If Ken or Allie or Joan had said that, it would have irritated her. But Phil wasn't trying to force anything on her. He was just offering comfort the best way he knew how. Oddly enough, the thought of someone praying for her sent more tears flooding into her eyes. Her insides were in such turmoil, she could use all the prayers she could get. She nodded and opened her car door without answering.

Alone in the silent interior of her car, Tori succumbed to a few minutes of crying. Not that her grief served any purpose other than making her feel sorry for herself. How ridiculous to cry over someone who didn't give a flip about her for the last fifteen years. The time for crying over losing her father was long past. Anger served her better. She could control that far more easily than sorrow.

And she had every right to be angry. She wadded up the dirty tissue and pulled a fresh one from the package Phil had pushed into her hand. When she stopped to think that Daddy hadn't cared enough to drive ninety minutes to see them, hadn't bothered to let them know where he was, she could feel her rage heating up. He'd apparently had a relationship with someone after leaving them. Patricia Ann Parker.

Who was she, this woman listed on the Internet as one of Daddy's relatives? Did she even know about his prior life? Tori blew her nose with force. Did Patricia Ann Parker know he'd deserted three daughters, let them grow up fatherless while he traipsed all over the country?

What *did* Patricia Ann Parker know?

Suddenly, Tori had to find out. Her hands moved quickly, before her brain could list the reasons she shouldn't go to Cincinnati. She shoved the key into the ignition, started the engine, and shifted into Reverse. Phil would tell anyone in the office that she wasn't feeling well. If Kate noticed her absence, let her assume Tori had gone home sick.

She was finally going to get some answers.

The neighborhood wasn't a wealthy one. The houses were small, and a little run-down looking. A few cars parked along the street, one with a flat tire that apparently hadn't been moved in months. Tori drove slowly, scanning the house numbers as she went. Thanks to a helpful convenience store clerk on the edge of the city, a printout from Mapquest lay beside her on the passenger seat.

There. The numbers above the door matched the ones she'd jotted down. She pulled her car to the curb and looked at the house. Not big. Dingy white siding. A single window to the left of the front door, the curtains pulled shut. No garage, and no car in the driveway. The yard needed to be mowed.

She shut off the engine, but didn't move. What was she doing here? Maybe Patricia Ann Parker didn't even live here anymore. And if she did, what would Tori say? "Excuse me, but do you know why my father ignored me for the last fourteen years of his life?"

The clock on the radio read 3:30. There probably wasn't anyone home anyway. Most people would be at work at this time of day.

Tori put her purse down on the floor, out of sight, and got out of the car. She locked the door, took a deep breath for courage, and marched up the empty driveway. Grass grew in long cracks in the blacktop. At the top of three steps, a worn welcome mat rested on the small square of concrete that served as a front porch. Planting her feet squarely on the mat, she rapped on the door.

Nobody answered. Out of the corner of her eye, she saw the curtains in the front window move and waited for the door to open. Nothing. She knocked again, harder this time. She did not drive all this way just to be ignored at the front door. Finally, the door cracked open and an eye appeared. A child's eye, partially hidden by a thick lock of dark hair.

"Hello." Tori pasted on a wide smile. "I'm looking for Patricia Ann Parker."

"She's not here right now." An adolescent voice.

"She does live here, though?"

The eye bobbed up and down as the girl nodded.

Well, at least she hadn't moved away. Tori was one step closer to getting answers to the questions that haunted her.

"I need to talk to her about something," Tori told the girl. "Can you tell me what time you expect her?"

The door edged open a bit more. "She gets off work at four. You can come back then if you want."

Stillness stole over Tori as she caught sight of a high cheekbone. There was something familiar about the curve of that cheek, the shape of that eye. Her tongue felt thick as she forced it to form words. "Is Patricia Ann Parker your..." She couldn't finish the question.

"She's my mom."

The door opened even further, and the child's whole face appeared. An unseen fist socked Tori in the stomach. Breath whooshed into her lungs in a gasp.

This girl looked just like Daddy.

Chapter Nineteen

"Are you sure you're okay? You still look sorta sick."

Tori took another sip from the glass of water the girl had brought from inside. She sat on the edge of the top step, unable to tear her eyes away from the pretty brunette who was undoubtedly her sister.

She managed a quick smile. "I'll be fine. I just felt a little faint for a minute."

"Maybe you should put your head between your knees. My teacher last year was pregnant, and she had to do that all the time when she felt like she was gonna faint." The girl examined Tori's slim frame. "Are you pregnant?"

Tori laughed. "No, I'm not." She took another drink from the glass and set it on the edge of the porch. "My name is Tori. What's yours?"

"Chelsea." She dropped down to sit cross-legged on the sidewalk, all skinny limbs and knees and elbows.

"That's a pretty name. And your last name is Parker?"

Chelsea scowled. "No, my mom's name is different, because she and Daddy weren't married." Not a hint of embarrassment. Just a statement of the fact, as though she'd explained it many times before. "I'm a Sanderson, like my dad."

Tori kept her smile in place with an effort. Daddy had acknowledged this girl as his daughter, had given her his name.

Their name. Not that he could have denied fathering her, since she looked so much like him. Some of the pictures she'd showed Ryan hovered in her memory. Chelsea's resemblance to Joan at ten or eleven years old was remarkable. How could Daddy have looked at her, watched her grow up, and not thought of the daughters he'd deserted?

"Chelsea Sanderson." The name tasted like bittersweet chocolate on Tori's tongue. "Was your father's name Tom?"

Chelsea's knees came up, and skinny arms encircled them. "Yeah, how'd you know?"

"I met him once. A long time ago." Pain twisted Tori's heart.

The girl's shoulders slumped. "He died, you know. Last year."

Tori nodded. "I heard. I'm sorry."

"I miss him a lot." She propped her chin on a knee.

Tori closed her eyes and, for a second, let sorrow wash over her. *Me too.* "How did he die?"

"He had a heart attack while he was driving."

A heart attack. He'd only been sixty. He should have had lots of years left. Years to watch this girl grow up. To make things right with his other daughters.

Tori forced a smile for Chelsea. "My father died too. The last time I saw him, I was a little younger than you are now."

The oval face tilted. "Can I ask you a question?"

"Okay."

"Do you remember him?" She hugged her legs tighter. "I mean, *really* remember him. 'Cause my friend Melissa says she can't hardly remember her grandfather, and he only died two years ago."

"I—" Tori stopped. The truth was, she'd concentrated on *not* remembering Daddy for so long. "I have pictures of him. That helps."

"I have pictures, too." Chelsea jumped to her feet. "Want to know how I make sure I'll never forget him? I'll show you. Wait here."

The girl leaped up all three stairs at once and disappeared into the house. Lead sat in Tori's stomach as she waited. The last thing she wanted to do was look at a bunch of pictures of Daddy with his new daughter. But she couldn't leave, not now. She drove up here to talk to Patricia, and she intended to stick it out until she'd done just that.

Chelsea returned carrying a cordless telephone. She sat down on the step next to Tori and pushed a series of buttons.

"Listen to this message."

Tori took the receiver and held it to her ear. When a familiar voice began speaking, it sliced like a hot knife straight through her soul.

"Hey, where are my girls? I'm calling to let you know I'm on my way home, and I'm in the mood for pizza tonight. Let's order one loaded with all the good stuff." He chuckled, and the sound set Tori's pulse to pounding. "Okay, we'll get two. One with just cheese for my little punkin' girl. Sound good? See you when I get home."

Painful tears pricked the backs of Tori's eyes. With an effort, she controlled them as she handed the phone back to Chelsea. She'd forgotten the sound of his voice. But now that she'd heard it again, it resonated in her memory.

She was in the bedroom she shared with Joan and Allie, Barbie dolls spread out around her. The front door slammed. Daddy's voice echoed down the hallway. "I'm home! Where are my girls?"

"That was the night before he ..." Chelsea's throat moved as she swallowed. "You know. I listen to it every night. It helps me have good dreams."

A car pulled into the driveway. Chelsea's face brightened as she jumped to her feet. "There's my mom."

Tori fought to regain a measure of composure as she stood. The woman stared at her as she climbed out of the car and came down the sidewalk. An attractive woman, tall and slim with curly dark hair. She wore a brown polyester dress that had the look of a waitress's uniform. A plastic tag pinned on the left side proclaimed her name: Patti.

Chelsea ran over to her. "Mom, this lady came to see you. Don't worry, I didn't let her inside."

"That's good, hon." Her expression held a note of suspicion as she examined Tori. "I'm sorry. Do I know you?"

Tori paused for only a moment. There was no way to ease into the reason for her visit, and she didn't really want to. She looked the woman in the eye, thrust out her hand, and said, "Hello. I'm Tori Sanderson."

Chelsea's eyes grew round. "Sanderson? You didn't tell me your whole name. Are you related to my dad?"

Patti didn't take her gaze from Tori as she snapped, "Chelsea, go in the house."

"But Mom, I—"

"Now!"

Chelsea obeyed, though she announced her frustration by stomping up the stairs and slamming the door. Another time, Tori would have thought that was funny. But at the moment, she couldn't look away from the angry stare on the face of … what was this woman to her, anyway? Not her stepmother. Just her father's girlfriend.

Patti's angry words took her by surprise. "How am I going to explain you to her?"

Tori's mouth dropped open. "Excuse me?"

The woman made a savage gesture toward the house. "Chelsea doesn't know about you. What am I supposed to say?"

Well, I didn't know about her either! But Patti seemed to know exactly who she was. Apparently Daddy had told her about his family.

"You could try the truth."

Patti's lips twisted into a grimace. "Why couldn't you just stay away? We're doing okay, finally. We don't need you butting into our lives. We don't want your interference."

"I want some answers about my father. I think I deserve that." Tori folded her arms and stood her ground as Patti's eyes narrowed into a glare.

"Tom made his choice. That ought to be enough for you."

Her words fell like blows. She was right. Daddy had chosen. He left her and Joan and Allie behind while he made a life with this woman and her daughter. His daughter. The one he called *my little punkin' girl.*

"I—" She swallowed, and tried again. "I just want to know why."

Patti seemed to grow taller as her spine stiffened. "You're too late. He's gone. Now please, leave us alone. Don't come back. We don't want anything to do with you."

She brushed past Tori and followed her daughter into the house. Stunned, Tori turned to stare at the closed door. She caught sight of Chelsea's face at the window for a moment, but then the girl was pulled abruptly backward and the curtain fell into place, shutting her away from view.

With a slow step, Tori walked to her car, climbed in, and drove away.

The ninety-minute drive back to Lexington seemed to pass from one breath to the next. Patti's angry glare was seared in Tori's mind; her words echoed. *"Tom made his choice. That ought to be enough for you."* But it wasn't nearly enough.

"Why?"

Her question punched through the silence in her car. It was directed upward, toward the gray, cloud-covered sky where she'd always considered heaven to be. Was Daddy there now? Was he looking down, watching her struggle to understand?

"Why did you stay with her, and not me?"

A sob choked off her voice on the last word. If Daddy was up there, he couldn't answer. Or maybe he chose not to, as he'd chosen all along.

Raindrops speckled her windshield, and she flipped on the wipers. The turnoff to her complex was up ahead, but Tori couldn't make herself take it. She'd go crazy sitting alone in her empty apartment tonight. Better to be around people who loved her. She'd go home, to Danville.

But where? Mom was at work at the hospital. Joan probably had plans with Ken. She would change her plans if she knew Tori needed her, but then the whole story would have to come out. Joan would be devastated when she found out not only that Daddy was dead, but that he'd chosen another family over them. And so would Allie. Tori's pain was still too fresh, too raw. Seeing their grief would send her over the edge tonight. She couldn't handle that. By tomorrow she'd have a grip on her own emotions, and she'd be able to stay strong as she delivered the devastating news to her sisters.

But not tonight.

"Good night, Gary. See you in the morning."

Ryan lifted a hand in farewell as he exited the store. He had just enough time to run home and grab a sandwich before his seven o'clock class. When the doors opened, he realized the rain predicted for this evening had begun. Hunching his shoulders, he dashed across the parking lot and slid into his car.

The light was still on in the dentist's office downstairs when Ryan pulled into the lot in front of his apartment. A couple of cars were parked outside, a BMW and a white Toyota. Dr. Patrick must have a late appointment tonight. He parked at the corner of the building, near the stairs. That's when he noticed someone sitting in the driver's seat of the Toyota. Someone who looked like…

Ryan shut off his car's engine. It *was* Tori. But what was she doing here? And why was she leaning over the steering wheel like she was asleep?

He got out of his car. When he slammed the door, she raised her head. Rain ran in rivulets down her window, turning her face into a blur. He splashed across the parking lot and arrived at her car at the same time she opened the door. She climbed out and faced him. That's when he saw that she hadn't been sleeping. She'd been crying. The skin around her eyes was red and puffy.

She looked up at him, and her face crumpled. Deep inside his rib cage, Ryan's heart gave a lurch. He opened his arms and, without a word, she stepped into them. Large drops of rain fell from the sky, wetting them both to the skin, while Tori cried in his embrace. He hugged her tight, trying to shield her from the downpour. Feeling more helpless than he ever had in his life, he realized he couldn't shield her from whatever had caused such deep, wracking sobs.

Lord, whatever it is, can't you help her?

"Come on." He steered her toward the stairs. "Let's get you out of this rain."

Wordlessly, she allowed him to guide her up the stairs, and stood with her sobs coming in gulps as he unlocked the door. Inside, he flipped on the light and ran into the bathroom for a towel. Thank goodness he had a clean one.

When he returned to the tiny front room, she stood exactly where he'd left her, right inside the door. He handed her the towel and then gently guided her to the worn couch, the only place to sit. From the way she avoided his eyes and mumbled her thanks, he sensed she needed a minute to regain her composure. He left her blotting her sopping wet clothes and crossed to the kitchen area, neatly tucked into a corner of the room, to put on a pot of coffee. By the time he returned, she seemed more herself.

No, not herself. Not the confident, flirty Tori he knew. Her head drooped, and her lips trembled as though more sobs were only moments away. He sat beside her, and she gave him a quick, embarrassed smile.

"Sorry. I didn't mean to do that."

"It's alright. That's what friends are for."

She ran her fingers through her disheveled hair in a self-conscious gesture. "I must look awful."

He'd seen her look better. Besides the puffy eyes, her nostrils were red and her skin splotchy. But a vulnerability he'd never seen before lurked in the depths of her blue eyes. It drew him irresistibly, made him want to protect her.

"You could never be anything but beautiful," he told her, and he meant every word.

The look she shot him was grateful. "I shouldn't stay. I know you have class."

Dynamite couldn't pry him out of here tonight if she needed him. "It's okay. I'm playing hooky."

The gurgle from the coffeepot ended in a loud hiss. Coffee dripped from the basket into the carafe, the sound magnified in the silent room. Ryan wanted to ask what had happened, but knew instinctively that he shouldn't rush her. She'd tell him in her own time. Instead, he poured two cups of coffee and brought them from the kitchen.

"Sorry it's not a latte." He handed her a steaming mug and took his seat again.

With a brief smile, she cupped it in both hands and sipped. Then she held it in front of her mouth and closed her eyes. "My father is dead."

Ah, so that's where the tears came from. "I'm sorry." He placed a comforting hand on her shoulder. "Do Allie and Joan know?"

She shook her head. "They're coming over to spend the night with me tomorrow night. I'll tell them then. But there's more."

He listened as she poured out her story, how she'd found her father on the Internet, discovered that he'd died, and that he'd lived in Cincinnati. How she'd driven to his house to confront the woman whose name was listed under the ambiguous label of "relative." And what she found there.

"You should see her, Ryan. Chelsea is pretty, and smart, and she looks just like Daddy." Tori shook her head. "She's got some great memories of her father. I should be happy for her. Instead, I can't stop wondering 'why her?' " She twisted on the cushion until she was facing him. "What does she have that I didn't?"

"You can't think that way. The problem was with him, not with you."

He might as well have kept silent. She didn't seem to hear him but stared vaguely at some point over his shoulder as she continued. "Chelsea adored Daddy. I could see it in the way her eyes lit up when she talked about him. If I'd been less of a mama's girl and more of a daddy's girl, maybe he would have loved me more. Then he wouldn't have left."

"You know that's not true."

Her gaze snapped to his face. "Do I?"

Joan's words in the store the other day came back to Ryan. Maybe she was right. Maybe all the expensive clothes, the perfect makeup, the flirting, were just a show. A way to cover up the insecure little girl who was trying to understand why her daddy left her. He'd never gotten a glimpse of that girl before tonight. And he was drawn to her even more deeply than before.

Lord, what can I say? I can't fix this for her. I can't answer her questions.

But he could do one thing. He could tell her how he felt. Ryan raised his hand slowly and let his finger trace the outline of her tear-streaked cheek. "I don't know why he left. But I do know one thing. His decision hurt him more than anyone else, because it deprived him of knowing you. I feel sorry for him. He missed out on seeing you grow into the amazing woman you are."

Warmth flooded her eyes, and for the first time all evening, a genuine smile played at the corners of her mouth. Acting more on instinct than thought, Ryan took the mug out of her hands and set it on the coffee table, his gaze never leaving hers. Then he moved closer on the couch and cupped her face in his hands.

"Are you going to kiss me?" Her question was a purr in his ear.

His hand slid to the back of her head, his fingers buried in the damp curls, and he pulled her gently toward him. "Do you want me to?"

In answer, her eyelids fluttered closed and her face tilted toward his.

The first touch of their lips was feather-light. And then Ryan pressed her closer and poured all the depth of his feelings into his kiss.

Emotions swirled in Tori's mind and snatched the breath from her lungs. All the tormenting thoughts dissolved as every sense in her body tingled with Ryan's kiss. When he pulled away her lips felt cold, bereft. She wanted that kiss to go on forever.

Wow. Was Joan right, or what?

When a second kiss didn't come, she reluctantly opened her eyes to find him watching her. "I'm feeling better now," she said with a coy smile.

He gave a low laugh and slowly backed away. "I'm glad." Then he sobered as he picked up his coffee mug. "But I need to tell you something important."

Uh oh. Didn't he want to go out with her anymore? Was that why he hadn't called her all week? To hide the deep disappointment that must surely be written all over her face, she turned away under the guise of retrieving her coffee. "Okay."

His words came out in a rush, as though he had to get them out before he changed his mind. "I'm not who you think I am. I don't drink designer coffee, and I don't know anything about marketing. I studied up on it so I could impress you. And I found out about your favorite flowers and your favorite pie so I could impress you too."

A suspicion slowly crept over Tori. She narrowed her eyes. "How did you find out those things?"

Blood suffused his face. "Allie and Joan. They've been giving me advice all along."

She started to laugh. Poor Ryan had fallen into the clutches of her matchmaking sisters.

"You're not upset?"

"Listen, on the scale of things that have upset me today, that's minor." She hesitated only a moment before slipping her hand into his. "Actually, I think it's sweet that you took their advice. Thank you."

He sobered. "Tori, I don't have a lot of money. In fact, I don't have *any* money. So I can't take you out to expensive restaurants and places like that. It's not that I don't want to, or that you don't deserve to be treated like a queen, it's just that I can't afford it right now."

"I know that." She squeezed his hand. "We don't have to spend money to enjoy each other's company. There are lots of things we could do that don't cost a penny."

His lips twitched. "You mean like picnics in the park or drives in the country?"

"Exactly."

"Your sister knows you better than I thought." His thumb traced circles on her hand. "Though I can't imagine why someone like you would want to go out with a farm boy like me."

"Because I've recently made an important discovery. I may not be crazy about farms," Tori leaned forward, and just before their lips touched, she whispered, "but I like farm boys."

Chapter Twenty

hen Joan and Allie arrived at Maguire's on Friday evening, Tori had already conducted more than a dozen interviews as early diners left the restaurant. She'd missed at least that many others, unable to talk to more than one party at a time.

"It's about time," she hissed at her sisters as they approached. "I've been here half an hour by myself."

"Sorry." Joan gave her a quick hug, then rolled her eyes in Allie's direction. "*Someone* couldn't pry herself away from her baby."

Allie's lip protruded, and she gave an audible sniff. "I can't help it. I've never left her overnight before."

"She'll be fine." The restaurant's door opened, and Tori whispered, "Okay, just listen this time so you know what to say."

Joan and Allie stood nearby as Tori approached the couple leaving the restaurant. They were happy to talk to her, and she recorded their answers on her survey form. A few minutes later, they left with their dessert coupons.

"That looked easy," Allie said.

"It is." Tori dug in her briefcase, then gave each of them a clipboard and a stack of forms. "Just smile, and make sure I can read your writing."

The next hour passed quickly, and Tori was sure she was getting some great data for her analysis. A few people weren't interested in taking the time to talk to them, but most seemed prepared to go on at length about the reasons they liked Maguire's.

She had just finished talking to a pair of businessmen when she turned around and got an unpleasant surprise. Kate stood on the sidewalk, arms crossed, glaring in her direction.

Busted!

Tori schooled her features and approached her boss. "Hello, Kate."

"Do you mind telling me what you're doing?" Her voice was chillier than Tori had ever heard it.

"I'm gathering data to help with my marketing plan."

"I thought we agreed that you didn't need to conduct any research."

Tori worked hard to keep her voice pleasant. "No, we didn't. You said I couldn't hire a research firm, and I haven't. I recruited my sisters to help, so it won't cost anything."

"No?" Her pencil-thin eyebrows arched. "Then what are you using as an incentive?"

Okay, yes, technically there was a cost involved, but not to Connolly and Farrin. "The Maguires agreed to a free dessert."

Kate's lips tightened. "Tori, does this have anything to do with our discussion about the location of their new restaurant?"

Behind her, both Allie and Joan stood quietly, waiting for the next customers to leave the restaurant. Probably listening to every word.

"Not only that," Tori said. "I'm collecting information to determine the customers' decision set. I've gotten some good responses on what they see as alternative choices that will help—"

Kate raised a hand to cut her off. "I don't care. I want you to know one thing. If you so much as mention the new location in front of the Maguires on Monday, you'll be looking for another job by Tuesday. Do I make myself clear?"

She didn't trust herself to answer. Her teeth clenched, she nodded.

"Good." Kate brushed past her and went inside the restaurant.

Allie and Joan approached.

"Wow." Allie's round eyes stared after Kate. "You said you worked for Attila the Hun, but I didn't believe you."

"I may not work for her much longer." Tori's lower lip trembled. Even if she didn't get fired on Monday, she'd blown her chance at the Account Executive position. No way would Kate promote her now.

Joan put an arm around her shoulders and squeezed. "Are you going to be okay?"

Tori nodded. "But let's get out of here. I've done enough damage to my career for one night. I don't want to be here when she comes back out."

And the worst part of the night still lay ahead of her.

Tori unlocked the door of her apartment and they all trooped inside.

"I hope you've got food in the fridge." Allie dropped her overnight bag on the living room floor on her way to the kitchen. "I thought we'd get to eat at Maguire's when we finished surveying people. I'm starving."

Laughing, Joan picked up the discarded bag and headed for the bedroom. "Careful, or you'll blow that diet you've worked so hard at."

"I can afford to take a night off." Allie's voice was muffled by the refrigerator door. "Hey, what is this?" She appeared in the serving window to glare at Tori. "Diet Dr Pepper? Baked Lays? Are you kidding me? This is a Sanderson Sister Sleepover. Where's the good munchies?"

"Allie, you've lost so much weight, I don't want to be the reason you fall off the diet wagon." Tori smiled. "But I got reduced-fat Oreos, and they're yummy."

Joan came back into the room. "Just remember, you have a bridesmaid dress to fit into in one month." She dropped onto the sofa. "What are we watching tonight?"

Tori picked up a stack of DVDs and waved them in the air. "Girls, tonight we're going to soak up the sights of Or-*lan*-do!"

"Oooh, Orlando Bloom." Allie returned to the living room with her hand stuck in a bag of chips. "I just love sexy pirates. And if you got *Troy,* we also get to see men in skirts."

"You bet I did." Tori set the DVDs on the entertainment center. Might as well get it over with sooner rather than later. "But before we start watching movies, I have to talk to you two about something serious." They exchanged a guilty look, and Tori knew what they were thinking. She fixed a scowl on them. "And it's not about Ryan, though he told me how you two have been feeding him information."

Allie put a hand to her collarbone and affected an innocent tone. "Who, us?"

Tori put a hand on her hip and stared her sister down.

Joan asked, "But if he told you, does that mean it worked?"

Even the memory of last night's kisses sent an answering flutter to Tori's stomach. She couldn't stop a dreamy sigh from escaping her lips. Her sisters grinned and high-fived each other.

"We knew it." Laughing, Joan clapped with delight. "You're perfect for each other."

Allie raised her nose in the air. "That's right. You just remember that from now on, Tori. Your big sisters know what's best." She tossed a chip in her mouth and crunched for emphasis.

"What-*ever*." Tori rolled her eyes, trying to hide a grin. "Do you know what Linus of the Peanuts gang says? 'Big sisters are crabgrass in the lawn of life.'"

"Yes, but he didn't have *your* big sisters," Allie answered with a smirk.

Tori could have come up with another barb, but instead she sobered. What she had to tell them wasn't funny. She drew in a breath and perched on the edge of the chair beside the sofa. "Seriously, I found out something last weekend that you need to know."

Their laughter died away.

"What is it?" Joan asked.

There was no good way to deliver bad news. She'd thought about it, tried to come up with some way to ease the blow, but finally decided the best thing to do was say it quickly and get it over with.

"Our father is dead. He died of a heart attack last March."

Their faces became mirror images of shock. Joan sank slowly backward until she rested against the back sofa cushion, and Allie's lips parted as her jaw went slack.

"How do you know?" Allie asked. "Did someone contact you?"

Tori shook her head. "I found him on the Internet. And that's not all I discovered."

She retraced her steps for them, how she'd paid to get his address in Cincinnati, and about seeing Patricia Ann Parker's name listed below Mom's. How she'd driven to Cincinnati yesterday, and what she found there.

Joan leaped to her feet. "Wait a minute. Are you saying we have a sister?"

"A half-sister," Allie said.

Joan gave her a quick look. "Whatever. There's another Sanderson sister living less than two hours from here?"

Tori nodded. "She looks a lot like you, Joan. The same dark hair, same bone structure. Even her eyes are shaped like yours. Like Daddy's." She smiled at Allie. "And she's a talker too. Like you. She opened right up to me about her feelings over losing…" She stared at her clasped hands, unable to finish the sentence.

Joan paced to the balcony door with a quick step, then whirled. "I want to meet her!"

"We can't. Her mother doesn't want us around." Tori swallowed, her throat tight. "She said Daddy made his choice, and we have to live with that."

Allie snorted like a bull. "That's who I want to meet. This *woman*. I think she owes us an explanation."

Joan's eyes widened. She took a step toward them. "Let's go. Tonight. Right now. It's eight o'clock. We can be up there by nine-thirty."

"She won't talk to us," Tori said.

"Oh, yes she will." Allie set her jaw, her eyes hard. "We'll *make* her talk to us."

Full dark had fallen by the time Tori pulled the car to a stop in front of the house. A light shone around the edges of the curtain in the front window. "This is it."

The silence deepened inside the car as they stared at the house. Finally Joan said, "It's not very big, is it?"

"It looks even smaller than my house," Allie said. "I wonder if Daddy left it to that woman in his will."

"I didn't do a property search," Tori said, "but I figured they must have bought it together. That's how come her name showed up at all. There had to be some official documentation that connected them."

Joan spoke up from the backseat. "It could have been Chelsea's birth certificate."

"I didn't think of that."

Allie slapped a hand on the armrest. "Well, girls, we're not getting anything done here. Let's go confront the Other Woman."

They climbed out of the car, and Tori let her older sisters take the lead, like the coward she was. She'd gone head-to-head with Patti before, and came away feeling bruised and bloodied. Besides, Allie was better at confrontations.

But even Allie seemed hesitant over this one. At the top of the stairs she paused and waited until all of them were in place. Reluctantly Tori joined her sisters on the small porch. When the three stood shoulder to shoulder, Joan knocked.

The curtains at the window moved, and Tori shrank behind Allie. If Patti saw her, no way she'd open the door. Breath caught in her lungs, Tori waited as seconds ticked by. Patti might even call the police. There wasn't a No Trespassing sign posted, though she'd made it clear she didn't want Tori to come back. Could they get thrown in jail?

A click sounded as the door was unlocked. It opened, and Patti stood inside. This time she wore jeans and a tank top, and her hair was pulled back into a quick twist. She looked less threatening tonight, and a lot younger. Her eyes moved as she looked from one of them to the other. Tori thought her eyes widened when she looked at Joan, but then they came to rest on her.

"I figured you'd come back, but I didn't think it would be this soon."

Tori stood straight, drawing strength from her sisters on either side of her. "I—" Her throat threatened to close. She swallowed and started again. "We just want to know about our father."

Patti broke eye contact first. Her head drooped forward as she stared at her feet. "I know. And I'm..." She took a breath. "I'm sorry I sent you away yesterday. It's just that I wasn't prepared. I didn't know what I was going to say to my daughter."

She looked up again, and her eyes begged Tori to understand. "She didn't know anything about Tom's past. And I don't want to ruin her memories of him. He was a good father to her. She deserves to keep that image of him."

Beside Tori, Allie stiffened. "But apparently we don't?"

Patti winced. "I know it's not fair. And it's my fault."

"Your fault?" Joan shook her head. "I don't understand."

A young voice came from somewhere in the house. "Mom, who are you talking to?"

Patti turned her head and shouted her answer. "Just some people at the door, honey." She turned back to them. "Chelsea's in the bathtub. She'll be out in a few minutes."

"Listen, we're not here to cause problems for Chelsea. We can come back another time." Tori started to back away, but Allie grabbed her by the arm and glared her into silence.

"No, it's okay," Patti said. "After you left yesterday, we had a long talk. She knows about you now." Her glance swept the three of them. "All of you. Do you mind if we talk outside for a minute?"

She stepped through the door and pulled it shut behind her. They retreated down the stairs and stood on the cracked sidewalk just inside the circle of light created by the porch light. Tori noticed that Patti's feet were bare, her toenails bright spots of pink in the grass.

"Tom and I met fourteen years ago in Las Vegas. He was working construction, and I was dancing at a nightclub."

Tori and Allie exchanged a glance. Fourteen years ago was a year after he left them.

"You must have been very young." Joan's voice was soft.

A sad smile curved Patti's lips. "I was twenty-four. He was thirty-seven."

Tori swallowed. Patti had been the age she was now. Younger than either Allie or Joan.

Patti continued. "I don't know if you knew this, but Tom had a drug problem. When we first got together he kept it fairly well hidden, but within a year he was out of control. He was in the carpenter's union, but he was let go from one job site after another. After a while he couldn't get a job anywhere. He couldn't stay clean long enough to pass the drug test. We paid the bills on the money I made dancing."

Tori couldn't imagine getting involved with someone like that. "Why did you stay with him?"

"I was almost as heavily into drugs as he was." Her face tilted upward as she looked at the house, and a faint smile curved her lips. "But then I got pregnant. I told Tom I was moving back home to Dayton to be near my family, and he could either come with me and get clean, or stay there and die."

Tori glanced at Joan. Mom had given him a similar ultimatum, only apparently he didn't make the same choice the second time. "He went with you."

She nodded. "I put down the drugs and never looked back. For Tom, it wasn't so easy. He finally did it when Chelsea was three years old, but it was hard for him, and he never stopped attending Narcotics Anonymous meetings. He was coming home from a meeting the night he died." The sadness in her eyes made Tori want to cry.

"But why didn't he contact us after he got clean?" Allie's question touched a painful place inside Tori. That's what they all wanted—no, needed—to know.

Patti didn't answer at first. She half turned away, and her face was hidden in shadow. "That was my fault." Her head drooped. "I was young. Selfish. Jealous. I insisted if he was serious about a life with me and Chelsea, he had to leave everything in his past behind him." She looked up, her eyes begging them to understand. "He wouldn't marry me because he said he'd already had a wife. I was afraid that meant he still loved her, that one day he might go back to her. So I made him choose. Her or me." She closed her eyes. "Her daughters, or mine."

What a terrible thing to do. Angry accusations battled in Tori's mind, but she still hadn't gotten all the answers she needed. "Why didn't you contact us last year? We had a right to know our father was dead."

Patti winced, then nodded. "You're right. I should have tried to find you. But the truth is, Tom died without a will. He didn't leave much, but he did have a little put back in annuities through the union, both here and in Nevada. And since Chelsea was the only heir they knew about…" She raised her head and looked directly into Tori's face. "I don't make enough money to support us. You three can't touch the social security payments we receive until Chelsea turns sixteen, but you could probably contest the annuity benefits. And you might be able to get half of this house."

"We wouldn't do that." Allie shook her head with a jerk.

"You don't know what you'd do if you had a child you couldn't afford to feed," Patti shot back.

Allie opened her mouth to answer, then fell silent. Tori knew she was putting herself in Patti's place, wondering what she'd do if she couldn't afford to feed Joanie.

Chelsea's muffled voice came from inside the house. "Mom? Where are you?"

Patti fixed a desperate glance on Tori. "Please don't mention the drugs. When you left last night, I told her that her father had been married before he met me, and that he'd had three daughters. But she doesn't need to know all the rest, does she?"

The door opened, and Chelsea appeared, framed by light from inside the house. "There you are. I didn't kn—" She stopped as her gaze fell on Tori. A wide smile broke out on the child's face and she raced down the stairs. "You came back! I said a prayer last night and asked God to send you back."

In the next instant, Tori was almost bowled over when Chelsea wrapped skinny arms around her in a fierce embrace. She'd never been the answer to anyone's prayer before. Her arms came up around the thin shoulders to return the hug. Her sister's hug. Over Chelsea's head, she looked at Allie and Joan through eyes blurry with tears. At a glance, she knew they were in agreement with her. This girl had already lost her father. Why put her through more pain?

She blinked back the tears, and gave Chelsea a firm squeeze. "I have a couple of people here who really want to meet you."

Chapter Twenty-One

Midnight was long past before they pulled away from the house. Tori waved out the window until she could no longer see Chelsea on the front porch.

"I love her." Allie turned from the passenger window to deliver her announcement as they turned off the street. "She's so much like Joan at that age."

"Can you believe she even wants to play the clarinet?" Joan asked from the backseat.

"She only said that after she learned you played." Tori smiled. "Just like she wants to be a cheerleader when I told her I was."

"And she was so excited to find out she's an aunt." Allie Pulled out her cell phone and stared at the screen. "I wish we'd thought to bring a camera so I could have gotten some better pictures. I never dreamed the visit would turn out so well."

"I know," Joan said. "I can't wait to tell Ken about her."

Tori steered the car toward the interstate. The night really had gone better than she expected. Patti even relaxed a little and told them stories about Daddy, like when he fainted at the hospital while six-year-old Chelsea got stitches in her forehead. The night ended with a promise to see each other again next weekend.

So how come she felt so down?

Because Daddy was there for Chelsea. She was his baby girl, his youngest. Where does that leave me?

And now, Chelsea was the youngest Sanderson sister. She had taken Tori's place, not only in her father's affections, but now in the family structure.

Don't be ridiculous. I am not jealous of an eleven-year-old child.

She kept her sigh soft, but not soft enough to escape her perceptive sister. Joan leaned up to squeeze her shoulder. "What's bothering you, Tori?"

No sense protesting. She knew her sisters. They had a ninety-minute drive ahead of them, and they'd nag her until she spilled her guts.

"Chelsea is great, and I'm glad we found her. But I can't stop wondering why Daddy chose her over us."

"The truth? Because he was a weak-minded man who couldn't stand up to his girlfriend." Allie dropped the phone in her purse. "If he'd had any sort of backbone at all, after he kicked the drugs, he would have married Patti so she had some security, and then told her he was going to contact us whether she liked it or not."

"You don't think it's because he loved Chelsea more than us, do you?" Tori's hands tightened on the steering wheel. "Or maybe, because she loved him more than we did?"

Allie's head whipped toward her. "What? That's crazy."

"No, I know what she's saying." Joan leaned forward so her face was beside Tori's shoulder. "Allie, your attitude was always, 'Our father left us. What's wrong with him?' But inside, I felt like, 'What's wrong with me?' "

"Exactly." Tori glanced at Joan. "Sometimes I worry that I didn't pay enough attention to him. Maybe he didn't feel like I loved him, and that's why he didn't think he needed to stick around."

Allie shook her head slowly. "That might have made sense when you were a kid, but you know it's not true now, right?"

Tori didn't answer. Did she? No, not really. Part of her was still that nine-year-old girl, wondering what she'd done wrong. "I just wish I'd looked for him sooner. Then I could have asked, and I'd know for sure."

"At least you still have a heavenly Father." Joan's voice rang with confidence. "Aren't you glad you don't have to be good enough for Him to love you?"

Here it came; the God-talk again. Tori almost scowled over her shoulder, but then the impact of Joan's words struck her. She didn't have to be good enough for God to love her. He loved her even when she didn't love Him. Even when she was too busy to think about Him.

Which was pretty much all the time.

And yet, He loved her anyway. Somehow, she knew that with a certainty she'd never felt before this moment. The air in the car seemed to snap, and the hair along Tori's arms prickled while, inside, the heavy feeling of depression lifted. She felt light. It really was true. Her Father loved her.

She met Joan's eyes in the rearview mirror. "I never thought of it like that."

Joan smiled and settled back.

Allie patted her leg. "And He'll never desert us, no matter what." She faced forward and pointed ahead. "Now, before you get on the interstate, can we go through that drive-through up there? I'm starving."

Chapter Twenty-Two

Ryan pushed his plate away and leaned back in his chair. "Mrs. Hancock, that was delicious. Those were the best rolls I've ever tasted."

Tori's grandmother blushed, obviously pleased with the compliment. "Thank you. They're a specialty of mine."

"She hasn't made them for us in a couple of months, Ryan." Tori's mom smiled at him. "I hope you'll come back so we can get them again."

Seated between Tori and her mother at the Sandersons' dining room table, Ryan felt like he'd passed some sort of hurdle. When Tori invited him to dinner after Sunday school, he'd been so nervous he could hardly concentrate on the minister's sermon. But since he walked through the front door, he felt like he'd been welcomed into the family. Allie and Joan had been unable to wipe the grins off their faces, and Eric had even clapped him on the back in some sort of unspoken congratulations. Apparently he'd received the stamp of approval.

Mrs. Hancock gestured toward the half-empty bowl of mashed potatoes. "We have a lot left over, I'm afraid. I hope it won't go to waste. I threw out last week's leftovers this morning."

"Don't worry, Gram." Tori laid her fork across her empty plate. "I'll take all the leftovers I can get. I have a feeling I'm going to need them."

Ken paused as he lifted his iced tea glass toward his lips. "Why is that?"

"Because I'm probably going to lose my job tomorrow." Her lips twisted into a crooked line.

Across the table, Joan leaned forward, her expression concerned. "Are you going to mention whatever-it-was your boss told you not to?"

"I'm going to try to avoid it, but I spent hours last night looking at the data we collected, and I really think they're making a mistake with that new location. I won't come right out and say it, but if they ask me ..." She shrugged. "I'm not going to lie."

"But what will you do?" Allie asked. "You said last week you didn't know of any other jobs like yours in this area."

"I'll probably have to take one that pays less. No more designer jeans." She gave Ryan a sideways grin. "I'll have to learn to live frugally."

Her smile made his insides do funny things.

"I can help with that," he told her.

Beneath the cover of the table, she slipped a hand into his and squeezed. "I'm counting on it."

"So I think you should give serious consideration to a scaled-down menu." Tori put as much confidence as she could muster into her voice and made sure she looked the Maguires in the eye. "Something that will appeal to the demographics of the area surrounding your new location."

A different menu was the only idea she could come up with for that new location to make sense. What she really wanted to do was tell them to ditch that building and keep looking until they found someplace on a main city thoroughfare. But she didn't dare say that outright, not with Kate sitting at the same table.

Mrs. Maguire was nodding, but Mr. Maguire didn't look convinced. He studied the document outlining her plan, his brow furrowed. Kate's expression remained completely blank, which worried Tori a little. During Mitch's presentation, Kate had smiled and nodded pleasantly.

And Mitch had come up with a couple of good ideas, Tori had to admit. He'd focused on designing a logo and a consistent advertising look that communicated the style and elegance people already associated with Maguire's Restaurant. And his sketches had been good.

But so were hers. If the Maguires were insistent on going ahead with a restaurant near campus, they would simply have to make some changes.

"I'm not sure I understand." Mr. Maguire picked up the paper and held it in front of him. "Our menu *is* our restaurant. You're basically saying we'd have to create a whole new concept that appeals to two different types of customers."

"Not entirely," Tori said. "You'd still have some of the same signature menu items, but each restaurant would have its specialties. And I'd recommend that you give the new restaurant a name that people associate with the existing one while still communicating its unique qualities. Maguire's Tavern, for instance, gives the impression of a more relaxed atmosphere."

Mrs. Maguire tilted her head, considering the suggestion. "I like that."

Mr. Maguire did not seem convinced. He leaned forward. "Why can't we just open a second Maguire's Restaurant? Was it the research you did that made you go in this direction?"

Tori clasped her hands beneath the table. "I didn't have much data to analyze, but what I did collect was fairly conclusive. Your customers are really loyal. You have a lot of upper management business people coming from nearby offices, but you also have a fair number of customers who drive from all over the city specifically to dine at Maguire's. And they tend to come back often."

He and his wife exchanged a smile, and he nodded. "We know that. It's one of the things we're proud of."

"You should be. But if you open a second restaurant that is exactly the same, you run the risk of diluting your existing location's customer base. Your loyal customers will stay loyal to you, but if the new location is closer to their homes, they'll go there instead."

He started to say something, and Tori held up a hand to forestall the interruption. "Yes, advertising will bring in some new customers, but I think you're missing an opportunity with that new location. It's not on a main thoroughfare, and you know what they say: out of sight, out of mind. The only new drop-in traffic you're likely to get is from the university. And you'll be competing with a ton of lower-price restaurants for them, all with higher visibility on the main road."

Mrs. Maguire spoke. "So what you're saying is, that building is so out of the way, nobody will know it's there except the college kids, who can't afford our prices?"

There it was, the question Tori had feared. She felt the weight of Kate's suddenly sharp stare. She didn't look in that direction, but kept her gaze fixed on Mrs. Maguire. "I don't have enough data to support that statement, but before you sign a lease, I do think you should look seriously at the reason three previous restaurants failed in that location."

Mrs. Maguire turned a triumphant grin on her husband. "I told you so! The one on Nicholasville Road is better, even if it is more expensive."

"Yeah, rub it in." He heaved a giant sigh and sat back in his chair before fixing a gaze on Kate. "Both these ideas are great, but we're going to have to take another look at our direction before we continue with an advertising campaign. So let's hold up for now, and we'll get back with you when we know more about what we're doing."

Tori's stomach sank. She could see it now. Their delay was going to push the account past this quarter's billing cycle.

Judging by the frozen smile on Kate's face, she knew it too. "I understand," she told Mr. Maguire. "We'll wait for you to get in touch with us when you decide on a course of action."

Tori joined Kate and Mitch by the door and shook the Maguires' hands in farewell.

"Good job," Mr. Maguire told Mitch. "I like your ideas."

Mitch's chest swelled. "Thank you, sir."

He shook Tori's next, but all he said was a brief, "You too."

Then Mrs. Maguire took her hand and squeezed. "Thank you. He needed to hear that from someone other than me."

Tori managed a smile, but she was acutely aware of Kate's hovering presence.

"I'll show you out," Kate told the Maguires, then hung back for a second as they left the room. The gaze she turned on Tori was icy. She spoke quietly. "Congratulations. You just lost the firm some much-needed revenue in this quarter."

She left, and Tori stared after her, her heart pounding in her ears.

I'm soooo fired.

Mitch stepped in front of her, shaking his head slowly. "That was gutsy, Sanderson. Not smart, but gutsy." His smirk widened. "After I'm promoted, we're going to have a serious conversation about corporate loyalty."

He wandered off in the direction of Kate's office, no doubt to enjoy the stunning view he'd have when he took her place as Account Executive. Nausea roiled in Tori's stomach. Kate firing her was probably a blessing in disguise. She couldn't work for Mitch under any circumstances.

She left the conference room, but headed in the opposite direction. What she needed right now was a friendly ear.

Phil looked up from his desk when she entered his office. His forehead creased when he caught sight of her face. "Tori, what's wrong?"

She closed the door and leaned against it. "I'm going to get fired."

"What?" He gestured toward one of the chairs in front of his desk. "Sit down and tell me what happened."

Tori sank into the chair. The story tumbled out, and he listened without interrupting.

"I tried, Phil, I really did." She folded her hands in her lap. "But that building is a mistake for them. When she asked me outright, I had to tell her what I thought." She gave him a look of entreaty. "Was I wrong?"

The tense muscles in her shoulders released when he shook his head.

"I think you did the right thing. I would have done exactly the same."

"You would?"

He nodded. "It's called integrity, Tori. And I'm afraid we're seeing less and less of it around this place."

"Well, I won't be seeing anything around here." She shook her head. "Do me a favor, would you?" With a gulp, she tapped on the framed Bible verse on the corner of his desk. "Say a prayer that I can find a decent job before too long."

A cautious look stole over Phil's face. "Are you saying you don't want to stay with Connolly and Farrin?"

She gave a short laugh. "I don't think I'm going to have a choice." Then she grew serious. "But even if Kate doesn't fire me, I can't stay here. I won't work for Mitch."

"I was hoping you'd say that." He grinned and rocked back in the desk chair. "How would you like to work for me?"

"Really?" Hope flickered at the edge of her gloom. "Do you think Kate would allow that?"

He shook his head. "You misunderstand. Can you keep something confidential for a few days?"

"Of course."

"I'm giving my notice on Friday." A huge grin flashed onto his face. "I'm going to open my own firm."

Stunned, Tori's jaw slackened. This piece of gossip would rock the office. Nobody saw it coming. Phil was a fixture at Connolly and Farrin. "Phil, that's terrific. Congratulations."

"Thanks. When you covered the commercial shoot for me on Friday, I was meeting with a loan officer at the bank to wrap up the final details on the financing. He called about an hour ago and told me I've got the green light." He held up a hand. "Now, it's not going to be nearly as glamorous as this firm. We'll handle small businesses, mom-and-pop places that don't have huge advertising budgets."

"Places like Nolan's Ark?"

He chuckled. "Exactly like that. I've got a list of potential clients that could never afford Connolly and Farrin, and I'm confident I have a shot at getting their business."

"And you want me to come work for you?"

"A talented young woman like you? Are you kidding?" He rocked forward and placed his folded hands on the desk, his expression serious. "I want you to know this didn't come about because of the decision to make Kate a partner. I've been thinking and praying about it for a long time. With the Lord's help and a couple of enthusiastic people like you, I think this thing has the potential to really take off. And you'd be in on the ground floor."

Without a doubt, the atmosphere at Phil's firm would be the polar opposite of this place. Imagine working for someone who prayed over his decisions.

Actually, that sounded like something she wanted to be a part of.

She sat straight up in the chair and gave him her widest smile. "I'd really like to work for you, Phil."

"Now, before you agree, I want you to know I won't be able to pay you what you're making here, not for a while. And we'll have to operate on a shoestring budget. No big expense accounts."

Tori couldn't stop the chuckle that gurgled up from deep inside. "I'm learning to deal with that in a lot of areas lately."

Chapter Twenty-Three

GOD HAS LED TWO LIVES TO TAKE ONE PATH

Joan Leigh Sanderson

AND

Kenneth Edward Fletcher

INVITE YOU TO SHARE IN THE JOY OF THEIR MARRIAGE
ON SATURDAY, JULY NINETEENTH
AT FOUR O'CLOCK IN THE AFTERNOON

Christ Community Church
DANVILLE, KENTUCKY

"You just had to have that ice cream cone this afternoon, didn't you?" Tori pulled two edges of silky fabric together on the back of Allie's dress and slid the zipper upward. "There. How does that feel?"

The Sunday school room in the basement of the church was barely recognizable. Articles of clothing lay scattered over every surface while the cords of curling irons snaked across the floor toward makeup mirrors lining the long table. A cloud of hairspray wafted their way from the direction of Karen, Ken's sister, and the minute she set the canister down, Mom snatched it up and applied it to an errant curl on Joan's head. Chelsea stood nearby watching, a miniature vision in a junior bridesmaid dress that matched the rest of them. The church sewing circle deserved a medal for getting it done so quickly.

"Ice cream has nothing to do with it." Allie tugged at the snug waist. "It'll be fine. Just tie the sash loosely."

Tori did, then stepped back to admire her handiwork. "There. You're stunning."

Actually, she wasn't. In fact, she looked a little green, and it had nothing to do with the mint colored silk of her dress. Her eyes widened, and a hand rose to cover her mouth. In the next instant, she fled from the room.

Great. Allie was coming down with the flu or something right before the wedding. Unless... A quick glance assured Tori that Joan hadn't noticed her sister's abrupt departure.

"I'll be right back," she announced, and followed Allie to the bathroom, where she wet a paper towel and stood waiting outside the stall.

"Thanks." Allie took it and dabbed at her forehead. "Now I have to do my makeup again. But I hope everyone's finished with the hairspray. One whiff and I'll lose it all over the bride."

Tori folded her arms and watched Allie closely. "Okay, 'fess up. Are you pregnant?"

After a pause, Allie nodded. "But don't tell anyone. This is Joan's big day, and I don't want to take any attention away from her."

Tori squealed and threw her arms around her big sister. "Congratulations! That's so exciting, Allie!" She drew back. "But it's really soon, isn't it? Joanie's still a baby."

Allie scowled. "Tell me about it. We're going to name this one 'Oops.'"

A giggle escaped Tori's lips. "That's what you get for losing all the weight and becoming sleek and sexy again."

"Come on. We'd better get back in there."

When they stepped into the hallway, Chelsea ran toward them. "Come see! She's got her dress on, and she's so beautiful."

She was. When Tori entered the room, the sight that met her stopped her in her tracks. Had there ever been a more beautiful bride than Joan? Her face really did glow as she stood in front of the full-length mirror they'd brought from home, gazing at her gown. Behind her, Mom was having a hard time not crying as she laced the corset back with long, silken cords. Tori blinked away her own tears and came to take Mom's place.

"Here, let me do that. I'm the maid of honor."

Allie piped up. "And I'm the matron of honor. I'll get the veil."

Tori concentrated on not twisting the cords as she criss-crossed them down Joan's back. Karen snapped a few pictures and then went to the other side of the room to put the finishing touches on her makeup.

"You know, there's still time to back out," Tori teased. "Say the word and we'll tell all those people to go on home."

Joan half-turned to grin at her. "Not on your life."

Tori smiled. "I didn't think so." She bit her lip as she threaded the cord through a silken loop. "I want you to know, I realize I was wrong about Ken."

Joan caught her gaze in the mirror. "You mean you don't think he's a religious nut anymore?"

"No. I think he's..." How was it Ryan had described Ken? "Genuine. And perfect for you."

"Of course he is." Allie approached holding Joan's wispy veil by the comb. "Who else would get so excited about such a crazy wedding present?"

Across the room, Karen turned, a mascara wand in her hand. "What did you get him?"

Tori rolled her eyes. "She bought him a herd of goats."

Chelsea's delighted laughter rang in the room, while Karen's mouth gaped open.

"Those goats will feed a poor village forever," Joan told her earnestly. "All their children will have plenty of milk and cheese and meat. It's a gift of life."

Karen grinned. "Yeah, Ken would appreciate that."

Allie whirled on Karen. "Do you know what Ken got Joan? He's been so secretive it's driving me crazy."

Karen's gaze connected with Tori's for an instant, then Tori busied herself by adjusting the already-perfect bow. Joan's secret suitcase lay in readiness in the trunk of Ken's car. If only she could be there to see her sister's reaction when he told her about their romantic honeymoon.

Karen shrugged and returned to her makeup. "Knowing Ken, it's probably something similar."

With a final tug, Tori stepped back and watched as Allie fitted the comb in the mass of Joan's dark curls. When she took her hands away, Joan turned toward them, her face radiant.

Mom lifted her glasses to dab at her eyes, then smiled at Chelsea. "I remember dressing her in her Halloween costume when she was your age. And now just look at her."

Tori slipped an arm around Mom's waist and squeezed. She'd been cautious at first, but she had swallowed her resentment and welcomed Chelsea into the family. Tori had never been prouder of her mother.

As for Patti … well, that would take a little more time.

In the sanctuary upstairs, the organ music changed to a different tune. Right on cue, Eric's voice called from the hallway.

"Is everybody decent in there?"

Joan gasped a breath, her eyes wide, as he entered. "Is it time?"

"Your groom is chomping at the bit up there." He stopped and gave a low whistle. "Wow. You're the most beautiful bride I've ever seen."

Allie punched him on the arm. "Nice, Eric. Hope you enjoy the couch tonight."

He laughed and made a display of rubbing his bicep. "She coached me on what to say, but you really are beautiful, Joan. It's an honor to escort you down the aisle." He crooked his arm toward her. "Are you ready?"

They gathered their bouquets and headed upstairs. In the narthex, three tuxedoed groomsmen waited. Tori's breath caught in her throat at the sight of Ryan, looking more handsome than she could have imagined. He was saying something to Gordy, but stopped when he caught sight of her. The admiration that lit his eyes set her pulse fluttering.

While Karen's husband escorted Mom to her seat, everyone else moved into the position they'd rehearsed. Tori and Ryan stood behind Allie and Gordy, the resident Guitar Hero who had agreed to act as the third groomsman.

Ryan leaned close to her and whispered, "It's in bad taste to outshine the bride on her wedding day. You look amazing."

She grinned up at him. "Thank you. So do you. You should wear a tux more often."

He stuck a finger in his collar and tugged at the bow tie. "Nah. It makes the customers at the hardware store nervous." Then his eyes softened. "The next time I wear one of these, I won't be walking down this aisle. I'll be waiting up at the altar."

A delicious thrill shot through her as heat flooded her face. Some day she'd have her turn. But today was Joan's day. She looked toward the end of the line, where Joan waited with her arm tucked into Eric's. The happiness in her sister's face stirred up a joy deep in Tori's soul.

She deserves to be this happy.

Ryan saw her glance and leaned over to whisper in her ear. "Is she sad that your father isn't here?"

"Oh, He's here." Tori covered Ryan's hand with hers and squeezed. "He's always here."

SISTER-TO-SISTER

"... this is the realm of happy endings, and readers won't be disappointed. The sisters are spirited and fun."

Publisher's Weekly

Books by Virginia Smith

Mystery and Romantic Suspense
Murder by Mushroom
Bluegrass Peril
Into the Deep
A Deadly Game

Classical Trio Series
A Taste of Murder
Murder at Eagle Summit
Scent of Murder

Falsely Accused Series
Dangerous Impostor
Bullseye
Prime Suspect

Available through
Annie's Book Club
Horse and Burglary
Triple Layer Treachery
Just Desserts
Thorn to Secrecy
To Hive and to Hold
Burning Danger
Web of Lies
Guilty Secrets
A Deadly Brew

Available from Guidepost Books
A Flame in the Night

Science Fiction and Fantasy
The Days of Noah
Sister of the Brotherhood

Biblical
The Last Drop of Oil:
Adaliah's Story
Raised for a Purpose: Talia's Story

Contemporary and Romance
Lost Melody★
The Zookeeper's Daughter
The Amish Widower

Tales from the Goose
Creek B&B
Dr. Horatio vs. the Six-Toed Cat
The Most Famous Illegal
Goose Creek Parade
Renovating the Richardsons
The Room with the
Second-Best View
A Goose Creek Christmas

Incredible Mayla Strong series
Just As I Am
Sincerely, Mayla

Sister-to-Sister Series
Stuck in the Middle
Age before Beauty
Third Time's a Charm

Historical Romance
The Heart's Frontier★
A Plain and Simple Heart★
A Cowboy at Heart★

A Bride for Noah★
Rainy Day Dreams★

For Children
The Last Christmas Cookie
The Last Easter Egg

★ co-authored with Lori Copeland

About Ginny

estselling author **Virginia Smith's** first novel was published in 2006. Since then, she's written more than fifty books and has collected a satisfying number of accolades and awards, including two Holt Medallion Awards of Merit. Ginny loves to introduce readers to her home state of Kentucky in her books (where the grass is green, not blue!) She loves Jesus, her family, writing, and geeking around on the computer, in that order. She and her husband live in the central part of the state with a feisty Maltese watchdog-wannabe named Max.

You can write to Ginny through the Contact page at www.VirginiaSmith.org. If you'd prefer to send a real letter, her mailing address is:

Virginia Smith
P.O. Box 4563
Frankfort, KY 40604-4563

Learn more about Ginny and her books at www.VirginiaSmith.org. She occasionally manages to Tweet @VirginiaPSmith, or you can really get to know her on Facebook, where she spends far too much time. Facebook/ginny.p.smith.

Made in the USA
Monee, IL
24 August 2023

41566882R00173